Praise for *The Cry of the Wind*

Kudos to this unlikely but undeniably successful alternate history.
- *Booklist*

Shows just what alternate history should be."
- *Robert A. Metzger, author of* Picoverse

Praise for *The Shadow of the Storm*

An undeniably successful alternate history.
- *Booklist*

The tale of One Who Flies becomes more compelling with each book in the series.
- *Locus*

Praise for *The Spirit of Thunder*

Quick plotting, good characterization, and great descriptions soon sweep the reader into the maelstrom.
- *Kliatt*

Praise for *The Year the Cloud Fell*

Fans of alternate history novels know they have a new hero.
- *Midwest Book Review*

A rousing good story...a great alternate history tale.
- *William Forstchen, author of The Lost Regiment series*

BENEATH A
WOUNDED SKY

Also by Kurt R.A. Giambastiani

Dreams of the Desert Wind
Unraveling Time

The Ploughman Chronicles
Ploughman's Son
Ploughman King

The Fallen Cloud Saga
The Year the Cloud Fell
The Spirit of Thunder
The Shadow of the Storm
The Cry of the Wind
Beneath a Wounded Sky

BENEATH A
WOUNDED SKY

Kurt R. A. Giambastiani

mouse road press
seattle

Beneath a Wounded Sky

Book Five of the Fallen Cloud Saga

1st Edition
A Mouse Road Publication
November 2012

mouse road press

16034 Burke Ave N
Shoreline, WA 98133
United States of America

Cover and book design © 2012 Mouse Road Press

ISBN-13: 978-1480165861
ISBN-10: 1480165867

First Mouse Road Press Edition: November 2012

DEDICATION

To Ilene,
my ever-fixed mark.

THE WORLD OF THE FALLEN CLOUD

Imagine a world that began much like our own.

Sixty-five million years ago, North America bade farewell to the islands of Europe from across the newly-born Atlantic, Australia stretched to separate itself from Antarctica, and the Indian sub-continent was sailing away from Africa, bound for its collision with the heart of Asia. In every place, Life abounded, and dinosaurs—some larger than a house, and others as small as your thumb—ruled the land, the sea, and the air, living out their lives in the forests and swamps that dominated the coastlands along the shallow Cretaceous seas.

Then the world broke open, unleashing a volcanic fury the like of which had not been seen for an æon. The Deccan Traps gushed molten lava, covering half of India with a million cubic kilometers of basalt. The ranges of Antarctica cracked, spewing iridium-laced ash into darkening skies. For 500,000 years, the planet rang with violence. Mountains were born, seas shrank, and Life trembled. Across the globe, resources of food and prey disappeared as the climate shifted from wet to arid. Populations competed, starved, and then collapsed. Over the next million years, half of all species died out, unable to adapt in time as habitats vanished in a geologic heartbeat[1].

In North America, the continental plate was compressed, thrusting the Rocky Mountains miles into the air. The inland seaway that stretched from the Caribbean to the Arctic began to recede, taking with it the moist marshes and fens upon which the last of the world's dinosaurs depended. The waters ebbed, revealing vast sedimentary plains, retreating for a thousand miles before they came to a halt. The sea that remained was a fraction of its former size; a short arm of warm, shallow water that thrust up from the Caribbean to the Sand Hills of Nebraska.

It was on these placid shores that a few species of those great dinosaurs clung to life. Reduced in size and number, the gentle sea gave them the time they needed to adapt and survive. Eventually, some species left the sea's humid forests for the broad expanses to the north, finding ecological niches among the mammals that had begun to dominate the prairie.

Life continued. Continents moved. The glacial ices advanced and retreated like a tide. In Africa's Great Rift Valley, a small ape stood and peered over the savannah grass. Humans emerged, migrated into Asia and Europe, and history was born. Events unfolded mostly unchanged, until the European civilization came to the Great Plains of North America.

In the centuries before the first Spaniard brought the first horse to the New World, the Cheyenne had been riding across the Great Plains on lizard-like beasts of unmatched speed and power. In defense against their new white-skinned foe, the Cheyenne allied with other tribes, and when the tide of European colonialism came to the prairie frontier, it crashed against the Alliance, and was denied. For a hundred years, the Alliance matched the Horse Nations move for move, strength for strength, shifting the course of history.

Then, through advances in technology and industry, the Americans, led by an officer named George Armstrong Custer, began to make headway and the Alliance was pushed

---

[1] For a more detailed analysis of this non-impact theory of the end of the Cretaceous Period, see *The Great Dinosaur Extinction Controversy*, by Jake Page and Charles B. Officer.

back beyond the Mississippi, beyond the Arkansas, all the way to the banks of the Missouri and the Santee. A few years later that same officer—now President Custer—sent his only son on a reconnaissance mission beyond those rivers, only to hear of his capture by the Cheyenne. In the three years since, young George has lived with the Cheyenne, and has sided with them against his own father's forces.

This is the World of the Fallen Cloud.

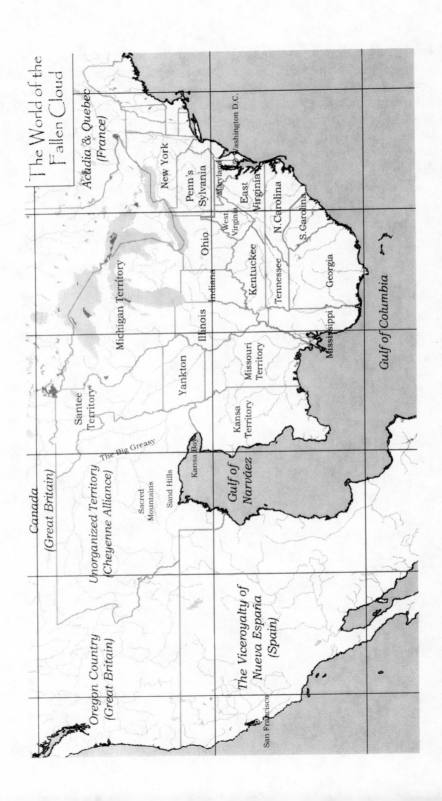

The World of the
Fallen Cloud

Acadia & Quebec
(France)

New York

Penn's
Sylvania

Maryland

Washington D.C.

West
Virginia

East
Virginia

Ohio

N. Carolina

S. Carolina

Indiana

Kentuckee

Tennessee

Georgia

Michigan Territory

Illinois

Mississippi

Yankton

Missouri
Territory

Gulf of Columbia

Santee
Territory

Kansa
Territory

The Big Greasy

Kansa Bay

Canada
(Great Britain)

Unorganized Territory
(Cheyenne Alliance)

Sacred
Mountains

Sand Hills

Gulf of
Narváez

Oregon Country
(Great Britain)

The Viceroyalty of
Nueva España
(Spain)

San Francisco

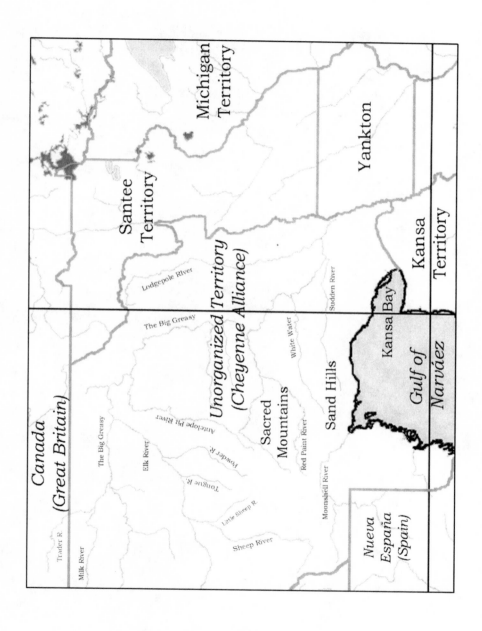

Chapter 1

Moon When the Cherries are Ripe, Full
Four Years after the Cloud Fell
Along the Red Paint River
Alliance Territory

Speaks While Leaving stood before the Council chiefs and waited for their stunned silence to break. It was her father, One Bear, who first recovered.

"What do you mean, 'No'?" he asked.

"I mean no," she answered. "I will not tell the Council of my vision."

This time her pronouncement was met with angry, disapproving murmurs. Chiefs spoke without regard for manners or propriety, and voices around the lodge increased in urgency and volume. The summer wind freshened and the dusty smell of dry grass swirled past the raised lodgeskins. The people sitting outside the lodge, hopeful for word about the new vision from Speaks While Leaving, began to stir as the story of what was transpiring crept toward them.

"She refuses?"

"She cannot!"

Inside, "She insults us," a chief said.

"She insults the entire Council!"

1

Tempers grew hot around her, knife blades glowing in the flame of her insolence, but from the tail of her eye Speaks While Leaving saw the one chief who remained cold as stone.

Storm Arriving—her husband until just a few days past—only stared at her. Back straight, fists on cross-legged knees, his rage was a focused heat in his eyes. The sharp edge of his disregard cut her heart, her soul, but his anger had nothing to do with her most recent vision or her refusal to share its content. No, her former husband's disapproval had begun months before, when they found themselves at odds about the future of the People.

She needed to be honest with herself: her marriage to Storm Arriving could have survived that schism if she had stayed at home with the People. But she had not. She had left, traveling across the Salt Waters to the kingdom of the Iron Shirts, widening the rift between them. When their infant daughter died of the red fever during the homeward voyage, it was the killing blow. Last night Storm Arriving struck the dance drum and threw away the stick—and with it his marriage. It had been a surprise to many, but not to her. She knew it was just the last breath of their union succumbing to a long illness.

Her actions now could do nothing to deepen Storm Arriving's disregard for her, but they would affect the Council's opinion of her.

All her adult life, Speaks While Leaving had been visited by *nevé-stanevóo'o,* the four Sacred Persons, guardians of the corners of the world, who brought her visions of the future, visions filled with advice and guidance for the People.

Dutifully, she had always described these visions to her elders. But four days ago she had been given another vision, and the power of it had been immense, shaking the earth, rattling rocks in the river bed, panicking the whistler herds, and waking people all across the mile-wide encampment of the People. It was a vision unlike any she had ever experienced, in both its clarity and its urgency, and it was perfectly clear that it was not to be treated like anything she had experienced before.

Her father stood to assert control over the growing tumult of the Council. He held out his hands to demand

2

quiet. Slowly, the chiefs complied. When order had been re-stored, he turned to his daughter.

"You have never refused to speak of your visions to the Council," One Bear said.

"No," she admitted. "I have not."

"Does this vision deal with the future of the People?"

"Yes," she said simply.

"Is it important that we hear this vision?"

"Yes," she said again. "Very important."

His voice rumbled with the constrained agitation that only a father of a recalcitrant, embarrassing child can feel. "Then why do you refuse to share it with us? This latest vision of yours...the ground trembled when the spirit powers visited you! That has never happened before. And yet it is this, the most powerful vision that you refuse to share? Why?"

Speaks While Leaving frowned. "You are not ready to hear it," she said.

Again the lodge was filled with a hubbub of disbelief and affront. One Bear struggled to remind the gathered chiefs of their manners.

Stands Tall in Timber, Keeper of the Sacred Arrows, rose to stand at One Bear's side, and together their silent example brought the meeting back to order.

"Speaks While Leaving," One Bear said. "You have made your position plain. You believe that you know better than the collected wisdom of the Council. During your lifetime, I have known you to be stubborn, headstrong, and full of ar-gument, but this is an arrogance I have never seen, even in you." He paused to give weight to his disapprobation. "Tell me, Daughter: when will the Great Council, with its grey heads and its many years of experience, when will this body of elders be worthy enough to hear of this vision?"

His rebuke hurt, but it was not unexpected, and she maintained her equanimity in the face of it. As arrogant as she had been—for she could not disagree with her father's assessment—she knew that handling this vision called for even more. She steeled herself for what she had to say.

"First, Father, answer me this," she said, looking around her. "Where are the chiefs from the Inviters, our greatest ally? I do not see them here." She saw her father's gaze narrow and his jaw jut forward as it did when he was holding his temper in check.

"And from the Cloud People, where are their chiefs? And the Little Star People? The Sage People? The Cut-Hair? Are we an alliance without any allies?"

She turned full circle and looked at the chiefs around her. Summer was the gathering time for the ten bands of the People; a time of plenty, of hunting, of story circles, and of sweetheart dances. But this summer there had been strife, and as Speaks While Leaving looked around the lodge, she saw many more were missing than just their allies.

"Where are the chiefs of the Hair Rope Band, my father? And the Flexed Leg Band? This is not the Great Council of the Alliance. This is not the Council of the Forty-Four chiefs of the People." She turned to make her argument to them all. "This is the Council of Those who Agree with One Bear."

"Daughter!"

"You have had your say, Father. Now I will have mine." She gestured to the empty places around the lodge. "Our Alliance is fractured. The Council is fractured. The *People* are fractured. Who should we follow? Should we follow men like him?" she asked, pointing to Storm Arriving. "Men who believe only in the rule of bullet and arrow, who want only to spill *vé'hó'e* blood? Or should we follow men like you, Father? Men who believe that piety and sacrifice alone will bring forth the changes we desperately need? You two—my father and my husband—you have not been able to agree on anything for moons. Do you think that today you will be able to agree on the meaning of my vision? Do you think you speak for all those who are absent?"

She turned as she spoke, addressing the body and no longer just her father. "The Council is split. We have no leader. The two factions are tearing us apart. You agree on nothing, and nothing gets done. When the day comes that both sides are willing to hear a voice other than their own, *then* you will be worthy of hearing from me!"

From his place among the war chiefs, Storm Arriving's voice cut through the silence, a growl made through clenched teeth.

"Just what do you think you are, I wonder."

She stared straight at him, affronting him, insulting him in front of the entire Council.

"I am the woman who was mother to your child," she said in a flat, even tone. "I am the woman who was your wife. I am the woman who you once loved, and the woman who loves you still, despite my pain. I deserve respect from you, but I think you have forgotten how to respect anyone, yourself most of all."

She glared at him until her resolve began to waver, then turned and walked past the chiefs to the doorflap. She stepped out of the lodge and into the throng of people who crowded outside. They gazed at her with that mixture of wide-eyed wonder and reluctant fear that had dogged her all her adult life. But with that fearful wonderment, she saw also a yearning, an earnest hunger for answers to their questions.

What will happen to us?
Who should we fear?
Who are our friends?
What should we do?

To her, the vision cleared the fog that shrouded the possible paths of their future, but the choice went against wisdom, against tradition, against her own judgment. The Council, split by interpretations of her previous vision, would surely splinter under the content of this one. And the people around her? They would be more lost than ever.

The breeze tugged at the ends of her short hair, brutally cut in grief after her daughter's death—was it only two moons since that awful day? Her grief was so fresh in her heart that, selfishly, she refused to cause others even more by giving them answers that would not soothe. She walked through the crowd and locked the secret of their salvation in her breast, praying that the time to reveal it would come soon.

George was nervous.

It wasn't your standard, everyday, giddy-laugh-and-get-on-with-it type of nervous, no. This was an entirely different breed of nervous. This was a gut-flipping, hand-rattling type of nervous that came nigh on to panic.

The blood sang in George's ears and his throat was tight and dry. He swallowed against the knot and glanced over at the two friends who had volunteered to help him through this ordeal, but the dour expressions they wore only accentuated his own misery. He took a deep breath of fresh evening air and let it out, slowly, through taut lips. He shook his head.

"Aw, Hell," he said, putting some brass in his backbone. "This is silly. What's the worst that could happen?"

Whistling Elk squinted into the distance, pondering the question. "He could throw the gifts back in your face, I suppose."

"Whip you down to the river," Limps said, his voice as somber as his features.

Whistling Elk nodded. "Yes. He could whip you down to the river, and then drag you through the camp, shouting to everyone how you took his sister to wife without his permission—"

"Against his word," Limps added.

"*Thank* you," George interrupted, stopping them. "Thank you, both of you. To be honest, I didn't really want to hear what the worst could be."

Limps frowned. "Next time, do not ask."

George chuckled, more to manufacture some nerve than out of any good humor. "After all, the *worst* would be if he killed me outright, eh?" He laughed again and regarded his friends.

"It is possible," Whistling Elk said reluctantly. "I heard that he was very angry after the Council..."

Limps stopped him with a gesture and studied George's features for a moment. "He does not want an answer to that question, either," he told Whistling Elk.

"Oh, for shit's sake," George said, switching to English as he always did when a good curse was required. Sweat started to trickle down the nape of his neck, despite the cool evening breeze.

The sun of the late summer's day was setting and the roiling clouds wore clothes of rose-pink and salmon-red, glowing brightly against the deep blue sky. Musky smoke drifted in the air as evening meals were prepared over fires of dried buffalo chips.

George's lodge stood nearby. A thin line of smoke drifted upward through the hole in the top and from inside came the quiet tune that Mouse Road—now George's wife—sang to herself as she went about her evening chores.

Outside, the three men stopped dawdling and prepared for their own chore. Each man had an item for the coming ritual.

At Whistling Elk's feet was a bundled pair of buffalo robes, each pelt thick with wintertime hair. Next to Limps, a stake was stuck in the ground and tied to it was a pair of whistlers—the large, lizard-like beasts that the People rode instead of the slower, less hardy horses that the Spaniards had brought to the New World. And, in George's trembling hands was a parfleche of folded rawhide painted with long diamonds and triangles in blue and white; inside the packet was a piece of red Trader's cloth, and swaddled inside that were four black feathers from the tail of a mountain eagle.

These items—the robes, the whistlers, and the eagle feathers—comprised the bride-price George would offer to Storm Arriving, Mouse Road's brother. It was not a rich price, but George was not rich in things valued by the People.

In the four years since he had come to live among them, George hadn't had time or opportunity to amass any personal wealth; not by Cheyenne standards, not by anyone's. His work first as a translator, then as liaison, and finally as an advocate for the People, had kept him travelling the world—to Washington, to Alta California, to Cuba, even to the royal courts of Spain—all in service to the Cheyenne Alliance in their struggle against the *vé'hó'e*, the men of the White Nations. During those years, the charity of his neighbors and friends had relieved him from the day-to-day struggle that was part of Cheyenne life. Their kindness had made it unnecessary for him to hunt all the bison, to husband all the whistler flocks, and to stalk all the eagles that would have allowed him to manage the wealth of a respectable bride-price.

And so it was with these meager gifts, some of which were gifts themselves, that George readied himself to cross the camp of the gathered bands, find Storm Arriving, and offer them as a price for an extraordinary woman.

To George, it seemed neither right to offer *any* price, nor proper to offer so little. Mouse Road was both un-buyable and priceless. In truth, the fact that such a ritual was even called for still amazed him; it was very far beyond any future he'd ever imagined for himself.

George and Mouse Road's courtship had occurred without their intention; it had grown with each furtive look and every trivial favor they had traded over the years. Their love had come upon them unsuspected, like the sun breaking through a clouded sky. George had been particularly unprepared, as his love for her had put him at odds with Storm Arriving, who when asked had denied George permission to stand as suitor to his younger sister. George had tried to honor the edict, but last summer, during the shipboard voyage home from Spain's royal court, the young couple's love strengthened and they realized that, according to the customs of the People, they had effectively eloped.

Unconventional was not the word George would have used to describe their romance. Unconventional was a word best suited to a widow who remarried too soon, or a man who took a bride ten years his senior. No, their romance was beyond unconventional; it was beyond all the established norms of his upbringing, and yet, it did not seem improper. In fact, as he listened to his wife's quiet humming, as he thought of her strength, her devotion, her clear-eyed view of the world and her powerful love for him, being married to Mouse Road seemed the most *proper* thing in the world.

And so he tucked his concerns away: this marriage might have come from the far side of convention, but it was well away from any taint of impropriety. He was satisfied, and glad of it. A smile crept over his lips, though, as he imagined his father's reaction to his new daughter-in-law. How would President Custer greet Mouse Road when she was presented on his son's arm?

The smile faded. Such a meeting would never happen, and George had a more immediate task before him.

Among the People there were many rules and customs. An elopement could be accepted if, after the fact, the husband brought the bride's family the price he should have offered beforehand. But, in bringing such paltry gifts to a brother who had explicitly denied the husband permission, well, George realized that Whistling Elk was wrong. Having his gifts thrown back in his face was probably the *best* of all likely outcomes, not the worst.

"Come," George said. "I've put this off for too long."

"Work grows no easier for waiting," Limps agreed.

Whistling Elk picked up the heavy roll of buffalo robes and hoisted them across his back. Limps untied the leader ropes that tethered the two whistlers. George, with his small parcel and its feathers, turned and spoke to his wife inside the lodge.

"Mouse Road," he said. "We are going."

Her humming continued.

"Mouse Road? Did you hear me? We are going."

Her quiet song neither stopped nor faltered.

"She ignores you," Limps said, patting George's shoulder.

"She is nervous, too," Whistling Elk said.

George understood. Storm Arriving's response would affect her as well, and more deeply than it could possibly affect him. He squared his shoulders and, with nods of readiness from the others, turned toward the center of camp.

The whistlers grumbled. A drake and a hen, they were a nesting pair, and more valuable for the fact, but nesting pairs had strong bonds and the drake flashed patches of color across his chameleon skin to show his displeasure at being moved so late in the day—dusk was when he preferred to see his mate settled in for the night, not a time for setting out on a journey. George smelled the cinnamon scent from the drake's skin and heard his notes of warning reverberate through the bony crest that curved back from the top of his head. Limps spoke a few calming words to soothe the animal, and the drake faded his display, his complaints quieting to a throaty flutter as he consented to being led away into the gloaming.

The gentle sounds of evening embraced them. In their lodges, families gathered in conversation and laughter. The prairie grass beyond the camp was alive with the music of sleepy songbirds and the shimmer of early crickets. A breeze brought the whisper of distant trees and the sound of water rushing along the rocks of the Red Paint River. The dusty air smelled of sun-dried grass, but the quickening of autumn promised a morning dew.

George considered his two friends as they walked.

Limps was a broad-shouldered man of mature years and rough-hewn features. In the twilight, his loose hair was a dark mass that shrouded his face. Only the ruddy glint of sunset in his eyes proved him to be substance and not made of shadow. To strangers, George had never known him to say a word, and even among friends he spoke little. But George had learned that when he did speak, his words had been carefully considered. Together, the two of them had seen births and deaths, war and peace, and George considered the older man a loyal and dependable friend.

On George's other side was Whistling Elk, and a man more different than Limps was hard to imagine. Whistling Elk was what the People called a Man Becoming Woman; a human possessed of both male and female spirits. In the culture of George's birth, a man like Whistling Elk would have been ostracized, an outcast; five years ago, George himself would have shunned such a creature. But here among the People, Whistling Elk was accepted, even revered for his dual nature.

Though male in body, in all outward manners Whistling Elk was a woman. He dressed as a woman of the People; his hair was braided and twisted into an elaborate topknot. His gestures were feminine, his voice high and lilting, and he was gentle in touch and word. A talented healer, he was also a cherished storyteller who could tie one story to the next until the evening fires were all burned out. But in one aspect, this unusual man was absolutely identical to Limps: he was a fearless and experienced soldier with many coups and victories to his name.

Together, the three of them also shared something else: a growing concern for their friend, Storm Arriving.

They walked slowly between the lodges of the Tree People band, the band of Mouse Road's family. On any other day, George would have described their pace as leisurely, but on this occasion he knew they were dallying. Limps was silent—not surprisingly—but so was Whistling Elk, which was a behavior unheard of in the loquacious storyteller. Their minds were all set on the man they were heading to meet.

George's relationship with Storm Arriving had been a marvel of extremes. They met as harsh enemies, each viewing the other as an uncivilized, incorrigible savage. But during George's time with the People—first as a captive and then by choice—they both learned the falseness of their prejudice. George had regarded Storm Arriving as kin long before his marriage to Mouse Road made them brothers. But kinfolk argue, and brothers fight, and in the last year their friendship had been strained.

Storm Arriving's refusal of George's suit for Mouse Road had been the first difficulty. The assassination of their revered chief, Three Trees Together, by a white man's bullet had been the second. The old man's death not only fractured the unity of the Council, but it also affected George and Storm Arriving in very different ways.

For George, the death of Three Trees Together had been a blow that sent him reeling into a pit of self-loathing and despair, whereas for Storm Arriving, it had been the fuel that fired him to an incandescent rage and hatred of the *vé'hó'e*. Both men were transformed by the event, but in divergent directions, and their disharmony increased.

Now, as George paced his way from the edge of camp toward its center, his heart traversed a darkened path toward unknown perils. His destination: a lodge at the middle of the People's encampment—the common lodge for soldiers of the Kit Fox society where Storm Arriving had been living since his divorce and his rejection of family and friends. But the distance felt much greater than what was described by the land over which he walked. To George, it felt a world away.

What reception would he receive from this man, a man he once knew nearly as well as himself but who now was almost as alien as he'd been on the day of their first encounter? And how would he react to that reception?

Their slow, silent passage drew undesired attention. Everyone knew the turbulent story of Storm Arriving and Speaks While Leaving and their long now-together-now-apart relationship. They also knew the story of Mouse Road and One Who Flies, as George was known among the People. The intertwined tales of these two couples—two sisters by marriage and two brothers in arms—had been told and retold around a thousand lodgefires, fodder for entertainment on cool summer nights and snowbound winter days. To many, tonight was just another part in the long saga that had been playing out for years—many years longer than George's time among them, in fact. As George, Whistling Elk, and Limps made their way through the camp, they accrued a following of the curious, young and old; people wanted to be there when this new chapter was tied to the tales that had already been told.

Brave stars peeked out over the massive heads of the Sacred Mountains. George watched the stars wink as the three men, with their whispering crowd of shadows, walked into the camp's circular heart. All around them, family lodges glowed like lanterns beneath the purpling sky, and before them stood the large lodges of the Council, the soldier societies, and the holiest of the People's artifacts: the Sacred Arrows and the Sacred Buffalo Hat. Unlike those of nearby families, these larger lodges were dark. It was late summer, and the season of hunting, of gatherings, of celebration, and of war was coming to an end. The People were starting to turn their attention to the serious business of surviving the prairie's harsh winter.

But one lodge was lit. The Kit Fox lodge glimmered with a thin, lonely light. As he approached, George could see the dark circle of the open interior; in its center, a small round patch of glowing embers. Seated cross-legged before it was Storm Arriving, his face a crescent moon of wavering firelight, his body half in light, half in deep shadow. He stared into the coals.

The whistlers, hoping they had finished walking for the night, crouched down near the staking post and made themselves comfortable. Whistling Elk unshouldered his burden and put the bundle of robes on the ground.

Go ahead, Whistling Elk signed to George. *Talk to him.*

George knew that Storm Arriving was aware of their coming. The approach of three men and two unhappy whistlers could hardly have gone unnoticed in the quiet camp,

12

even without the entourage of onlookers. George was also sure that Storm Arriving knew exactly who stood outside, and why. The soldier's studied disregard of them spoke with sharp eloquence.

"Storm Arriving," George said softly.

Silence.

"Storm Arriving," he said, a bit louder. "I would like to speak with you."

Silence. George looked at Whistling Elk.

Again, Whistling Elk signed.

George cleared his throat. "Storm Arriving, please. I would like to speak with you."

Storm Arriving continued to stare into the coals.

Whistling Elk sighed theatrically. "He's going to be stubborn," he said, loudly enough to be heard by the group of followers. A few chuckles peppered the circle around the lodge entrance. "I think we should change his name to Eats Rocks for Supper."

More laughter rolled through the gathering.

What are you doing? George asked him in signs.

Whistling Elk mimed prodding the nearby whistlers with a stick. "But it puzzles me," he went on. "He has been in there for days and nights, all alone. He talks to no one. I would think that a man who divorced his wife at a public dance would be glad to be rid of her. But not this one." He turned to speak directly to the people who had tagged along. "Not Eats Rocks for Supper. No. He just sulks."

George could see smiles through the twilight, and heard the change in tone as Whistling Elk turned to goad his target.

"And he sulks for good reason. Here is a man with much—a voice often heard in Council, the highest regard of his brother soldiers, a loving and respected wife. True, he lost his daughter to the red fever, but who here has not lost a young babe or sibling to illness? Is that reason enough to turn your back on your friends? No," he said, echoing the murmurs of the crowd. "No, that is the time when friends can be of the greatest help. But what does Eats Rocks for Supper do? He sulks. He feels sorry for himself, day and night, night and day. I feel sorry for him as well, and you should too! For he is probably the sorriest—"

"Enough."

Storm Arriving stood in the opening to the lodge.

"Ah, you *do* speak," Whistling Elk said. "Good." He nodded to George and took a step backward.

"I need to speak with you," George said.

Storm Arriving stared at him, impassive, unaffected.

"We have nothing to say.

"You are wrong," George said. "We have a great deal to say."

"Then say it," Storm Arriving responded. "But do not expect me to listen." He began to walk past them but George put a hand on his chest to stop him. Storm Arriving looked down at the hand in disbelief, shocked at the affront.

George and Storm Arriving were of a similar height, but Storm Arriving was by far the more powerful man. George's gentle, academic upbringing among the elite of the White Nations, his youth spent in light farmwork and his early manhood spent in heavy bookwork could not compete with the world that had formed Storm Arriving.

Decades of riding whistlers and hunting buffalo had given Storm Arriving a muscular torso. Hard work and quick fighting had made his legs and arms strong and agile. Long winters had inured him to the privations of his tribe's nomadic life, stripping him of every ounce of fat, hardening every soft line.

His dress was common to warriors of the People: long, fringed deerskin leggings; a breechclout of red cloth; a tunic of elkhide, decorated with shells and beads in geometric patterns. The right side of his head was shaved clean to showcase the seven silver rings that hung all around the pierced fringe of his ear, and the rest of his hair was pulled back into a single braid, tied at the nape with red leather and two eagle feathers. His dark skin was like teak, and when his black eyes looked up from George's hand, they flashed with anger.

If he wanted to, he could have thrashed George in the time it took to draw a single breath, and they both knew it.

George had a choice, a choice he'd been considering during the long walk to this place, and he knew it would mark their relationship forever. His mind whirled, considering once more all the possibilities, judging the ramifications, gauging each possible outcome. Humor, anger, passivity, command; these choices and others he discarded. Storm Arriving had changed in the last year. His tireless campaigns against the U.S. Army had wiped away everything kind and friendly from his soul. As George met this new man's gaze, he saw nothing but the soldier, the strategist, the ruthless victor of terrible encounters. If George was to have the barest chance of being heard, if he was to have a hope of penetrating the bitter armor that Storm Arriving now wore around his heart, there was only one path.

"I come to you humbly and with great respect," he began, allowing his voice to reach the gathered crowd. "I come to apologize for having disobeyed your directions, and for eloping with your sister against your wishes. I come also to bring these gifts, and beg you to accept them as a bride-price."

"Gifts," Storm Arriving said. "Insults. I should throw them back in your face."

"How funny," Whistling Elk interjected. "That's just what I told him you would...do." The glares of both men stopped further remark from the storyteller.

George opened his hands before him in supplication. "I know that these gifts are insufficient, but they are all the wealth I have. I know that you are too respectful of me to ignore my request to consider them."

Storm Arriving growled and pushed past, but George reached out again to stop him.

In a blurred heartbeat, Storm Arriving grabbed George's arm, yanked him sideways across his leg, and dumped him on the ground. He slammed a knee into George's chest and cocked his fist before a shout from Whistling Elk halted his blow. Storm Arriving was not breathing hard; George was not sure he was breathing at all.

"Yes," George said, as calmly as he could with a man kneeling on his ribs. "You are too respectful. We have been too much to each other for you to ignore this request. I know that you will do the honorable thing and give these gifts full and proper consideration."

The cold hard gaze lost none of its razor edge as Storm Arriving looked at the robes, the whistlers, and at the parfleche that lay in the dirt a few feet away.

"What is in that?" he asked.

"Eagle feathers," George managed to say.

"How many?"

"Four," George said.

"A sacred number," Whistling Elk said quietly.

Storm Arriving shot the storyteller another glare and Whistling Elk turned away as if two men grappling in the dirt was a regular occurrence.

"Who gave you these feathers?" he said, and then suddenly grunted. The pressure on George's ribs relented and Storm Arriving was lifted up.

Limps had grabbed Storm Arriving by the scruff of his tunic. He hauled him to his feet and then struck him backhanded across the chest. Storm Arriving stared at his Kit Fox brother, dumbfounded.

"One Who Flies caught the eagle himself," Limps rumbled. "He asked me how. I told him how. I watched him build his blind. I saw him lay the bait. From afar, I watched. He waited. Two days, without food or water, and from the sky above the eagle watched him, too, judging him. On the third day, the eagle saw that One Who Flies was worthy, and that his sacrifice would be honored. He came down, and he gave One Who Flies a chance to take his life."

Storm Arriving, George, Whistling Elk, everyone gathered was stunned. It was more than anyone had ever heard Limps say at one time. Limps, his eyes flinty with anger, struck Storm Arriving again across the chest and pointed at George.

"He did not beat at the great bird as a boy might. He took the eagle's wounds like a man. Talon and beak tore him as he fought for the proper hold. And he killed the bird well. One thrust of his knife." He turned to the gathered crowd. "*One* thrust." And then to Storm Arriving again.

"*He* caught the eagle. *He* chose the finest of the feathers. *He* chose their number. For you." He took a step away, then turned. "For *you.*" Then he folded his heavy arms across his chest and appeared as if he would never utter another word.

The shock of Limps, speaking in sentences, wore off

16

slowly, but Whistling Elk brought them all back to reality with a gentle cough.

Storm Arriving looked around at the assemblage. He looked at the gifts again, then at the men who brought them, and George thought he glimpsed a flash of embarrassment cross the soldier's face.

"Leave the gifts," he said. "I will consider them." Then he stalked away, his long strides taking him into the evening gloom.

Whistling Elk walked over and extended a hand to George.

"That," he said as he helped George to his feet, "could not have gone better. Very well done! And you!" He turned to Limps and took him by the shoulders. "You told a story!" His voice was filled with amazement and pride.

Limps' grin shone in the gathering dark.

"So," George said, brushing himself off. "What happens now?"

"Now?" Whistling Elk said. "Nothing. We are done."

"What? But...but he didn't accept the gifts. He just said he would consider them."

Whistling Elk patted George on the back. "It is the same. No one returns such gifts afterward. It is his way of expressing his displeasure. In the morning, he will still have them, and thus accept them."

George looked around. Everywhere he looked, he saw a smile. What Whistling Elk described was true.

"Then, we are done?"

"We are done," Whistling Elk said. "Shall we go tell your wife?"

Chapter 2

Monday, September 1st, AD 1890
Palacio del Gobernador
La Ciudad de la Habana, Cuba

Alejandro sipped his port, tasted honeyed plums, and frowned.

"Wine gone sour?" Roberto asked from the dark leather divan that dominated the center of the smoking room.

"Eh?" Alejandro said, distracted from his thoughts. "Oh. No. It's excellent, as always."

"What, then?" Roberto asked.

Roberto's years as governor of Cuba had greyed his hair and rounded his belly, but they had not dulled his wits. His brother-in-law was still as sharp as the day they'd met, back when they were both soldiers of the Crown in the highlands of Alta California. Despite his sleepy, after-dinner torpor, Roberto could still discern Alejandro's mood from the slightest clue.

"Go on," Roberto said, waving his cigar. "Tell me. Good money says I already know."

Alejandro smiled and went to the humidor. He selected a long *puro* and stepped to the candelabra. He took a thin wooden spill from a silver cup and touched it to the flame.

The strains of the string quartet playing a Mozart sonatina resonated from the room to which the women had repaired after dinner. He knew Victoria's taste ran more toward the new French composers, but Roberto's Olivia was the more conservative of the two sisters and, as hostess, she set the tone for the household.

"If you are such a clairvoyant," he said as he puffed the cigar to life, "then you tell me."

"Very well," Roberto said, sitting up a bit taller. "You're anxious. Impatient."

Alejandro laughed and walked the perimeter of the smoking room, regarding the oil-brushed landscapes that studded the dark-paneled walls. "Hardly insightful," he said, inspecting the *Shepherds in the Hills at Aix-en-Provence*. "My daughter could have told me that."

"All right then," Roberto said, lofting a cloud of smoke toward the Tiepolo-inspired ceiling. "You want to act. This quiet after the storm in the harbor; it eats at you."

"Hm," Alejandro said in grudging acknowledgment. It had been a month since the explosions that had ripped through Havana's harbor, sinking three Spanish ships of the line and two freighters. He had never been comfortable with his involvement in the plot to blow up the ships and frame the Americans for the deed. Even more distasteful was the loss of life the act had caused—two score and twelve had perished in the explosion or the ensuing fires. But without a doubt, the worst of all was the fact that the tragedy, manufactured as it had been, as costly as it had been, had not brought about the desired effect. The portside fires had been cold for weeks, and still there had been no word from Madrid. The Crown, the Premier, even the Viceroy in San Francisco, were all uncharacteristically silent. When Alejandro thought of the charred bodies he saw floating off the quay, the pall of oily smoke above the exposed keel of an overturned warship—

"Each day that passes without a call to arms is an affront to Spanish honor," he snarled. "Sagasta and Cánovas! Those ministers should be put down like the sick old mares they are. And María Cristina! How can she stay silent?"

"Oh!" said Roberto playfully, rising and leaning forward to inspect Alejandro's expression. "So you are on personal terms with Her Majesty, now?"

Alejandro reined in his emotions. He had never told Roberto about the private audience their Queen Regent had granted him, nor had he breathed a word of the intimate regard and favor she had bestowed upon him. That night she had gone against the advice of her chief ministers, elevated Alejandro to the post of Special Ambassador to the Cheyenne, and authorized him to forge an alliance with the natives of the American Interior.

Sow us a friendship, and we shall reap a nation, she had told him, and then had caressed his cheek. It was a memory that still made his heart pound.

Roberto would laugh the incident aside and call him an old fool for reading too much into the attention of a young and lonely widow, starved for allies in a hostile government—an interpretation that had also crossed Alejandro's mind a few times as he struggled to understand her actions. But more than Roberto's ridicule, Alejandro feared any embarrassment the knowledge of that night might cause his wife. He knew that anything he told Roberto, Roberto would tell Olivia. Olivia, in turn, would of course tell her sister, and Victoria deserved much better than to be the subject of family gossip. Victoria had stood by Alejandro through his past disgraces—both military and political. He was not going to sully this latest triumph if he could avoid it.

No. The kind and tender touch of his Queen would forever warm his heart and fuel his loyalty to the Crown, but there was no reason to speak of it to anyone.

"Our Royal Queen Regent and her ministers," he said, composed once more, "waste precious time. Spain must respond to the Americans' scurrilous attack—"

"Which we orchestrated."

Alejandro glared at Roberto. "Do you believe they know this?"

Roberto shrugged and went back to his seat on the sofa. Leather creaked and sighed. "They must suspect." He sipped his port. "The next message from Madrid will either be a commission that sends you to your Cheyenne, or a summons that will take you—take us—to the gallows."

"*¡Dios mío!*" Alejandro breathed. "May it be the former."

Roberto laughed. "You *are* eager to leave my house! Is the wine so bad?"

Alejandro chuckled and was grateful for Roberto's eternally sunny outlook. "Of course not," he said. "But I can do nothing from here. I *must* be out there, among those savages, if I'm to—" He caught himself again. "—forge this alliance and restore our family fortunes."

Roberto reached for the cut-crystal decanter of port and refilled his small glass. "I remind you," he said, "that you are hardly a frontiersman." He held out the decanter.

"What do you mean?" Alejandro said, setting his glass down for another splash of port. "I was a field general, on the march for months at a time."

"Ages ago," Roberto reminded him as the crystal stopper clinked into place. "And your general's tent with a full support staff was much homier than the conditions you experienced last time you were among those 'savages,' as you call them."

"True," Alejandro admitted. "But this time I will be among them as an Ambassador of the Spanish Crown, not as a fever-ridden shipwreck survivor."

"You hope," Roberto said with a wink.

Alejandro nodded.

Indeed, he thought. *I do hope that.*

The two men drew on their cigars and enjoyed a moment of shared quiet. The scent of hibiscus wafted in from the patio beyond the open French doors. With it came the sounds of the city that lived beyond the garden walls. The sun was setting, and as the day's oppressive heat was coaxed offshore by the easterly trade winds, the populace prepared for the last act of Havana's lively day.

Like most of the great cities in Europe, the governor's mansion was in the heart of the capital city, surrounded on all sides by her vitality. As he walked to the open doorway, Alejandro could hear two guitars and a violin playing an old folk ballad in an alcove down the street—a dissonant counterpoint to the more courtly melodies that drifted in from the sitting room. Farther out, a young woman sang a love song, a dog barked, and laughter rose and fell as townsfolk emerged onto the still-warm cobblestones. Seagulls slipped past overhead, mewing in the cooling air, and beyond all

21

came the bells of churches calling the worshipful to vespers. Havana was such a mix of contrasts—Spaniard, Creole, Indian, and Negro; an *olla* filled with faiths and classes and professions that put pirates and nuns, doctors and canefield workers all shoulder-to-shoulder on the narrow streets. Alejandro used to marvel at Roberto's ability to govern such a place until Roberto himself explained.

"Havana has been here for three hundred years," he had said. "Do you think it needs *me* to keep it running?"

A shout from the courtyard interrupted his thoughts, and the sound of hooves on gravel announced the arrival of a messenger. The two men stood just as the door opened and Gutierrez, Roberto's butler, entered with a tray in his hand. On the tray was an envelope.

"My apologies, sir," Gutierrez said to Roberto, and then turned to Alejandro. "This telegram just arrived for you, Excellency. From Madrid."

Alejandro and Roberto shared a look.

Was this the commission?

Or the summons?

Alejandro took the red-bordered envelope.

"Thank you, Gutierrez," he said, and the butler bowed and withdrew.

Alejandro's name was written on the front in block letters, and the back was sealed with wax. He cracked the seal and unfolded the telegram. He read.

SPAIN DIRECTS U.S. TO CEDE TERRITORY TO
OUR NATIVE ALLIES. VICEROY TO STAGE
FORCES AT CIMMARON. YOU MUST PREPARE
THE WAY. HONOR NOW THE TRUST I PUT IN YOU.
  MC

Alejandro stared at the words, reading them a second time, then a third.

"Looks like good news."

Alejandro started at the voice by his side and turned to find Vincent D'Avignon reading over his shoulder. Alejandro stepped away from the man and put the telegram back in the envelope.

Vincent D'Avignon was a wiry man of indeterminate age

who had come into Alejandro's life via a long road of questionable repute. He had arrived in Havana as a hanger-on and sometime-aide to young George Custer and his native allies. Alejandro had never heard the whole of their history, but it was clear from the attitude of George's companions that D'Avignon was neither trusted nor liked. "Tolerated" was the word that Roberto had used to describe his own opinion of him, and lately, "useful" was also an applicable term, for it was D'Avignon who had executed their gambit of the portside explosions. And it was D'Avignon, too, who had given Alejandro the motive for war: gold, and lots of it, tucked away in the heart of Cheyenne Alliance Territory.

Yes, Vincent D'Avignon had proven himself extremely useful to gentlemen who wanted to keep their hands clean. It was not difficult, however, to remember that he was also an unmitigated scoundrel.

"Who's MC?" D'Avignon asked, studiously innocent.

"MC?" Roberto said, nearly spilling his drink. "You're not serious." He stood and held out his hand. "Let me see."

Alejandro tucked the envelope inside his coat.

"Well, at least *tell* me!"

Alejandro crossed the room to the French doors. He glanced over at D'Avignon. "Her Majesty has demanded the United States cede the Interior to the Cheyenne," he said. "She is sending an army into Tejano to underscore the point."

Roberto sat down again. *"¡Dios mío!"* he breathed. "She intends to invade?"

"Heh!" D'Avignon laughed. He hooked his thumb in Alejandro's direction. "And wants him to lead the way!"

Alejandro glared at the man. "Where the devil did you come from?" he asked, nettled.

D'Avignon shrugged. "I was in the garden. I heard a horseman. That means only one thing around here: news. So, I thought I'd drop in to see if it was the news we've been waiting for. It seems like it was." He smiled his long-toothed rogue's smile. "You *were* going to tell me, weren't you?"

Alejandro nodded. "Of course," he said.

"Naturally," Roberto agreed. "Wouldn't leave without his chief prospector. That's the whole point, isn't it?"

Alejandro looked from man to man, unsure of which was

annoying him the more. "Perhaps you would excuse us?" he said to D'Avignon. "With this sudden change in plans, there is some family business I'd like to discuss with my brother."

D'Avignon raised his hands. *"Certainement,"* he said, backing toward the garden door. *"Je comprends tout."* He stopped at the humidor, opened it, selected a *puro,* brought it to his nose, and inhaled its aroma. "There are a thousand details to be settled before so grand an expedition." He took a box of matches from his pocket and, striking one, lit the cigar. "Just remember to reserve me a bunk." He bowed to the two men in turn—"Your Excellency. Governor."—and strolled out into the garden, scarved in smoke.

Roberto watched him disappear into the evening gloom and tsked. "Something about that man..." he said.

"Something?" Alejandro said, tossing the stub of his cigar into the fire. "Everything!"

"Hush," Roberto said, rising his seat on the divan. "He's a necessary evil and has proven himself quite useful. Now—" He waggled the fingers of his open hand. "Let me see that telegram."

Alejandro considered it. Hiding it at this point would raise more suspicions than would revealing its contents. He produced the envelope and handed it to Roberto.

Roberto perused it at arm's length. "MC," he said. "Not 'Her Majesty,' not 'Queen Regent María Cristina,' Just MC." He folded the telegram and looked to Alejandro.

"You read too much into it," Alejandro said, turning his back and walking to a bookshelf.

"Do I?"

"Yes," Alejandro snapped over his shoulder.

"Then look at me."

"What?"

"Look at me," Roberto said. "Look at me and tell me what happened at El Escorial."

Alejandro faced him and let his perturbation show on his face. "Don't be an ass, Roberto."

"That is *not* an answer."

Air escaped Alejandro like water from a tipped bucket, all in a rush. He searched for the words to describe the private audience their Queen had given him. He quaffed his port and set the glass down on a marble-topped table. "It was nothing like you are thinking, I mean." He began to pace the room. "It was just a moment of...of extraordinary personal favor."

Roberto raised an eyebrow.

"You mustn't speak of this to anyone," Alejandro said.

"Now I *am* concerned," Roberto said, and Alejandro tried again.

"It was...it was nothing," he said.

"Hardly that, it seems."

"We just had a quiet talk. She spoke to me as an equal. She held my hand. She stroked my cheek. It was all perfectly innocent."

"Innocent?" Roberto said, incredulous. "And this took place where?"

Alejandro shrugged. "In her apartments."

"Her *private* apartments?"

"Yes," Alejandro said, eyes flashing at the insinuation. "With the door open and with a guard outside."

Roberto nodded and eased himself down onto the divan. "A guard who heard everything, no?"

Alejandro nodded.

"And who could report every word to Ministers Sagasta and Cánovas?"

Alejandro took a sharp intake of breath as Roberto's point struck home. He sat down heavily next to Roberto. "She intended all along..."

"Yes," Roberto said. "And you, so long out of favor, failed to see it for what it was."

Alejandro did not know what to think, what to feel... She had *used* him. And he had been a blind goose and eaten it up. He felt anger, shame, utter embarrassment, and even a wistful sense of honor, all at once. Roberto had enough empathy not to chide him for his silly naïveté—after decades as a soldier and a diplomat, to be taken in so wholly, and by a woman, no less.

"*Ai-ai-ai,*" he sighed. "I have been masterfully played. She has used me as a rook to challenge her own two bishops of state!"

Roberto clapped a meaty hand on Alejandro's shoulder and stood. "You used each other," he said as he went over to the side table. "She got a wedge to drive between Sagasta and Cánovas, and you got an ambassador's post and the oversight of an invading army." He splashed cognac into two glasses and handed one to Alejandro. He raised his own glass.

"To being bested, and still coming out the winner."

Alejandro raised his glass as well.

"Amen."

Chapter 3

Wednesday, September 3rd, AD 1890
Outside Taneytown
Maryland

The carriage bucked, jarring its passengers.

"Mother of God," Custer cursed.

Libbie scolded him. "Keep a civil tongue, Autie."

"I just bit my civil tongue," the president said, sucking at the wound. "Only the uncivil half is left."

"Then keep it quiet altogether," his wife said.

Custer looked out the window and kept silent. Libbie had been in a petulant mood since that morning when they'd set out from the White House.

The carriage broke out from among the trees and into a field where the heat of the midsummer's day pressed a bright haze from the ground. The onion grass wilted and the catalpa trees drooped beneath the heat. The air was humid and suffocating, thick with the scent of moist decay. The road—little more than two ruts through a meadow—was guiding them across the countryside of Penn's Sylvania and toward a meeting neither of them wanted to take.

"Hat in hand," Libbie groused under her breath.

After twenty-six years of marriage, Custer knew his wife

well enough to discern her tactics. Libbie never talked to herself; it was just her way of starting a conversation without being the first person to speak.

"Something troubling you, Sunshine?" Custer asked as he stared out the open window.

"I just don't like it, Autie; your coming out here to him, hat in hand."

"I'm not coming to him 'hat in hand,'" he said, turning to face her.

"Oh, yes you are," she said, eyes flashing. "The President of the United States, bumbling around the back-country, searching for a little flea bite farm miles from nowhere."

He chuckled. "We're only five miles from Taneytown."

"And Taneytown is *nowhere*," she said.

"Well, we're hardly 'bumbling,'" he said, trying to mollify her. "Samuel gave very specific instructions on how to get there."

"Don't jolly me along, Autie," she said, slapping his thigh. "You're out here a-begging. And you can't paint it any differently than that."

Her dark pin curls, so meticulously coiffed to frame her pretty face, stuck to brow and temple like leeches, but he knew it was more than just the heat had riled her. Her blood was up; he could see that plainly in the pulse along her neck, the hands balled into tiny fists, in the taut line along her jaw, and in the way she would only look at him with fleeting glances from the tail of her eye.

He put on a pouty face, made more comical now by the lingering paralysis from last year's stroke. She glanced over, saw him, and hit his leg again. He pouted harder, putting his shoulders into it, looking up at her like a palsied pup.

The lilt at the corner of her mouth told him he'd won. She struggled to maintain her anger, but knew as well as he that the effort was futile. A giggle escaped her, and she slapped his thigh a third time, though more gently, as she conceded defeat.

"You know what I mean," she said, unwilling to surrender without concessions. "You know exactly what I mean."

Custer smiled and took her hand in his. "Yes, my dear, I do. But I need him to do this."

"Then order him to do it. You are the President, are you

not?"

He patted her hand and looked out the window. "You know it's more complicated than that," he told her.

There was a split-rail fence, now, running alongside the road and keeping zigzag pace with the carriage. The air was redolent with manure. They were getting close.

"He's a capable man," Custer continued, "but prideful in that way Southern gentlemen sometimes are. I need him to do this, but more to the point: I need him to *want* to do this."

Libby tsked and shook her head. "Men," she said, as if it explained everything. "And they say *women* are vain." She unfolded a fan of bone and white lace and tried to cool herself. "I still don't see why you insisted on bringing me along on this...errand. You would have done just as well alone. I feel like a stage prop."

Custer coughed up a surprised laugh and turned toward her. "At times you understand me completely, but at others...I'm amazed that you still find me such a cipher." Libbie's expression did not change. "My darling girl," he said. "*I* am the stage prop on this trip, not you." He chuckled at her perplexity. "You'll see."

The carriage swung around to the right and showed them a deep grove of walnut trees. The fence kept formation, curving alongside the carriage until they slowed and turned in through a gap in the rails. The road worsened as they drove between the thick boles with their large, green-husked fruit strewn like old cannon-shot across the pathway.

Custer pointed as buildings came into view. A low barn, a stable, a tall house, all river-rock foundations with white clapboard siding above.

"Nearly there," he said. As they continued, he could see that the silvered shingles on the roofs of the outbuildings were covered with splotches of green moss and grey lichen, but the shakes of the main house were orange and freshly split. As the carriage slowed to a stop in the yard, Custer smelled new cedar and mown hay. The sound of hammering peppered the air.

Custer and Libby waited for the presidential security detail to debark and inspect the area. One guard, Hancock, went to the house to meet the woman who had come out onto the shaded porch. She was a tall, spare woman in a plain white frock and blue work apron. As Hancock spoke, her expression changed from curiosity to horror, eyes wide, hand over mouth. She turned and disappeared into the house. Custer heard her calling out.

"Charlie! John!"

Hancock came over and put his hand on the carriage door.

"What did you tell her?" Custer asked.

Hancock, red hair blazing in the sunlight, shrugged. "I went with the 'just in the neighborhood' line, sir. I told her that we were hoping to beg a glass of sweet tea for the First Lady, who had become a bit overheated."

"Oh, Autie!" Libbie said. "She didn't know we were coming? That's just cruel."

Hancock opened the door and extended his hand to assist Libbie. She took the offered help and, with a backward glare at her husband, stepped out into the yard. Custer stepped down after her and leaned on his cane.

The yard was quiet now—the hammering had ceased. Custer could hear hurried footsteps and the clinking of glass from within the house. A round-bellied man appeared in the doorway. He wore dusty denims and was pulling suspenders up over his hastily misbuttoned shirt. He raked a quick hand through dark but thinning hair, and bustled toward the carriage.

Hancock moved to intercept the eager fellow but Custer stopped him with a muffled cough.

"Mr. President," their breathless host said. "Charles Tarbox, at your service!" He extended his hand, then half-withdrew it, unsure of the protocol.

Custer reached out and gripped the re-offered hand. It was rough from recent work and moist from a hasty wash-up.

"Mr. Tarbox," Custer said. "A pleasure. This is the First Lady, Mrs. Custer. Libbie? Mr. Charles Tarbox."

Tarbox lightly clasped her extended fingers and Custer continued as Libbie took his arm. "Please forgive our intrusion. We were traveling nearby and with this heat, well, John spoke so often of this beautiful farm of yours, I

30

thought we might stop in and impose upon you for a glass of water."

"Just a glass of water?" Tarbox said, suddenly deflated. "We were hoping you might stay a bit longer. To supper, perhaps?"

"Well..." Custer felt Libbie pinch his arm as she interrupted.

"We wouldn't dream of imposing upon you and your family. In fact, I told Autie"—another pinch—"that we really needn't have stopped at all."

"Ah," Tarbox said, looking back at the house. "Gussie will be so disappointed. She's an avid reader of your books, Mrs. Custer."

Custer watched as Libbie's placid, well-practiced smile went slack, then returned, reinforced by her girlish dimple.

"Why, Sunshine," Custer said. "I do believe you're blushing." This earned him yet another pinch.

"How charming," Libbie said, trying to cover her embarrassment. "And Gussie is...?"

Tarbox winced. "Beg pardon, ma'am. I mean Augusta, my sister."

There was a clatter from the house and the tall woman they'd seen earlier came out and, with the housemaid's help, set up a table and tray with glasses and a pitcher of dark tea with sliced lemon.

"Oh, here she is—please, ma'am," he whispered in an aside. "Don't let on I called her Gussie in front of you. She'd never forgive me." Hands clasped in supplication, the man's anguish was almost palpable.

Libbie relinquished her husband's arm, reached out and slipped her hand under her host's. "Our secret," she said. "And now, Mr. Tarbox, why don't you introduce me to your sister."

"With pleasure!" he said, grinning broadly. He gestured toward the house. "Though I must say, I am surprised you two haven't met. After all those years on the Kansa prairie, and with you knowing her husband John so well. But then again, she was always more of a 'home front' wife. Not the 'front line' sort like you were, ma'am." He looked back at Custer. "John is here, by the way, Mr. President."

"Is he?" Custer said, and he knew by Libbie's glare that

he'd escaped another pinch.

Tarbox introduced the Custers to his sister and, judging by Augusta's rapt attention to Libbie's every word, Custer guessed that they would stay to supper after all.

It wasn't long before Augusta's husband appeared at the doorway to the porch.

General John Meriwether's last tour in the Territory had put some grey in his hair and taken some weight from his frame, but instead of making him appear old or frail, Custer thought it gave his old comrade-in-arms the appearance of having been honed, whetted like an well-used hunting knife. His eyes were deep-set and his cheeks high and hollowed.

"Apologies for my tardiness," he said in his clear baritone voice. "While Charlie was banging on shingles I was on the downhill side of a manure pile. It took me a bit longer to make myself presentable."

His grip, when Custer shook his hand, was still firm, and by the corner of a smile he saw tucked up underneath the bushy mustache, Custer knew that though the brother and sister had been gulled by the fiction surrounding the First Couple's arrival, this old soldier knew better.

"Libbie," he said, bowing and taking her hand. "I'd say you never looked lovelier, if I did not fear of making my wife jealous." His Carolinian accent was relaxed and comforting. "I'm glad that you two have finally had a chance to meet. Augusta esteems you above all other women."

"John, hush," Augusta said, self-conscious.

They talked of easy things, of farms and horses and the improvements underway on the house. Libbie's unpretentious manner and Meriwether's long familiarity dispelled any odd feelings Augusta and Charlie had about the impromptu gathering with such celebrated company. And then, after a pleasant half-hour's chat, Meriwether caught Custer's glance and stood.

"Come along, Mr. President," Meriwether said. "There's a horse I think you'll be interested to see."

Tarbox looked up. "Oh? Which one?" He began to stand.

"No, no, Brother," Meriwether said. "Don't deprive the ladies of your company. We just have some catching up to do."

Tarbox said, "Ah," comprehending fully, and sat down with a sheepish smile.

"Mr. Tarbox, I hope you will forgive the rudeness a pair of self-indulgent old blades." Custer rose and took his cane in hand. "Ladies," he said with a bow. Then he turned to join Meriwether.

They stepped down from the verandah and walked around the house. The late summer sun paled every hue, from the yellow-green of leaves overhead to the bleached wood of the nearby fence rails. Cicada calls shimmered through the day's heat, and the two men walked slowly. They did not speak for a time, but Custer saw Meriwether's appraising look.

"Am I changed so much?" Custer asked.

Meriwether chuckled. "Actually, you are remarkably *un*-changed. The papers—"

"Bah!" Custer said. "They always exaggerate."

"All the same, I expected something more than a cane and a slight hitch in your enunciation."

Custer nodded, recounting his injuries from the near-assassination. "There's much that doesn't show," he said. "Writing is hard. Eating in polite company is a challenge, as you'll see. There's a ghost in my vision, and the pain makes me short-tempered. But it's all...manageable."

They entered the stable and Meriwether headed toward the far end.

"I was glad to read that young George had been found innocent of any wrongdoing in that affair. Ah, here we are."

He gestured to the last stall along the row, and when Custer saw the horse within it, his heart shuddered and began to pound. The horse was a bloody sorrel, shiny, with copper-penny mane. There was a white blaze on his face, and white socks on all four feet.

"I'll be damned," Custer breathed. "It's Vic."

Of course, it wasn't. Vic had fallen at the Battle of Kansa Bay, but this horse was the very image of that brave old steed, even down to the look in his eye.

Custer reached out his hand, let the horse settle, and stroked the velvet warmth of his muzzle. The horse breathed out and in, moist heat testing the air, and Custer was filled with a sudden melancholy, a lightning flash of hot grief. The memory of Vic's death cut through his mind: he felt again Vic's stuttered step as the arrows pierced his breast, saw his wide-eyed fear as they both fell, and heard the animal's panicked scream cut short as Custer's bullet turned his dying friend into a protective bulwark. The memories were sharp, unexpectedly so, and Custer's eyes stung with emotion.

"Mr. President? Are you all right, sir?"

Custer frowned and cleared his throat. "It's nothing," he said. "Ghosts. Just ghosts."

"I'm sorry. I didn't mean—"

Custer waved a hand, dismissing the issue. He gave the horse another pat and tucked the memories away. Time for business.

"I need your help, John."

"I reckoned this wasn't an accidental visit. What can I do for you? Does Jacob need help in the War Department?"

"No," Custer said. "Well, yes, of course he does, but that's not what I need from you. Nothing so...mundane."

Meriwether leaned back against the stall's door and skewered Custer with a glare. "Mundane?" he said. "That's a word chosen to intrigue me, isn't it?"

"Did it work?" Custer asked with a sidelong glance.

Meriwether shrugged. "I'm still listening."

Custer turned and walked slowly back the way they'd come. "We're in a difficult spot," he said. "The nation, that is. I need your expertise and your experience."

"Anything I can do," Meriwether said, joining him.

Custer looked up and squinted into the sunlight as they emerged from beneath the shaded eaves. The sharp tang of split wood danced atop the base aromas of hay and manure. A breeze freshened, caressing the distant meadow and sighing through the walnut branches.

"We're in a pickle, John. What Morton started, Congress is determined to finish. They're forcing us into a confrontation with Spain—not a good thing under the best of circumstances, but it's all the worse for the fact that it's just what Spain wants."

He kept his measured pace, leading them back toward the verandah, timing his words to the ground ahead of them.

34

"Between the sinking of those ships in Havana and the schoolyard diplomacy of this Congress, we're headed into a war. There's nothing quite so inevitable as a war that both sides want to wage. The Senate has demanded a full blockade, but you and I both know it will be just a sideshow. The real theater is in the Territory."

"Either way," Meriwether said, "at least it's going to happen in your own backyard. Better than halfway around the world."

Custer shrugged. "True. But that backyard isn't without its own...challenges."

Meriwether laughed. "That's a mild assessment."

"Indeed." They were nearly back at the front of the house. Custer could hear the quiet conversation and the clink of glass and china. He took another two steps and stopped at a place where he could be overheard without being seen.

"That's why I need you," he went on. "Your experience, your judgment, your *mind,* they're priceless to me at this juncture. I need you, John. I need you, back out in the field. I don't think we'll succeed without you."

Meriwether stared at him. "What? You need me *where?*"

Custer returned his gaze. "You heard me."

Meriwether raised his eyebrows and stared off into space. "Back in the field?"

Custer went in for the kill. He could hear that the conversation and sounds of convivial refreshment had stalled. He stepped over to Meriwether and gripped his arm.

"We will not succeed without you. I'm convinced of it. All my other generals—Herron, Stant—they all failed. But it wasn't really their fault. They didn't know the land, and more to the point, they didn't know those people. But you do. You are the only man who ever made any progress out there; you know the Cheyenne."

Meriwether's gaze came back to Custer. "I thought we were talking about the Spanish."

Custer acquiesced the point with a nod. "We were, but the Spanish are merely the catalyst. The *Cheyenne* are the key. I know you see that."

Meriwether's brow furrowed as he saw the map Custer knew was still fresh in his mind. The Gulf of Narváez, the

35

Kansa Plains, the rivers reaching northward, westward, thirsty for their mountain headwaters. And with each place, each river, each hill: a memory. It was Meriwether's turn now to relive his years on the prairie, and to drink again the intoxicating alienness of the place and its people. He shook his head to clear away the flood of recollection.

"But back in the field? I can't make any more difference now than I did before."

"Yes you can," Custer argued. "You still see it. You still know the land. And you know how best to use it, especially against the Spanish." He put his cane before him and leaned on it with both hands. "It's a critical time, John. Augusta will understand."

Meriwether jerked as if stung. He looked at Custer and then over his shoulder toward the house. Custer heard a sudden clatter of tableware and knew that their conversation had been overheard.

Meriwether's gaze drifted back to Custer's face. *"That,"* he said, "was dirty pool."

Custer did not flinch. He spoke in a low, quiet voice that only his old friend could hear. "I need you, John. I know you retired during that ugliness with Morton, and I can't press you into service. I can only ask. You can refuse me. That's your prerogative, and I know you want to. But if having to explain your refusal to Augusta makes it harder for you to say no, I'll take it. Dirty pool or not."

Meriwether stood there, the sun beating on the back of his neck, his eyes locked on Custer's face, the muscles of his jaw knotting, teeth grinding as he chewed on the matter. Custer let him ruminate. The decision—no matter how lopsided the argument had been—had to be Meriwether's. He would have to wait as Meriwether tested all the feints and stratagems, playing the game out in his mind.

The supper that followed was hearty and unprepossessing. A thick barley and onion soup, corn bread, and pork chops with apple sauce provided sufficient food to surround their idle chatter and fill any awkward pauses. Throughout the meal, Custer watched Meriwether and Augusta exchange glances, and several times they excused themselves to "see to something" in the kitchen. Each time they returned, Augusta's eyes were more red and the line of

Meriwether's mouth was drawn more taut.

When the meal was done, Libbie said, "Mrs. Meriwether, have you read the latest from Mr. Wilde?"

"Oh, yes, in Lippincott's. The story about the young man in the picture frame."

"Yes, that's the one. He read it to us when he visited us last spring."

"Visited!"

"Yes; let me tell you all about it." And with that, Libbie and Augusta retired to the sitting room where they would wait until the men had completed the day's business.

The three men glanced at one another across the table. Tarbox, as their titular host, laughed uncomfortably and rose from his chair.

"If you would rather I—"

"No," Meriwether said forcefully, surprising both Tarbox and Custer himself. The general smiled and motioned with his hand. "Please, Charles. Sit. Stay." He took the brandy bottle by the neck and poured a splash for Tarbox and then one for himself, knowing well enough not to bother with one for his president. He stared at the glass.

"If I do this," he said, "I do it properly."

Custer frowned. "What are you trying to say?"

Meriwether looked up. "I won't be hamstrung. We fight this my way. Cheyenne or Spaniard, red or white. You set the goal, but I make the field decisions."

Custer nodded. "All right," he said.

"And this time, if your son gets in my way, I'll crush him. Just like any other combatant. No special treatment for the President's wayward boy. Agreed?"

Custer was acutely aware that Tarbox was witness to the negotiation, and that the answer he was about to give would be recalled and corroborated, should it become an issue. If he refused, he'd lose the most capable and experienced Indian fighter he had, but if he agreed, he'd put his own son in peril for, if there was to be a war in the territory, young George was sure to be in the thick of it, fighting for his misguided principles. Meriwether's repugnance for George's treason would grant no quarter.

"Just like any other combatant," Custer said. "No special treatment, but neither will you single him out. You won't go gunning for him."

Meriwether chewed on the counter-proposal for several moments before he nodded and stuck out his hand.

"I'm your man," he said.

As Custer shook on the deal, he tried to convince himself that he hadn't just consigned his son to death.

Chapter 4

Tuesday, September 9th, AD 1890
Muelle de Caballeria
La Ciudad de la Habana, Cuba

"Hurry!"

Alejandro held the small lantern to guide his wife and daughter down the dark gangway to the pier. The rustle of the women's skirts echoed the sound of the nighttime waves lapping against the sea wall. Behind them came Roberto and Olivia. D'Avignon brought up the rear.

"Come along, now," Alejandro urged them. "No time to waste. The tide has already turned."

The cool air was thick with the scents of kelp and harbor mud. They made their way past net-draped barrels and shadowed stacks of crates, heading toward the lights of the tall triple-masted steamer at the pier's end. Alejandro noted its name with approval—*Emperatriz del Océano.* Men at fore and aft were readying the lines and the stack was belching smoke. Alejandro reached the boarding ramp and beckoned to his family.

"Pardon, sir," D'Avignon said, coming forward. "Not that one." He pointed to the other side of the pier. "That one."

Alejandro peered through the gloom toward the darkened ship across the broad dock and stepped closer, lantern held high, to get a better look.

The *Reina Caribeña* was a small, two-masted steamer with stains of rust discoloring her hull's cracked and peeling paint. The deck, where it wasn't cluttered by cargo and unkempt lines, looked slick and slippery. Most troubling to Alejandro's eye were the crew, standing idle, uninterested in making any preparations for departure, but who paid great attention to the newcomers, especially Alejandro's wife and daughter.

"No," Alejandro muttered to himself, then turned and said the same to D'Avignon. "No! I forbid it."

Roberto came up to his side. "Forbid what?"

"Forbid—" He gestured toward the crew, the disorder, the rust and peeling paint. "—that," he said.

"His Excellency," D'Avignon said with the barest of sneers, "is too fine for such a vessel."

"Don't you start that game with me," Alejandro warned, and the wily prospector raised his hands and stepped back.

"It's not a concern for me, Roberto," Alejandro continued. "It's the women. We can't subject them to such...conditions."

Roberto put a hand on his brother-in-law's shoulder. "We must. It's necessary. D'Avignon says—"

"'D'Avignon says,'" Alejandro mimicked, exasperated.

"Yes, D'Avignon says," Roberto went on. "He says that a ship of no apparent value has the best chance of running the blockade, and I agree. You would, too, if you would listen to reason." He pointed to the larger, finer *Emperatriz del Océano*. "She is our decoy."

"And this scow?" Alejandro said with a nod to the other ship.

"She's ugly, but she's fast. And D'Avignon made sure the crew made her presentable below decks. Look at her! Would you expect to find a Governor and Special Ambassador on that?"

Alejandro didn't like it, and he liked even less the fact that it made sense. *And* the fact that it was D'Avignon's plan. D'Avignon smiled and nodded when Alejandro looked his way. The man was becoming insolent. He would have to be watched in the coming days. Alejandro needed to remind him who was in charge.

"Hmph," he said, and left that as his final verdict on the entire subject.

The accommodations below had indeed been made suitable for female passengers. Floors were scrubbed to gleaming, linens were fresh, and the stale tobacco smoke that permeated the rest of the ship was only a vestigial scent among the perfumes of soap and rose water in the staterooms. Alejandro gave up his sleeping berth to Isabella; he would be spending the entire voyage at the rail, anyway, so it was no inconvenience to him. Isabella would be more comfortable with her mother in this strange place than on her own.

After seeing his family settled into their stateroom, Alejandro went above deck to get some air. The *Emperatriz* and the *Reina* set sail under a starry sky, the larger ship taking the lead. Alejandro's stomach was already queasy by the time they passed the fortifications at Castillo el Morro, and as they headed out to sea, he stared up at the immensity of the heavens. The pale swathe of the Milky Way was like a silver shawl draped across the sky. He picked out a few constellations—the square of Pegasus, the cross of the Swan—and noted the blue eye of Vega hanging in the northwest, but the distraction was only momentary; he was unable to ignore the relentless, unemotional power of the black ocean that surrounded him.

The *Reina* began to pitch and rock as she rode through crest and trough, and her smaller size only added to Alejandro's anxiety. When you set out to sea, he thought to himself, you roll the die and neither prayer nor riches can save you. On a larger ship like the *Emperatriz,* he might have been able to fool himself through some of the voyage, as her oaken sides and disciplined crew extended the illusion of safety. They might even have sighted the Tejano coast before he had to admit that they were little more than a bobbing cork on the restless water. But in a rusty bucket like the *Reina,* the truth was inescapable. Wind, storm, or a simple leak could spell their doom. At least the clear, moonless night meant calm weather, for a while, anyway.

Crewmen appeared and doused the lights along the bulkheads and rails. Alejandro looked around in alarm.

From fore to aft, lights were going out; the *Emperatriz*, too, was going dark, leaving only a single lamp off her stern for them to follow. He heard a footfall beside him and smelled smoke from a cigar.

"Excellency," D'Avignon said in greeting.

"What is it? Why are they doing that?"

"Oh, the running lights? Nothing to worry about, sir." The glowing tip of his cigar wove a gesture toward the *Emperatriz*. "We'll be sailing in her shadow until we pass the quarantine line. Hopefully, we'll slip past without an encounter."

Alejandro didn't want to know the other side of that wish. "How long until we pass the blockade?"

"Not long," D'Avignon said. "We want to get through before dawn." He put the cigar between his teeth and even in the dim light Alejandro could see his rakish smile. "Easier that way."

"Undoubtedly," Alejandro said and then felt his stomach begin its rebellion. "I wonder if you might do me the favor of taking that cigar downwind."

Alejandro was at the rail, suffering his second episode of nausea, when they heard whistles from the *Emperatriz*. The *Reina*'s crew appeared from the shadows, starlight gleaming from rifle barrels.

"Warship. Starboard bow," came the call from a speaking-trumpet off the *Emperatriz*'s stern. Crewmen relayed the information to the wheelhouse.

Alejandro crept forward, staring wide-eyed into the night, but he could only see the dark bulk of the *Emperatriz*'s sails against the shimmering starlight. The two ships ran in tandem, forequarters into the easterly wind, sails drawn taut as they plowed the waves. He felt a shudder in the rail as the captain ordered the engine room to build up steam. The crew were quiet, as intent on their study of the darkness as was he.

Then a bang, a pop, and a new star exploded to the north, bathing the *Emperatriz* and the *Reina* alike in its harsh, white light.

"Flare," one man cried, and bo'suns' whistles pierced the

sounds of wind and wave with piped orders.

Crewmen slung riflery over shoulders and put calloused hands to sheet and line. Alejandro could see no other ship, but in the swinging light of the falling flare, he saw a crewman aboard the *Emperatriz* signaling cryptic instructions. The *Reina* responded and came forward along the larger ship's port side to hide behind her bulk. Another flare burst in the sky, doubling the sharp shadows and deepening the night around them. Then Alejandro heard a distant siren, a mechanical wail that the wind could not produce. The signalman from the *Emperatriz* returned to the rail and drew his thumb across his throat and pointed north in a gesture that even Alejandro could comprehend.

Cut. Run.

The crew of the *Emperatriz* set about lighting her lamps as she turned her bow into the wind. Alejandro felt the deck tremble as the *Reina*'s captain commanded the engineers to engage the drive and bring her to ahead full. The ship veered to port, and while the crew moved smartly to reef the sails, the ship began to put distance between herself and her sacrificial lamb.

D'Avignon appeared at Alejandro's side.

"*Quel dommage,*" he said. "But that's why they are here."

Alejandro nodded toward the *Emperatriz,* her crew now shouting with mock surprise and outrage. "What will happen to them?" he asked.

"Eh," D'Avignon shrugged. "Nothing, *peut-être.* They have nothing of real value—just some light cargo of cloth and tobacco. Most likely they'll be turned around. The Americans haven't begun freebooting...at least not this close to Havana."

But then another set of flares lit the sky and all of them—*Emperatriz, Reina,* and the approaching American warship—were all as plain as bugs on a tiled floor. Bells rang and the warship's siren whooped. Smoke spewed from its stacks and it hove off from the *Emperatriz* and came before her bow in pursuit of the smaller quarry.

"Smarter than we expected," D'Avignon said of the American commander. "Now we'll see if our skipper was just bragging about this old girl's speed."

The *Reina* put her nose into the wind and lunged forward with all the rumbling power her engine could provide. The crew lashed every inch of sail tight against the spars, making her as sleek as possible.

Behind them, the American ship, broad of beam, bounced across the oncoming swells, her searchlight swaying up and down, side to side.

The captain of the *Reina* powered his ship across the troughs and split the crests with his narrow bow. He had not lied to D'Avignon; his "old girl" was fast, and within a quarter hour the warship was just a bright light stabbing into the darkness behind them.

The *Emperatriz,* far astern, had escaped as well. The American commander, having reached for what he guessed was the greater prize, had lost both.

"I wonder if he's cursing his decision," Alejandro asked aloud.

"Probably not," D'Avignon said. "I think he's savvy enough to see he made the right choice. Not his fault we were the fleeter vessel."

"Best choice in a bad situation."

"Mais oui."

Alejandro stared into the night and actually felt a moment of calm. A false dawn glowed in the east and the Milky Way was studded with tiny rosettes of pink all along its length. In the west, where the dark was deepest, stars hung like gemstones—diamonds, rubies, sapphires, topaz. He relished the sight, smelled the salt air, felt the cool wind on his face and neck. After the hectic and unsettling events that followed his audience with the Queen Regent, he finally felt at ease. The pieces he had been juggling where falling into place. He had a royal commission, he had been restored in society, his family and his name had been revived, and he now had the authority to regain his honor and his fortunes. And all for the glory of God and Spain as well. Everything was staged for success, and he was confident of achieving his goals.

When the nausea returned, he went to the rail with a happier mood.

At La Puerta De Luna, Alejandro entrusted his family to Roberto's hands.

"I'll see them safely home," Roberto promised, and Alejandro knew he would.

"Be careful," was all that Victoria said when they made their goodbyes. He kissed the fine, pale skin of her perfect hands and regretted the months that would soon separate them.

"I shall make you proud," he said.

"You already do," she assured him.

Roberto took the families westward, toward Albuquerque and eventually to the vice-regal court at San Francisco, while Alejandro headed north along the Tejano coast toward Cimmaron, Apishapa, and the staging grounds along the frontier.

Hours later, he was seated in a stifling hot carriage, re-reading the telegraph messages that he had picked up at port.

D'Avignon peered over at them in interest. "Do you know this general?" he asked as whips cracked and the carriage swerved along the rough coastal road.

"Pereira?" Alejandro shook his head. "No. I've never met him. Roberto told me that he is one of the viceroy's protégés; young, well-favored, but relatively inexperienced. I know the priest, though." He pulled out another telegraph message. "Father Velasquez is an old warhorse himself. He and I campaigned together, during the Tejano conflicts."

"Still a priest?" D'Avignon asked. "Not a bishop by now?"

Alejandro smiled. "Some men are born soldiers, even if they choose the path of God."

The carriage rattled along, and Alejandro enjoyed the ride as much as possible. It was infinitely better than being on the high seas, and it would also be his last bit of comfort before the miles of hard riding that were ahead of him once they reached the frontier. The future would be full of rough living and few amenities, but he reminded himself of all he would achieve. D'Avignon, in the seat across from him, posed a much greater challenge. He was critical to the success of Alejandro's financial goals, but he had to be controlled. Alejandro eyed the telegrams and smiled. With Velasquez in the picture, reining in this "useful" man might

45

be a much simpler task. Velasquez could put the fear of God into anyone, even a scoundrel like D'Avignon.

Alejandro closed his eyes and began to plan.

Chapter 5

Plum Moon, Waxing
Four Years after the Cloud Fell
Headwaters of the Red Paint River
Alliance Territory

George dug his heel into the walker's side. The massive beast banked in a sharp, turf-tearing curve and powered back toward the herd, legs pumping, ribs heaving beneath her rider's thighs. The walker had grown lean during George's trip to Spain and now they both needed to hunt— and hunt well—to prepare for the coming winter.

The bison were pounding down the hillside, hooves clicking as they ran. The cows and their calves were deep in the dense heart of the herd while young males and old veteran bulls ranged along the dusty fringes, eyes alert, heavy heads ready to turn and rake horns along an attacker's flank.

Yips and hunting cries slashed through the bisons' thunder. Whistlers trumpeted as they dashed in and out of the fleeing herd, bringing their riders in range for a killing shot. Some of the older riders still used bow and arrow to bring down their buffalo, but the *pop-pop* of rifles was everywhere this season. War and politics had made it a difficult year for hunting and the younger men opted for what worked over what was traditional. Their families need-ed meat for the winter, and they could sing praise over the spirit of a bison shot dead by a bullet just as easily as over one brought down with an arrow in his heart.

George worked the lever on his own repeating rifle and slapped his walker's flank. The walker bellowed—the blast of an angry locomotive—and pushed her bulk in pursuit of the retreating herd.

They rode into the thick cloud of dust, crossing dark earth shredded by a hundred thousand hooves. Two young bulls trailing the herd panicked at the monster's approach, peeling off from the rest to gain room to maneuver. The walker roared again and turned to follow.

Barrel level, knees tight against the wicker saddle, feet in the taut riding ropes, George readied himself for the mo-ment when the two bulls split up. The walker put on as much speed as she could—a final burst to close the gap. The nearest bull saw her coming and leapt completely over the back of the other bull to escape. The second bull fal-tered, stumbled. The walker lunged. Tooth-filled jaws snagged the second bull's hind leg while George tracked the first. He aimed, fired, and the first bull went down as well. George leapt to the ground and both he and his walker moved in to finish their kills.

Within minutes the herd was gone, a rising cloud of choking dust and a wide path of torn earth marking their route west. Over the rise, whistlers appeared carrying the families who would butcher the kills, celebrate each bison's sacrifice, and sing their fallen spirits into the next world.

George spied Mouse Road as she topped the rise. Speaks While Leaving was with her, and the two women rode down to greet him.

"She took one for herself," George said, pointing to his walker as she crouched on the prairie grass, bloody jaws working on her gory meal. "And I brought down another. Over there."

"Two for us, then?" Mouse Road smiled and threw her arms around his neck. "That is very good news." He held her tight, flushed with pride, and dizzy with love for his new wife. She slapped his hand when it roamed too far from propriety and laughed as she spun out of his grasp.

Later, she signed. Then she motioned to her former sister-in-law.

"Speaks While Leaving wanted to help, since she has no other family, now." She sounded unsure of herself.

Speaks While Leaving peered at him through her short, unruly hair. She glanced around at other women from the Tree People Band who were riding out onto the hunting ground, meeting husbands and brothers.

Speaks While Leaving had been detached recently. Whenever George had seen her she had been silent, alone, almost as if she was avoiding her neighbors. For years she had been a problematic figure due to her gift of prescience; men avoided her company, fearful that her great power would overwhelm their own and leave them defenseless in battle. Now, cast aside by her husband, in mourning over her daughter's death, and in contempt of the Council's demands, she was bad luck personified. George realized that her isolation during the past weeks had not been completely self-imposed.

He reached out and put a gentle hand on her shoulder. "You are most welcome," he said. "I am glad to see you back among us."

Her smile was tentative and sad, but it lingered. Then she set her jaw. "My thanks," she said, and turned to join Mouse Road and begin the work at hand.

They worked at the first kill, splitting the hide down the spine to get the tenderest meat, and then skinning the carcass, setting the organs aside for special attention. At each task, they sang to the spirit of the bull, thanking him for the sacrifice that would keep the family fed, clothed, and sheltered through the winter ahead. George heard such songs across the hunting ground, grateful voices laying down respectful words beneath the joy and celebration that followed successful days of hunting.

But a dissonant chorus of yipping shouts cut across the prairie, and everyone looked up from their work. George shaded his eyes against the sun as he saw a half-dozen soldiers ride up on the low spine of the eastward hill. They were patrol riders, and their sudden appearance here was not good news. The group separated as they headed out onto the plain, each man seeking a different target. One rode

49

toward George.

"One Who Flies," the rider called to George. "You must come."

"What is it?" George asked.

"The Iron Shirts," he answered. "They ride toward us. You are wanted."

The Spanish, George thought to himself. *Here? Now?*

He did not know what this sudden appearance meant, but if Spaniards were involved it could easily go very wrong. He needed to be there, if only to provide diplomatic translation. He turned to Mouse Road, but she anticipated him.

"Go," she said. "My other mother and her daughters will help us. But take your walker. We need the whistlers."

George started to argue, but she was right. The women needed the whistlers to roll and move the carcasses as they were butchered, and then to cart everything home on a travois. He looked over at his walker. She had finished gorging on her kill and lay nearby, basking in the sun, her eyes half-lidded in gluttonous stupor. She was not going to be pleased.

He walked over to her. The ground was soaked with blood and gore, as was her head, maw, and the hind feet she had used to hold down the body as she tore it apart. Her belly was distended with her meal, and gobbets of dark flesh hung from her teeth. She was grotesque.

Four years ago, George knew he would likely have pissed himself if he'd been within ten feet of such a creature, but now he walked over to her and kicked her in the ribs.

"*Nóheto,*" he said.

The white membrane across her eye slid down and she skewered him with her yellow-eyed gaze.

"Now," he said, and beckoned her up with a lifted hand. "Let's go."

If she wanted, she could have reached out and bitten that hand clean off or disemboweled him with a twitch of her outstretched foot. But she did not. Such was the tie between rider and walker.

George had bonded with her years ago. Her old bond-rider had died during the Battle of Cumberland Gap, leaving her bereft in the midst of war. The image of that day was still etched in his memory: she stood ten feet tall, breathing hard from the climb up the mountainside. At her feet lay the bloodied body of Dull Knife, her rider, shot dead in an ambush by the bluecoat soldiers. Oblivious to the fighting all around her, she leaned down and nosed her rider's lifeless body, breathing in the scent of blood and death. Then she lifted her head to brush the lower limbs of ancient maples and roared; a harsh, howling sound that chilled George's blood and brought the battle to a sudden stop. To the trees that towered above and the sky beyond she bellowed out her rage and grief, and then, with a quick eye, she spied the nearest bluecoat, ran forward, and tore him in two. The fight was rejoined, but did not last much longer.

After the fight had ended and the walkers were exhausted, Storm Arriving grasped George's arm and shoved him to stand before her.

George stood there as Storm Arriving slowly backed away.

"Face her," Storm Arriving whispered. "Meet her eye. Show her your resolve."

A walker was an immense presence, even when bonded to a rider, but the animal George stood before was now a rogue; a free being, unbound, in pain, wounded in body and spirit alike. His reflex was to turn, to run, but he decided to trust Storm Arriving instead of his fear, thinking not of what the beast could do, but of what they had come to do, of their goal, and of his desire to see justice done for the People.

The walker was lying down, breathing heavily from her exertions. Even though she was on the ground, she could still look down at him, glaring at him first with one eye and then the other like some gargantuan raptor. She opened her mouth. George heard her intake of breath and braced himself. She growled at him, a deep, resentful sound, and he felt her anger in his own heart. He stood his ground, letting her grief and rage wash over him, his skin vibrating with the strength of her pain, and his breath shortened by impassioned empathy.

She extended her neck, coming closer to him. Her knife-bladed teeth were before his shoulder. She blinked, the white membrane flicking across the great yellow eye that was close enough to touch. At Storm Arriving's instruction, George scratched her dusty skin, staring into that eye, his heart pounding, sweat sudden on his skin. The walker breathed in, then out, her breath bathing George, her exhalation warm in the cool forest clearing. And then the tight knot in George's stomach just...went away. The walker made a rumbling sound in her breast and lifted her head.

"Good," Storm Arriving said. "She is yours now."

George had never asked what might have happened otherwise.

Since that day she had been bonded to George and he to her; two individuals with one purpose. According to tradition, she had been given no name, but was merely "the walker bonded to One Who Flies," or, as Mouse Road had said, simply "your walker." But George knew that no ownership or mastery was implied by that label. She may have been "his" walker, but only so far as that distinguished her from all other walkers. She was still an individual and as such deserved respect.

Which she now demanded.

George looked to the clouds above. "Yes, you're right," he sighed. He walked around her small upper arms with their three-inch long claws and gently rubbed the silk-haired skin of her shoulder. "I know you have just eaten and don't want to move, but I need you. The Iron Shirts have come." He let all his anxiety at the situation bubble to the surface; his fears, his hopes, and his emotions made his heart pound and his skin flush. His walker sensed his mood, and in a moment she rolled to her feet and stood, ready to ride.

George stepped up onto her thigh and settled onto the wicker and ropes that formed the rudimentary saddle that kept him from sliding down her spine. Her breathing was labored from such activity so soon after gorging, but she did not fight his will as he directed her to move.

"Let's go," he said, and she stepped into motion, taking him up the ridge toward the patrol riders. One Bear was there, as was Two Roads, war chief of the Kit Fox soldiers, and several other chiefs of the bands that were still in residence. The other riders were not bothered by the close presence of a walker, for she was obviously sated and would not pose a problem for their whistlers. For some, though, their feelings about George were not as benign.

"I suppose you must come," Two Roads said with condescension. "After all, you are the reason they are here."

George frowned but did not otherwise react to the sting. It would serve no purpose. Besides, the remark was, for the most part, true.

They headed off at a trot. The walker lumbered and huffed as she worked to keep pace, but the whistlers slowly pulled ahead. A few miles from the hunting site George spied other patrol riders who rode in to join them. The massive drake ridden by Storm Arriving was unmistakable.

They rode for many miles, the whistlers always about a bowshot ahead, until they stopped short. George caught up to them just as he saw, emerging from a shallow vale a league distant, the Spaniards.

It was a large group, more than just an expeditionary force. Two files of cavalry flanked a company of infantrymen, and coming into view were wagons, some with men and many with supplies.

Storm Arriving spun his whistler and came up to where George's walker stood. "Was it not enough that we had the bluecoats to fight?" he asked. "Did you need to bring us yet another enemy?"

George looked to the side in respectful deference. "They come as allies, not enemies, if you will receive them as such."

Storm Arriving snorted in derision. "You have been gulled by the Trickster," he said. "He has drawn webs across your eyes, and now you see light as dark, and call the moon sun." He raised a hand in exasperation. "Between you and my former wife, we are surely lost."

George toed his walker a step closer. "If you approach them in this way, you will create the thing you fear."

Storm Arriving glared at George, an eye-to-eye challenge that George refused to meet. "Hunh," was all the soldier said, and then turned his whistler to rejoin the others.

They waited for the Spaniards to see them. Finally, they did, and a small group of riders detached from the main force and rode in their direction. Cavalrymen escorted officers and a few civilians up to the hilltop, but the Spaniards had obviously never met with Alliance riders, before. Their horses pranced and shied as they approached the lizard-like mounts of the People. When they were within fifty yards Storm Arriving's drake stretched out his neck and delivered a low, trumpeting call that made the hair on the back of George's neck stand up. The horses of the Spanish cavalry immediately halted, some rearing. A half dozen men were thrown and several horses—with or without riders—spun and tore up the turf in retreat.

The patrol soldiers and chiefs chuckled, but George knew that humiliation was a bad start to this relationship. "Stop it," he said in a harsh whisper. "You only make it more difficult."

Storm Arriving did not respond.

The Spanish cavalrymen got their horses under control and the troop split into two groups, each wheeling to take a flanking position twenty paces from the chiefs as the officers and civilians came forward to meet the delegation.

The military officers approached first; a colonel with a brace of lieutenants, all resplendent in their pale blue uniforms despite the dust of travel. The civilians came up behind them.

First was an older man with grey hair and the black cassock of a clergyman. Around his neck hung a rough leather lanyard with a simple wooden cross, but the heavy gold ring on his finger spoke of his true power and position.

Next to ride forward was another man in black, but this face George knew well. Alejandro looked uncomfortable in the saddle, though he tried to hide it with a straight back and a pleasant smile. George did not know if the ambassador's discomfort came from his days in an unaccustomed saddle or from lingering guilt for his part in the treachery at the Havana harbor, nor did he care; the mere fact that he was uneasy was good enough for George.

The men remained on their horses as the colonel moved forward and in a loud, clear voice, made the introductions.

"My name," he began, speaking in French, "is Colonel Baltazar Rolando, and I bring greetings from Her Glorious Catholic Majesty, María Cristina Deseada Enriqueta Felicidad, Queen Regent of Spain, to the indigenous leaders of the Cheyenne Alliance. She presents to you His Excellency

Señor Alejandro Miguel Tomás Silveira-Rioja, Special Ambassador to the Cheyenne Alliance; and the Reverend Father Domingo Alberto Simeon Velasquez, envoy from the Mother Church in Rome, with the hope that together we may build peace and a lasting friendship between our two nations."

George said nothing, but waited. When One Bear signed, asking him to translate, George passed on the introductions for the chiefs who did not speak the Trader's Tongue.

"Ask them what they are doing here," Storm Arriving said.

"You know what they are doing here," George said.

"I want to hear it from them."

This first meeting required a deft hand, and Storm Arriving was spoiling for a fight.

"I am not translating your words," George said. "I speak for One Bear, who speaks for the Great Council."

Storm Arriving glared back over his shoulder at George, then looked to One Bear. "Ask them," he said, his anger putting a hard edge to his words. "Make them say what it is they want here." Then he pointed to Alejandro with his war club. "Especially that one. Ask *him* what he really wants here."

Alejandro's face blanched at being singled out with such vehemence. The colonel frowned and his officers began to look edgy. George tried to keep calm, but his walker sensed his agitation. Horses whickered in fear as the bloodstained monster took a step forward. Lines on both sides wavered; horses danced, whistlers fluted, and then George saw the face of a man behind Alejandro, a familiar face with a familiar smirk. Fury filled him, and he forgot about diplomacy, first impressions, and new alliances. He could think only of that face, and of the betrayals, pain, and loss that always followed the man who owned it.

Vincent D'Avignon.

Before George could control his emotions his walker reacted. She pulled in a massive breath and bellowed it out in an ear-splitting roar. The parley broke apart; horses scattered, whistlers bounded away from the raging walker. Alejandro kept his saddle as his mount fled the scene, but D'Avignon fell from his plunging horse and rolled as he hit the ground. The walker took two steps and lunged.

"No!" George said, putting all the restraint he could manage into the command. "Leave him!"

The beast held her strike, halting just above the prostrate form. D'Avignon whimpered as he lay face down in the dirt, hands curled over the back of his neck. George slipped down off his walker's back, pulled his knife, reached down, and grabbed a handful of D'Avignon's hair.

"What in blazes are you doing?" someone asked in a loud, imperious voice.

It was a moment before George realized that the voice was speaking in English. He looked and saw Father Velasquez standing, fists on hips, eyes ablaze with righteous indignation.

George squinted at the man.

"Well?" Velasquez said. "I demand an explanation."

"Au secours!" D'Avignon cried.

"Shut your mouth," George ordered with a tug that pulled his victim's head back. He looked over at the priest. "I am not interested in providing you with an explanation."

"I can see that," Velasquez said. "Nevertheless, you will provide one."

George brought his knife around to D'Avignon's throat. D'Avignon's lips moved as he whispered pleading prayers. George smiled. "All right, Father. Do you want it before I kill this cur? Or after?"

"You will not kill him."

"No?"

"No."

George heard the rumble in his walker's throat and his smile tightened. "And you know this how?"

"If you intended to kill him," Velasquez said, "you would not have hesitated. You want him cowering, not dead. You want his terror, not his head."

Slowly, George took his blade from D'Avignon's throat. He straightened and put the knife in its sheath. With a motion he told his walker to keep her prey from leaving, and D'Avignon whimpered as the beast leaned down and glared at him with a large, unblinking eye.

George walked over and stood before the priest. They were of a height, though the Spaniard was stockier and silvered at the temples. There was a great discipline in the priest's steady-eyed composure; George had met this type before, during his years in the Army of the United States. A "true believer" George's father would have called him, though this man seemed to temper his ideals with realism.

"This man is not to be trusted," George said. "He is a betrayer, a liar, and a thief."

"None of which is a capital offense," Velasquez countered.

George forced himself to relax. "True," he said. "Though as you said, I probably would not have executed him. He is guilty of much more, but those crimes were not against me or my people."

"Your people?" Velasquez asked.

George met his gaze. "Yes," he said, and pulled aside the yoke of his tunic and pinched at the exposed pale skin. "Do not make the mistake of thinking that this makes me one of you." He motioned to the chiefs and soldiers who had gathered again behind him. "*Those* are my people. Not you." He spat toward D'Avignon. "And definitely not that. Understood?"

Velasquez nodded. "I understand you."

George returned to his walker and leapt to thigh and saddle. "Please, sir," he said once more in the Trader's Tongue. "Please extend my deep apologies to Colonel Rolando and His Excellency. My walker became unsettled and, well, I fear horses do not herd well with our mounts. I hope that they will forgive this...interruption, and that we may continue our introductions under calmer circumstances."

Velasquez nodded, and George noted the hint of a smile.

Yes, George said to himself. *You have played this game before, and better than your homespun appearance suggests.*

"I will pass along your apologies," Velasquez said, speaking also in French. "Perhaps you can provide a few riders to guide us to a place we might make our camp?"

"I will pass the request to our Council." Then he slapped his walker's shoulder and toed her around so fast her tail cracked the air over D'Avignon's head. He urged her toward the knot of chiefs.

One Bear frowned, though both Two Roads and Storm Arriving grinned broadly.

"You have given Long Teeth a proper welcome," Storm Arriving said, referring to D'Avignon.

"It was shameful," One Bear scolded. "I do not understand you, One Who Flies. You and Speaks While Leaving, you force us toward an alliance with the Iron Shirts, you tell us to treat them like friends, and when they arrive you treat them like old enemies!"

George signed his agreement. He didn't want One Bear to replace him with another interpreter, so he acquiesced. "I have apologized to them, and now I apologize to you and the other grandfathers. I was surprised to see Long Teeth again, and my anger bested me. It will not happen again."

One Bear could not argue with such an abject confession of regret. He signed acceptance and turned to ride back to camp.

"The Iron Shirts would like some of our soldiers to show them where to camp."

One Bear thought, then turned to Two Roads. "Keep those domesticated elk they ride away from our whistlers," he said. "And keep them all downwind and downstream. We don't want them fouling our water. They are a dirty people with no thought for others."

The chiefs headed back toward camp and Two Roads took his Kit Fox soldiers to show the Iron Shirts where to camp.

George watched them go in their separate directions— leaders of the People and of the Iron Shirts—and wondered if this was a good thing or a bad thing that had happened today. He was not convinced that the Spanish were necessary to the ongoing safety of the People, but Speaks While Leaving was, and managing their presence here was going to prove quite a challenge. Seeing D'Avignon, though, had tinged it all with a darker hue, and now George saw much more of the cloud's shadow than he could of its silver lining.

Chapter 6

Wednesday, September 24th, AD 1890
Advance Camp
Spanish Expeditionary Forces
Near the Red Paint River
Alliance Territory

Alejandro didn't remember it being like this.

His memories of army life were fond ones: days in the saddle, the fresh breeze in his face, the scent of leather in his nostrils; evenings around warm campfires, eating hearty meals; nights under starry heavens, cozy beneath a taut tent that kept off the midnight dew. Somehow, in his mind, traveling with a cadre of soldiers through open country had acquired a favorable patina, like the craquelure of an old painting that fogs and obscures the actual details of the scene.

But now those details were apparent in sharpest clarity. The bug bites, the smell of sweat and smoke and manure, the grit that embedded every wrinkle and crevice, the cold nights, the disagreeable food with its even more disagreeable indigestion. He experienced it all again, anew, and wondered why his memory had lied to him.

Rainclouds had shadowed them into the Territory, and the clouds opened up just as they had started to make camp, turning a difficult task into a misery. They were a half-mile from the nearest pickets of the main encampment, a distance that put the Cheyenne's lack of trust into physical perspective, but Alejandro had not expected to be welcomed as an old friend among these people. The history between Spain and the natives of the New World had been violent and ugly, and only the past century of relative quiet between the Crown and the Cheyenne allowed him to even contemplate this alliance. And so he sat on a camp-stool in his sagging, sodden tent, wrapped in a musty-smelling blanket of rough wool, listening to his guts gurgle, and looked out at the gloom of the early morning while he contemplated what needed to be done first.

The decision was made for him, announced by the approach of sloshing footsteps. Alejandro stood as a handful of black-frocked men appeared: Father Velasquez and four of his fellow clergymen. Along with them, standing to the rear like a magpie among the crows, was D'Avignon.

"Excellency," Velasquez said with a respectful nod. "May we come in?"

"Certainly," Alejandro said, and beckoned them inside.

His tent was not large, but was ample for a small meeting. Stool, cot, and trunk were arranged around his camp desk to provide seating for his guests. The priests entered and sat, and then D'Avignon poked his head inside the tentflap.

"Tea for your guests, Excellency?" D'Avignon asked in rough Spanish.

"Yes," Alejandro said; the man's ubiquitous presence was annoying, but hot tea would be very welcome. As D'Avignon left, Alejandro turned to Velasquez. "I'm glad you've come. We must discuss our next steps. Your mission here, as I see it—"

"Respectfully, Don Alejandro," Velasquez said, "I already know our mission here. It is quite plain." He turned and checked with his fellows, all of whom nodded sagely. "We are here to bring these savage heathen into the glory of God's light and comfort. It is a task we have performed before and, with His grace, will be able to perform many times in the future."

"Yes, I see. Thank you. You have put it quite succinctly," Alejandro said. "I wanted to tell you, though, how important this mission is to us."

"Excellency, the importance you place upon this mission is irrelevant. We would work to bring these unfortunates to Christ with the same fervor, even if you considered it to be the height of folly."

Alejandro eyed the priest and was about to speak when D'Avignon returned with a kettle and a stack of tin cups. Tea was poured and served. Alejandro breathed in the aromatic steam and let it calm his nerves.

"Reverend Father," he said after a moment, putting a pleasant smile on his face. "Perhaps I wasn't clear. When I said I wanted to tell you how important this mission was to us, I did not mean to myself alone, or even myself and your superiors in the Church. I meant 'us,' as in 'Her Majesty and I.'" He let that sink in for a moment, but Velasquez did not register any change in expression, so he continued.

"Father, you and I have known one another a long time. We have seen many campaigns together. I won't mince words with you. Her Majesty has taken a special interest in these people; a personal interest, in fact. So let me warn you now: if she hears of any activities such as occurred among the Yaqui or the tribes of the Tejano, she will never forgive you. Not ever." He raised a hand to forestall the priest's rebuttal. "And before you tell me how unimportant our regent's earthly forgiveness is to you, I shall say that regardless the state of your immortal soul, a royal disapprobation such as she can bestow will make your remaining years here in this world a trial indeed. Especially when it can be easily avoided by reining in the more—energetic—methods your fellows have been known to employ." He leaned back and sipped his tea.

"I hope I have clarified my meaning, Father."

Velasquez's demeanor had not altered, though Alejandro noted the pulse stronger in his neck.

"You tie our hands, Excellency."

Alejandro chuckled. "Not at all," he said. "I'm confident that you and your colleagues can devise sufficiently persuasive measures that do not include beating, flogging, or any of the harsher techniques you have used in the past. The rest of our force arrives soon. They bring with them ample supplies—food, liquor, tobacco, and such—to ensure the natives' full and enthusiastic cooperation. Look at it this way, Father," and he leaned closer to imply a conspiratorial tone. "We don't expect you to drop the stick, just to use more carrots." The priest's dour expression remained, and Alejandro leaned back again.

"We need these people on our side. Willingly on our side. Neither Her Majesty nor I will countenance anything that puts this alliance in jeopardy." He stood and his guests all rose in response. "I appreciate your coming to chat with me, Father, and I hope you will accompany me today when I go to speak with the chiefs of the Cheyenne Council. Ostensibly, I go to request riders to help guide our army northward, but I also hope we can discuss topics of more interest to you. There are many souls here that need our help in finding the way to salvation."

At last Velasquez's expression lightened. "I am glad to hear you say so, Excellency. I feared you were only interested in the more...temporal aspects of this expedition."

Alejandro reached out and put a hand on Velazquez's shoulder. "Believe me, I place equal importance upon our spiritual goals. I have made a solemn vow, Father—a vow to our Lord in Heaven—to bring as many souls to his Church as possible."

And finally Velasquez's deeply-lined features turned upward into a grin. "That is good news, Excellency. Very good news. I am sure that, together, we can achieve great things."

Alejandro nodded and saw the clergymen out. He heard them talking enthusiastically as they squelched their way through the rain-soaked grass, and he sighed.

One worry down, he thought to himself.

"D'Avignon," he said.

"Yes, Excellency."

"You have chosen your men?"

D'Avignon came up close behind Alejandro. "Yes. Ten strong backs await your orders."

"And they can be trusted?"

The trader laughed his rogue's laugh. "Definitely, Señor. These men love their country, but gold sways them, too. And your offer carries the best of both worlds—to get rich in the service of Spain."

"Good," Alejandro said. "Very good." He smiled toward the rain and the mountains hidden behind the low, grey clouds. "Prepare to take them out soon. I'd like to keep you away from One Who Flies and avoid further...complications. Do you have any locations in mind?"

"Oh, yes," D'Avignon said. "I prospected this area with One Who Flies years ago. Up in those hills—" He giggled like a boy. "The creekbeds glitter with gold dust."

Alejandro shook his head. "No," he said. "Those hills have been interdicted by the Council. They are...holy...or something to the natives."

"Then it's perfect!"

Alejandro frowned. "What do you mean?"

D'Avignon winked. "Don't you see, Excellency? One Who Flies will never think to look for me up there."

Chapter 7

Plum Moon, Full
Four Years after the Cloud Fell
Borderlands near the Moonshell River
Alliance Territory

Storm Arriving rode to the top of the ridge and called the squad to a halt. Around him, the forty Kit Fox soldiers reined in and awaited his command. He pulled his knees out from under the first-rope and stood, balancing on his whistler's back to get a better view.

The coastal lands were grey with drizzle from a low roof of clouds that brought visibility down to a dozen bowshots. He shielded his eyes from the mist with his hands and peered into the distance.

The land rolled away from him. Scrub dotted the slopes with dark hummocks, like tassels on the uneven prairie blanket of gold and green. Close by, patches of blood-drop flowers stood out like fresh wounds on the land. Farther away, somewhere beyond the veil of weather, lay the Moonshell River and the army of the Iron Shirts.

Behind him Grey Bear, his second-in-command, griped about his empty stomach, which encouraged the men to grumble themselves. Storm Arriving cleared his throat and everyone—man and whistler alike—fell silent once more.

The mist whispered as it fell on the sodden grass. The southerly breeze was warm and flavored with salt from the inland sea. Ahead, a quail shifted in her hiding spot beneath a bush and, to his right, a toad creaked. Then, faintly from within the melding of grey cloud and gold grass, he discerned a sound that did not belong: a rhythmic metallic clang.

"There," he said, pointing. "Half a hand's ride that way."

He sat down, slipped his feet in the loops and his knees under the first-rope, and touched his whistler into motion. The others followed without question or word, the only sounds the creak of rope and the gentle thud of whistler's feet in the wet grass. Grouse and quail flushed from hiding on drumbeat wings, curving away from the party's path through the unmarked land.

They neared the crest of a rise and Storm Arriving held up a hand to bring the group to a halt once more. They could all hear the clatter of equipment and the chaos of voices that typified *vé'hó'e* movement.

"Slowly," he said to the others. "We do not wish to startle them." A few of the men chuckled, and they all followed him as he nudged his drake to walk up and over the hilltop.

The Moonshell River was a twisted plait beneath the clouded sky, its banks festooned with swaying stands of cottonwood, birch, and sweetgum trees. Draped like a dark cloth through the flatland on the near side of the river was the army of the Iron Shirts: a long, dark stain of men, horses, and wagons that churned the ground with their passage. Storm Arriving and his guide party lined up on the crest, making themselves visible against the sky to the soldiers on the flat below, but the army trudged on, oblivious to their arrival.

"And we need the help of these?" Grey Bear asked.

Storm Arriving understood the resentment, but also saw something that his fellow Kit Fox did not.

"Look," he instructed the others, pointing to the columns of men below them. "Upon each shoulder. Do you see? Repeating rifles. Each man has his own. And there." He pointed toward the rear where men pushed large-wheeled wagons. "Look closely, and you will see mounted rifles, just like the bluecoats have."

Grey Bear shook his head. "But look at them. The ones on foot are nearly asleep, and the ones on horse are too few."

"I agree," Storm Arriving said, and smiled at their surprise. "But follow my eye, as I look at all these sleepwalking Iron Shirts, from the first man carrying their flag to the last man pushing a rolls-along, and imagine with me the many bluecoat bullets it would take to bring them all down. And now, imagine how angry that would make the Iron Shirts, and how many more sleepwalkers would come to stand above their dead."

He regarded his Kit Fox brethren. "All my life the People have fought and bled against the bluecoats. All my life, all my father's life, the life of my father's father, and beyond even that time. We have met them head on, hit their flank, and taken their rear guard, but still we bleed, and still the bluecoats continue to come. We have fought them alone and with the help of our brother tribes. We have joined with old rivals like the Crow People and the Wolf People, and still we bleed, and still they come. There is only one nation who hates the bluecoats as much as we do." He waved a hand toward the army below.

"Let *them* bleed for a while."

A bugle sounded, and the Kit Fox turned their attention back toward the valley.

"Finally, they see us," Red Wing said.

"Stow rifles and bows. Spears up. Move with me, slowly. We are expected, but *vé'hó'e* can be very stupid."

The Iron Shirt officers bellowed orders and soldiers moved to take up defensive positions. Ranks of riflemen stood or knelt as they made weapons ready, cavalrymen cantered their mounts to take posts on either side of the approaching Kit Fox. As Storm Arriving walked his forty soldiers to within a bowshot, he noted the condition of the force before them. Their faces were tired and besmirched with soot, and their pale blue uniforms were muddy from marching through the first rain of autumn. The men with the roll-alongs halted and leaned against the shoulder-high wheels, watching with yawns and sleepy eyes. All around, Storm Arriving saw faces that were older, with grey at chin and temple, while other faces were wide-eyed and unsure;

hardly anywhere did he see the set, steady eye of a true warrior, and this was especially true of the riders with the tall hats and gold braid on their uniforms.

"This is what they send to face the bluecoats?" Storm Arriving said under his breath.

"These are only good for catching bullets," Grey Bear groused.

"They'll surely do that," said another.

"Halt," Storm Arriving said, both to stop their words and their progress. He'd allowed himself to become distracted by the condition of the Iron Shirts' army and now refocused on his duty.

The Kit Fox were ranged in a single row, well within range of the riflemen, and they were downwind so the whistlers caused no problems with the Iron Shirts' mounts. Their position was a statement of trust, but Storm Arriving could not be sure the message was understood. He raised a hand in greeting and toed his drake a few steps forward from the squad. Three of the Iron Shirt officers nudged their mounts a few paces in advance of their line.

"*Soyez les bienvenus à notre pays,*" he said in the Trader's Tongue. The Iron Shirts glanced at one another. "*Est-ce que vous comprenez ce que je dis?*" Storm Arriving asked. "*Parlez-vous le français?*" Uncomprehending stares were the only reply. Storm Arriving felt his temper begin to rise.

The young officer with the most gold on his uniform waved a hand as if brushing away a fly, and began to speak rapidly in a language that was filled with burrs and odd lisping hisses. To Storm Arriving, it sounded like the Iron Shirt's tongue was too big for his mouth; he had heard the Iron Shirts' language before, but never heard it spoken so fast. The officer's face was unwrinkled, his moustache thin, and his hands were soft and pale. His body was untested by combat, but his demeanor was one of confidence and superiority. He completed his speech with a gesture toward Storm Arriving and then stopped, obviously waiting for a response.

"Spirits give me strength," he said, biting down on his anger, and then spoke to the Iron Shirts in signs that even a drunken idiot could understand.

"You," he said, pointing at the officer. "Follow." He made

his fingers walk up his forearm. "This," he said, and pointed to his drake's hind end. Then he turned his mount and nudged him into motion. His soldiers followed suit. They moved a few strides ahead and Storm Arriving looked back. The Iron Shirts hadn't moved.

"Come!" he ordered with word and gesture. "This way!" He kicked is drake into motion and didn't really care if the Iron Shirts followed them back to the Council or not, but the shouted commands and the *ton-ton-ton* of bugles told him his point had been made.

The Iron Shirts moved slowly and no amount of gesticulation or pointing to the cloud-banked fire of the descending sun could urge them to a greater speed. At evening, still with a hand's worth of light remaining to the waning day, the Iron Shirts called a halt. They had covered only a fourth the distance Storm Arriving and his own party could have traveled on foot, and it became clear that this was going to be a long, tedious journey back to where the People had camped along the Red Paint River.

"Send two riders home," he told Grey Bear. "The Council should know of this delay. And send scouts out to the east. I do not want to be surprised while rolling this stone across the prairie." Grey Bear appointed soldiers to the tasks, and then ordered the others to gather wood for an evening fire. Storm Arriving watched the Iron Shirts set up their own encampment.

"Do they do everything so slowly?" Grey Bear asked, coming up beside his war chief.

But Storm Arriving had noticed something. "Watch them," he said, and pointed to individuals, first this one, then another. "It is like a dream dance," he said. "It is slow, but each step is repeated. Look." He pointed. "That one with all the gold rope starts it all. He speaks to one of those men with the feathered hats, and they speak to the men with the many brass buttons, and they speak to others. Each man is told what to do; no man thinks for himself."

Grey Bear laughed quietly. "It is like they have never camped the night before."

"And they look like they intend to stay until the next moon." He pointed to the Iron Shirts being set out as picket guards. "Pass the word: do not wander toward the Iron

Shirts in the night. They'll shoot at anything."

Grey Bear laughed again. "You think they could hit anything?"

Storm Arriving shrugged. "With that many rifles, even a blind army could hit a bull's eye, just by luck alone."

Chapter 8

Plum Moon, Waning
Four Years after the Cloud Fell
North of the Sand Hills
Alliance Territory

Before dawn on the third day, Heron in Treetops brought a scouting party to Storm Arriving with news.

"Bluecoats," Storm Arriving said to the others. "Break camp. Heron in Treetops, you and the scouts will follow me." They rode toward the Iron Shirts at once. The shell of the world had just begun to pale, but the sky was clear. The Iron Shirt pickets at the camp perimeter had learned not to shoot at their new allies, so Storm Arriving kicked his drake up to top speed. They sped into camp, clods of mud flying from their whistlers' feet. Sentries scattered and horses tested their tethers as the group slid to a halt near the command tents.

"Wake up!" Storm Arriving called out to them. "Wake up!"

Angry voices came from all sides as Iron Shirt officers emerged from their tents, buttons undone and sleep still crusting the corners of their eyes. The young commander of the Iron Shirts came out, wiping lather from his face. His gaze was narrow and his jaw was set in a thin line beneath his moustache. He spoke to Storm Arriving in sharp sylla-bles, obviously upset by the abrupt termination of his morning ablutions. Storm Arriving was just glad to see that he at least had not been still asleep.

When the commander was finished complaining, Storm Arriving slipped off his drake and walked toward him. Again, he spoke as if to the simplest of minds. He crouched and cleared a spot in the moist soil at their feet.

"You," he said with a finger toward the officer, and drew a circle in the dirt.

"I," he said, indicating himself, then the direction of his camp. Another circle, to the north of the first.

"Bluecoats," he said, and drew a third circle, to the east of the first two, and then finger-walked from the bluecoats to their own position. "Boom," he said, miming a rifle shot.

The *boom* and pretended aim of a rifle were understood immediately. The commander leaned closer, pointed, and asked a question. Storm Arriving had no idea what was be-ing asked, so he just repeated the information in word and sign.

"Bluecoats. Coming here. With weapons."

Another question, and the commander pointed to his foot and then to one of the horses that whinnied nearby.

"On horses," Storm Arriving said, and signaled a count of five times ten. "Five tens, at least."

More gestures, and pointing to the sky.

Storm Arriving understood and lifted a hand to point from where the sun would rise to where it would be after a few hands passed.

"Soon," he said. "You must prepare."

The commander called out to his officers and immedi-ately began issuing orders. The older men snapped into motion, shouting orders of their own, and the Dance of the Iron Shirts began again with barked commands that made men leap into action.

"He is young," said Heron in Treetops, a strong, sharp-eyed young man who liked to wear a black *vé'ho'e* vest and a round black hat he picked up on one of their southern raids. "But they do listen to him."

"That's a good thing," Storm Arriving said. "But what is he telling them to do? That is what worries me."

71

General John Meriwether dismounted and held out his horse's reins. McGettigan, his second-in-command for this excursion, swapped him reins for a pair of heavy binoculars. Meriwether leaned up against the trunk of a tree to steady his view and peered through the lenses.

The Spanish army was spread out west-to-east in a sloppy tumult of mud and tents along the cleft of a creekbank. Between the main camp and Meriwether's eastern vantage point was a plain of low grassland flanked on the north by a curving line of rumpled ground forming a long shallow bowl. This would be his first testing ground.

It had been sheer luck that they caught sight of the Cheyenne scouting party the day before. Under normal conditions, the Cheyenne would have outmaneuvered them within hours, but the Spanish forces were like a Judas goat, limiting the scouts' mobility and guiding Meriwether's expeditionary force straight to the object of their search.

And now he had them in his sights. It was a sizeable force—the cluster of command tents alone spoke of at least two brigades—but he could see at once that the Spanish commanders were inexperienced in this terrain.

Infantry outnumbered cavalry by at least ten to one; a classic ratio, but men on foot were slow and exposed in this theater. In addition, the rifled artillery they had brought was heavy and cumbersome, and the soil, especially in the coming season, would not support such large ordnance. It was as if the Spaniards were planning to establish a permanent presence. That thought made Meriwether uneasy, and as he scanned the gathered host below, it was clear that this was indeed more than just an invasionary force. This army was here to establish a foothold, and that meant the wind was blowing from a very different quarter than he and the President had expected. The Spanish goal was not to support, but to occupy.

He considered recalling his men, but decided against it; regardless what the Spaniards long-term intentions were for this army, a lot could be learned from this first encounter. Already, he could see that the Spanish commander was green, his tactics learned from battles fought in Europe almost a hundred years ago. Meriwether smiled. The tutelage of enemy generals in the realities of war was one of his favorite pastimes, and he was glad for the chance to take it up once more.

Storm Arriving squatted on the elevation north of Crazy Woman Creek, gritting his teeth and feeling helpless. The commander of the Iron Shirts had wordlessly but unmistakably dismissed him and his scouts after the news of the bluecoat presence had been understood, and no words or signs would make a difference. The Iron Shirts did not want their help.

So they had ridden back to the rise on which they had camped the night before and watched as the army roused itself like a hibernating walker disturbed from its winter sleep. Clumsy, slow, heedless of any danger, the Iron Shirts buttoned up their sky-blue tunics and wiped down their rifles with a deliberate calm that Storm Arriving found maddening. As the sun rose, he watched the bluecoats take up positions just beyond view of the camp, taking full advantage of the land's limited topography. The Iron Shirts had been oblivious to it all.

Now, the sun two hands into the morning sky, the Iron Shirts ordered their men onto the plain. Their foot-soldiers were deployed in massive squares bristling with swords, rifles, and bayonets, and their horse-soldiers were split into two groups to the side and rear of the infantry. On a strip of hard land near the creekbed, Iron Shirts had wheeled out the large iron guns and pointed them at the field. Small wagons stood nearby, ready to resupply them with shot and powder.

Meanwhile, mounted bluecoats formed a skirmish line along the far limit of the battlefield. Beneath the trees to the east, Storm Arriving could see the glint of brass and steel worn by their commanders, but there was something he found more disturbing. Herons in Treetops noticed it too.

"Where are the rest?" he asked.

"Our scouts said they numbered five tens, at least," Storm Arriving said. "I see half that, at most."

"Where are the rest?" Heron in Treetops asked again.

As the bluecoats began to advance down toward the battlefield, Storm Arriving knew the answer. He knelt and squinted into the distance, scanning the terrain beyond the Iron Shirts' far flank.

"There," he said, pointing, and Heron in Treetops cupped hands under the brim of his hat to get a clearer view.

"Yes," he said. "I see them."

Crazy Woman Creek ran fast, cutting a smooth, steep-sided cleft through the land. In a land generally devoid of hiding places, the trees and brush that grew along the creek provided a perfect opportunity. As they watched they saw shapes flitting through the deep growth and now and again a head surreptitiously peering through the scrub.

As the Iron Shirts advanced their formations of men toward the oncoming line of skirmishers, the other half of the bluecoat force was creeping up along the defile, preparing to take the artillery from the rear.

Storm Arriving picked up his rifle and fired a shot into the air. Several heads turned at the sound, including the commander. Storm Arriving shouted and pointed toward the creek beyond the artillery, but his gestures were ignored and the commander turned his attention back to the approaching bluecoats.

Orders were bellowed across the plain. A bugle sounded and the advancing square of Iron Shirts stopped and re-formed into four rows. The bluecoat skirmishers moved erratically across the field, keeping the enemy's attention on the battlefield. They were within range of the riflemen, but only barely, and the Iron Shirts did not raise their weapons.

Storm Arriving saw the artillery soldiers, positioned along the creekbed, load their cannon and adjust their aim. How the Iron Shirt commander expected them to hit the skirmishers was unclear—to Storm Arriving it was like throwing stones at hornets—but it was obvious the commander's orders were never going to be tested. The flanking bluecoats had moved up through the underbrush along the creekbed and were only a stone's throw from the artillery.

"The bluecoats are going for the wheeled guns," he said aloud.

Grey Bear laughed. "You said you wanted the Iron

Shirts to bleed."

Storm Arriving ran to his whistler. "Not all at once!" Then he shouted to the others. "Mount!"

Soldiers leapt onto their whistlers and slapped them into motion. They streaked down the slope and hit the flatland just as the flanking bluecoats burst upward from the creekbed and fired a volley. The Iron Shirts manning the cannon went down screaming. The entire army's attention was suddenly drawn away from the plain, and that was the moment the skirmishers turned and fired into the ranks of riflemen.

Chaos spread like a stain across the field. Shouted commands competed with bugle calls and wails of the wounded and dying.

Storm Arriving sped straight through the Iron Shirt rearguard. He drove his men past the cavalry, heedless of the panic they sowed among the horses. They swept around the rear of the commanders who stood in a knot shouting at the top of their lungs. He did not have to give his own men orders; they knew exactly what was to be done. A child could see that the threat lay at the wheeled guns, now in the hands of the bluecoats.

A couple of his men had rifles in hand, but like him, most opted for spears or long-handled war clubs. Storm Arriving grinned as they approached the line of artillery. The bluecoats were turning the loaded cannon toward the main body of the Iron Shirts, and the sight of a cannon's swiveling maw set Iron Shirt foot soldiers running. Storm Arriving gripped the leather-wrapped handle of his club and lifted its heavy stone-weighted head. Beneath him, his drake flashed battle colors across chameleon skin, bars of red and white that pulsed and gyred. Storm Arriving and his Kit Fox soldiers let loose a war cry.

They flew in. Rifles fired. Storm Arriving swung his club in a crushing, upward arc. His whistler leapt a caisson, butted a man with its crested head, its feet pushing through the line with claw-toed strides. One cannon fired in a gout of smoke and noise. The ball ripped a tear through the frantic mass of Iron Shirt soldiers. And then the bluecoats were on the run, diving back into the underbrush and down toward the rushing creek. The scrub was too dense for the whistlers to charge through, so Storm Arriving signaled his men to halt.

They reined in at the end of the artillery line. The flanking bluecoats had escaped up the creek and the skirmishers had retreated from the plain. Storm Arriving inspected his squad. There were smiles and sweaty brows and chests filled with the thick breath of battle, but they were all there and all untouched.

"Two," Heron in Treetops said, enumerating his coup with a grin.

"One for me," Storm Arriving said. "The same for this big boy here," he added, patting his whistler's flank. The drake's head and neck were still striped with battle colors, but the patterns had slowed and now barely crawled across his skin.

It had been a good encounter; a decisive outcome with several coups and no injuries. A Kit Fox couldn't ask for more. Storm Arriving lifted his head and looked over toward the snarl of men that surrounded the commanders like bees in a disturbed hive. The Iron Shirt commander caught sight of the Storm Arriving's smile and his eyes went cold and hard. Storm Arriving laughed all the more and the commander looked away.

Then Storm Arriving looked eastward, across the plain where Iron Shirts were picking up their dead and wounded. There wasn't a bluecoat on the field; their only casualties had been dealt by the Kit Fox among the artillery. He squinted and shaded his eyes, peering at the trees on the ridgetop.

Meriwether steadied himself against the aromatic bark of the sassafras tree and studied the group of natives astride their lizard mounts.

"That has to be him," he muttered.

"Sir?" McGettigan said.

"That Indian, the laughing one on that huge drake." He handed the binoculars over to his second. "Right side of his head shaved, four black lines beneath his right eye. That's the one they call Storm Arriving."

"The bastard that attacked all those homesteads last

year?"

"I'd swear to it," Meriwether said.

"He's a savage. A vicious monster," McGettigan said. "What's he doing here with the Spanish?"

"Monster?" Meriwether said. "Is that what they think of him out here?"

McGettigan looked genuinely surprised at his general's question. "Sir, that...." He took a breath and got his emotions under control. "That brute kills innocent people. Women and children, sir. He torched homesteads in Westgate and destroyed New Republic. He's a mindless killer who's responsible for more murders than I can count!"

Meriwether nodded. "I see," he said. He patted McGettigan on the shoulder. "Now let me paint you a different picture, and pay attention, because this will be the portrait that will govern our actions in regard to this man."

He walked out from beneath the shade of the sassafras and gazed out across the battlefield. He saw the litter bearers running the wounded toward the surgeon's tent. He saw the command structure still trying to assert control over the frenetic infantry. Horses ran wild, dead lay scattered near and far, and across the entire scene the only circle of calm he could see was centered on the natives and their war chief. There they were, stolid and resolute on their lizard mounts, watching him just as he was watching them.

"That man," he said, "is the most brilliant strategist on the prairie."

"Sir, I can't believe—"

"You will believe," Meriwether said with the tone of command. "Or you'll pay the price for it. That man has thwarted our every attempt at controlling this territory, and ruined the careers of several generals in the doing. He is ruthless, to be sure, and yes, he has killed women and children, but if you think that we are innocent of that crime, think again. He uses the best tactics of his culture and everything he has learned from us as well. And just in case my words aren't enough to convince you, think about this: that man just turned a devastating slaughter by our inferior force into nothing more than a costly mistake. In short, he just saved that Spanish commander's ass."

The smile on Storm Arriving's face faded as his gaze returned to the small knot of bluecoats that watched from beneath the branches of the green-twig trees at the edge of the battlefield.

"What do you think?" Grey Bear said, riding close.

Storm Arriving nodded up toward the stand of trees. "See the man in the center."

"The one who remains still while the others move to do his bidding," Grey Bear said. "What of him?"

"I know that man," Storm Arriving said.

Grey Bear chuckled. "You are an eagle, now, and can see a man's face at such a distance?"

Storm Arriving smiled once more. "No," he said. "But I know him. He is clever. He is patient. He tests the bow before he puts an arrow to the string."

A rider sped in from the perimeter, his whistler's skin rippling with angry bars of white and scarlet.

"News from the Council," the rider said breathlessly. "The Iron Shirts want to press the bluecoats in battle, to push them back toward the Big Greasy. The war chiefs agree, and are sending us more soldiers. We are to assist them in this war."

Storm Arriving looked back at the bluecoats.

"Are they at least sending us someone who can speak their gibberish?"

"Yes," the rider said. "That, also."

Storm Arriving could feel the bluecoat war chief's gaze on him, could feel the challenge. It took no eagle eye to sense it. Storm Arriving hefted his war club, lifted it, pointed it at the bluecoats, and let his smile widen into a grin.

"Good," he said. "This is good."

"We go!" he said, and they rode off to meet their incoming reinforcements.

Chapter 9

Plum Moon, Waning
Four Years after the Cloud Fell
Along the Red Paint River
Alliance Territory

Speaks While Leaving walked quickly away from the twi-
lit camp, frowning, her gaze darting from side to side. She
was on an errand for Mouse Road—what was it? A message? A delivery? She could not remember, could not focus
her mind. She stepped briskly past an outlying lodge, head
down, eyes searching the growing gloom, heading through
the trees toward the river. She heard a step behind her and
spun.

No one.

Again.

She turned back toward the river and yelped as a man
half-emerged from the trunk of a tree. He was misshapen,
crudely formed, his skin bark, his hair a snarl of twigs and
leaves. His eyes, dark, peered at her. She heard the creak of
wood as his lips twisted into a smile.

She ran.

She left the trees behind her, felt the forest mulch give
way to dry grass beneath her feet. Heart pounding, she
wove through scrub-brush, pushing herself to a clearing

along the riverbank, then stopped to lean against a lichen-clad boulder and let her breath catch up with her.

Be calm. It will pass. It has before.

Truth, but not the whole of it; each episode during the past moon had eventually faded, but each one had grown more intense, as well. From the day she walked out of the Council meeting she had been haunted during the twilight hours by spirits shadowing her throughout the camp. She saw more and more each night, and they stayed longer into the dark, almost until moonrise.

They did not come with the familiar pressure of an on-coming vision, and her sight was not flooded with the mind-filling light that always accompanied a visit from *nevé-stanevóo'o*. If anything, as twilight approached her sight dimmed, as if her eyes refused to adjust to the encroaching darkness. But, as she looked back at the camp and saw her neighbors at their lodges, talking with their relatives, visiting around small story fires, she saw each figure glowing with an unearthly light, and as they moved, ghostly streamers trailed after them like moonlit smoke.

The breeze off the river was cool and moist and smelled of slick river rocks and sun-cooked mud. She closed her eyes and concentrated, trying to block out the other world, the spirit world that was bleeding into this one. The wind rustled the leaves in the trees behind her, and she heard the creaky call of diving lizards in the banks at the river's edge. She felt the rough hardness of the boulder. Her heart began to slow.

Then the solid stone shifted beneath her hand and she leapt backward. She did not wait to see what form might emerge from the rock. With earth spirits to one hand and ghost-wrapped people to the other, there was no pleasant choice. At least among her people there was a chance of a friendly face.

She headed back toward the outlying lodges, nodding to neighbors, trying to keep calm and ignore the glimmering cloaks that covered them all. She saw Blind Eye Woman working a buffalo skin from the recent hunt, and noticed that her ghost seemed to be a half-motion behind her in every movement. Both flesh and spirit form alike nodded in greeting as Speaks While Leaving walked past.

Farther on, the elderly Two Guards and his wife Black Tree Woman were sitting at their fire. Two Guards was carving a pipe to trade and Black Tree Woman was mixing some dried meat into a thin stew made with suet and pine nuts. Speaks While Leaving saw that both of their ghosts had short-cut hair, like she herself had done as a sign of grieving. And the ghosts were busy with tasks quite different from their counterparts.

What are you trying to show me? she asked the spirits.

The spectral images shimmered as the night began to deepen and Speaks While Leaving found that instead of wanting the night to come, suddenly she wanted the gloaming to linger. She studied everyone intently, determined to discern as much as she could while the ghosts still walked beside her neighbors.

Close to home she met another elderly pair, Wolf Robe and his wife Sun Walking. They too were without grown children to help them in their advancing years, and depended on charity to make it through the winter months. Here, though, it was the people who had blunt-shorn hair while their ghosts still bore their braids. Wolf Robe and his spirit self sat cross-legged on the ground, one beside the other, but Sun Walking was making fry bread while her spirit shadow seemed to be stripping meat for the drying rack.

"Greetings," she said to them as she walked closer. They both nodded and Sun Walking beckoned her closer.

"Come," she said with a smile. "Sit." She skewered a triangle of fry-bread and lifted it out of the sizzling suet. She let it cool in the twilight breeze a moment, its aroma a mixture of sweet and savory, and then offered it to Speaks While Leaving. "Have a piece. We have plenty."

Fry-bread was a treat reserved for special feasts and dances, as milled grain was hard to come by. For Sun Walking to be making it at all was unusual, but in a time of grief?

Speaks While Leaving took the offered piece. It was warm, and had a light crust that promised a moist, flavorful interior. "My thanks," she said. "I see you are mourning someone. I apologize for not coming to see you sooner, but I had not heard of recent deaths."

"Ah, this?" Sun Walking touched her short, grey hair and gave a low, cunning laugh. Her ghost flickered, put more meat on the drying rack, and dimmed beneath the deep of night.

"Do not apologize. No one has died. It was the Iron Shirts."

Speaks While Leaving's expression told all.

"I did not believe it either," Wolf Robe said, looking up from the fire. "The Iron Shirts! When have they ever been a friend to the People?"

"It was the Ravens," Sun Walking said, referring to the black-frocked priests that came with Alejandro and the others. "They offered us sacks of food, and all we had to do was cut our hair."

"They wanted us to give up our clothes, too, for those *vé'hó'e* swaddlings they wear," Wolf Robe added.

"And promise to worship their man-ghost-on-the-cross," Sun Walking said.

"And you did?" Speaks While Leaving asked, unable to hide the shock she felt.

"Well," Sun Walking said, plucking at her deerskin tunic. "We drew the line at wearing clothes of Trader's cloth."

"But you promised? You promised to worship the ghost god of theirs?"

Sun Walking chuckled again. "You know that *vé'hó'e* promises only last as long as it takes to say the words. Why should ours be any different?"

"But your braids!"

Sun Walking picked another piece of fry-bread out of the fat and handed it to her husband. Wolf Robe juggled it until it cooled and then bit into it with relish. "Hair grows until we die, dear one," he said. "If two cut braids help us through this winter, I'll give them one every year."

The humor on Sun Walking's face faded. "But some are not as sensible as we are," she said, inclining her head back toward the lodge of Two Guards and Black Tree Woman. "I worry about them. This has been a difficult year for many, with bands leaving early for the winter camps, and there has been little trade with the other peoples. Some will not be with us in the spring."

"The Ravens will not help them?"

"Not until they promise, as we have."

Speaks While Leaving shook her head. "That is not right," she said, standing. "It is not what we agreed."

"They promised you, did they?" Wolf Robe said around a mouthful of bread, and laughed.

"Take a piece to little Mouse Road," Sun Walking said, handing her another piece of fry-bread. Then she laughed, too.

"I thank you," Speaks While Leaving said. She took the steaming fry-bread and headed for home.

The last of the twilight had faded, and all the ghosts were gone from the camp, but the paired stories of real and spirit lingered. Some pairs were similar, some different, but everyone had more than one story to tell. The earth spirits were speaking to her through them, she was sure, though as usual their language was difficult to decipher. As she walked the winding paths between the glowing lodgefires, the answer began to form in her mind. It stayed elusive, though, furtive, like coyotes beyond the firelight, nothing but glowing eyes and the sound of padded feet. It had something to do with the vision the spirits had given her, but she could not force the knowledge of what it all meant.

And right now, there were more pressing matters.

She found Mouse Road at home.

"Here," she said, giving the fry-bread to Mouse Road.

Mouse Road stared at the still-warm treat and grew puzzled. "But who is having a feast? Who is having a celebration?"

"Wolf Robe and Sun Walking," she said, letting the information sink in.

"But what do they have to celebrate?"

"Nothing." Speaks While Leaving felt her belated anger arrive. "Nothing at all."

"Then why..."

"The Ravens from the Iron Shirts. They are handing out food to the needy, but only if they cut their hair and promise to act like *vé'hó'e*."

"But that wasn't—"

"No," Speaks While Leaving said. "It wasn't."

They heard a step outside the doorflap, and One Who Flies came in. He looked at them both with a frowning face.

"What?" he asked as he sat down at the fire.

Speaks While Leaving told him.

He shook his head, and took out his knife and a whetstone. He spat on the stone and began to hone the blade. "More to bring to Alejandro's tent in the morning."

"Why?" Speaks While Leaving asked. "What else is there?"

He did not look up from his work, but slowly drew the blade across the flat stone in long, grating arcs. "A group of boys were hunting deer up in the Sacred Hills. They saw some *vé'hó'e*. Arrows were loosed. Shots were fired in return."

Mouse Road sat down beside him. "Were they hurt?" she asked.

"No, the boys are fine. They came back to get their fathers' rifles so they could go back up there. They nearly did, too, but Crazy Whistler's son made a mess of it and nearly shot his own foot off." He laughed, but there was more bitterness than humor in the sound. "It took all I had to convince the fathers to wait until dawn. We'll go to Alejandro first, but I doubt we'll be satisfied by what he has to say."

Speaks While Leaving was still standing, her brain a-whirl. She thought of her father, of Storm Arriving, of Alejandro, and felt them pulling each in their own direction, each determined to follow their own path. Images sped past her mind's eye—ravens flying up from barren trees, blood spattered on golden grass, the sounds of heat and battle, the chanting of *vé'hó'e* prayers. She saw pathways in her mind, choices, and then she understood.

It was coming. Her vision was coming. For good or ill, it was coming.

George headed out early to find his walker, taking ropes and saddle before the sun was up and while his breath still smoked in the air. He wanted her with him today both to bolster his confidence and to put the fear of God into the men he was to meet. She was out with the other walkers, nested down in the tall grass to the south of the encampment.

He wound his way through the field of monsters, feeling each presence more than seeing the beasts themselves. They lay in sleeping trenches clawed into the soft earth, the hump of each spine rising above the seed-heavy heads of waist-high grass like a living barrow mound. He walked for a bit, then listened with his heart to the somnolent creatures. Never fully asleep, they were all aware of him, but recognized him as a rider and so did not bother to wake fully.

Pity the poor fool who rides into this field unaware, he thought, and not for the first time.

He felt a shift in his heart and heard a deep snuffle from his right. He turned and saw his walker, her head just cresting the level of the grass for a better look. She saw him, and he heard her groan.

"Sorry, sweet one," he said as he came close. He scritched her brow and sleeked back the gossamer hairs that covered her neck. Dew had collected on the feathery filaments and as she rose, she shook her head and shivered the skin across her torso and down to her tail to rid herself of the chill drops. The sun crested the horizon as she stood, limning her in an aura of pale fire.

He patted her flank and bade her prepare, then picked up the harness and tack that would keep him from sliding off her bony spine. As he assembled the rope-and-wicker saddle, she breathed gouts of air across him, warming him, mingling their scents, strengthening their bond. She would die for him, he knew, either to protect him or to avenge him, without fear or concern for her own well-being. Some days—like this morning—he took little comfort from that knowledge. Today, even a twenty-foot long monster at his side would make little difference.

He did not expect anything from Alejandro, at least nothing satisfactory. Given that expectation then, it was a fair bet that a war party would soon head up into the Sacred Hills, and with them would be the young boys who encountered the *vé'hó'e*—untried youths eager for their first blood. George might be able to steer them clear of the worst, to persuade the soldiers to send a smaller, more seasoned force that could strike the intruders hard and with sharp precision. He might even avoid the situation entirely by convincing Alejandro—through plain talk and some walker-assisted intimidation—that it was in his group's interest to keep his people out of the Sacred Hills. But in the end, what would it buy?

The People's way of life, their very survival, was pinned on the willingness of their men and women to defend their families, their traditions, and their territory. By stopping today's conflict, he would only delay what had to happen. Boys left behind today would try to count their first coup tomorrow, kill their first man tomorrow, die tomorrow. They were eager for it, eager to grow up, to be men. Fevered by the immortality of youth and educated by four centuries spent beating back wave after wave of European settlers, how could it be different?

And what would the Spaniards do if he stopped it all? That was easy to answer. Whatever George was able to thwart today, they too would try again tomorrow. Just like those young boys.

He sighed as he mounted up onto his walker's back. He felt her ribs expand and contract with a sigh of her own. She felt his frustration, and that wasn't a good thing. The walker would amplify anything he felt—a powerful tool in battle, where the symphony of blood and adrenaline, man and walker, created a formidable weapon. He needed to focus his mind in order for her to be an advantage in negotiation.

It was a difficult spot, but George had to admit his own part in bringing it about. The Spaniards were here because George had asked them to come here. No getting around that fact. But it also seemed that his role only advanced what was surely inevitable. The worlds of the People and of the *vé'hó'e* had been rushing toward this conflict for centuries. If it did not come today, it would have come soon enough. No adjustment of history, no quirk of the past could have changed the course of this storm that was about to break upon them.

He wondered, as he toed his walker into a slow trot, how this all reckoned with the vision that Speaks While Leaving had been given. He could not see the method in the madness.

As he rode off to meet the others, he wondered if there

was any method at all.

Alejandro heard voices raised outside his tent and put down his cup of coffee to listen. Horses whinnied from the corral to the south, then soldiers barked orders to halt and be recognized, in Spanish—moronic fools. How many times had he told them that unlike the tribes of the south, very few of these natives spoke Spanish? The flap to his tent opened and Luis, the lieutenant he'd impressed into service as his aide stepped in, fear on his face. Alejandro lifted a hand for quiet. Then he heard the dull thump of massive footsteps.

"Don Alejandro," came a voice from outside his tent. "I need to speak with you. I do not have an appointment."

Alejandro smiled despite the situation. Young Custer remembered well his previous life among the elite of Washington. He picked up his cup and saucer, rose, nodded to his aide, and stepped outside.

A nervous-looking escort squad stood outside. Behind them, One Who Flies sat astride his gargantuan lizard. He was backed by a chevron of native warriors bedecked in skins and feathers, mounted on chameleon-skinned whistlers. They were all armed with clubs and spears, but Alejandro saw carbine sheaths, too. In all, they each looked as fearsome as One Who Flies and his beast.

The appearance of walkers had always turned Alejandro's guts to water. Just their size alone was enough to test the mettle of an average man, let alone seeing one in motion, seeing the power, the intelligence, and the—the *menace,* that imbued them. The man who met those creatures on the battlefield never forgot the experience. It took all Alejandro had to keep hold of his coffee cup and take a calm, measured sip.

"How can I help you gentlemen?" he asked, all nonchalance.

"Down, chick," One Who Flies said coolly, and his walker slowly lowered itself to the ground. As he stepped down, the beast tilted its head back and yawned. A few soldiers actually gasped and one took an instinctive step backward. It didn't help when the walker began to clean its back teeth with the claws on its short forearm.

"We have a problem," One Who Flies said. "Two, actually, and they need your immediate attention." One of the natives was translating the French they spoke for the others.

"Of course," Alejandro said, wanting to get back onto familiar ground. "Shall we step inside?"

"Thank you," One Who Flies said, "but no. This not a negotiation."

Alejandro kept the smile on his lips but let his eyes grow steely. "I see," he said. "Then what is it, if I may ask?"

One Who Flies was still relaxed, his features pleasant, nonchalant. "Your priests; they have been withholding aid from those who refuse to abandon their traditions."

"As we agreed," Alejandro said, "the priests are here to bring the souls of these people closer to God."

"As we agreed," One Who Flies parroted, "they may convert whom they can, 'through peaceful and non-coercive means,'" he finished, quoting from the charter written back in Madrid.

Alejandro laughed. "A gift is not coercion," he said.

"A bribe is not coercion, I'll grant you. But extortion is. Aid all, or aid none. Your choice. Item two..."

This was not the way Alejandro wanted things to go. "One Who Flies," he said, in English.

"*In français, s'il vous plaît, Excellence.*" One Who Flies raised an eyebrow and his walker snorted, head up, eyes suddenly alert.

Alejandro took a deep breath and let it out slowly. "I will pass your instructions to Father Velasquez," he said, in French once more.

"Item two. Our scouts have sighted some *vé'hó'e* up in the Sacred Hills. This area was specifically forbidden to you and your soldiers, even for hunting. We have only one question. Are they your men?"

Skillfully played, Alejandro said to himself. Any answer—yes, no, or even an I don't know—would back him into a corner. Say "Yes," and he would admit he knew that Vincent sent men up there. "No," and he might as well go up into the hills and kill those men himself. Say "I don't know," and he would admit the possibility that they were there and the fact that he didn't have control over his own forces. It was well-played, all right, but Alejandro had been a diplomat for twenty years, had negotiated with royalty and with reprobates—sometimes with both in the same person—and in that time he had learned that sometimes it was best not to answer, but to obfuscate.

"Your reports are incorrect, One Who Flies. There are no white men up in those hills."

One Who Flies blinked, confused by the unexpected answer. "What do you mean?"

"Surely your patrols would have seen any group from this camp sneaking across the river and up into the hills. Surely your people are watching us that well, at least. And how could they be from anywhere else? How could a group of white men infiltrate so far into Cheyenne-controlled territory? And for what reason?" He shook his head. "No, your scouts are mistaken. There are no white men in your sacred hills."

The French he spoke was translated to the rest of the whistler riders, but their faces did not show any of the uncertainty he had hoped to sow there. So, the men up there were dead men and Alejandro's only solace was that he could deny all responsibility of them with total confidence.

Provided, he said to himself, *that D'Avignon has done as I—*

"Where is Vincent?" One Who Flies asked, as if reading his mind.

"What?"

"Where is Vincent D'Avignon?"

"I—I do not know," he said, and cursed himself for answering without forethought.

One Who Flies nodded to the other riders. In two leaping strides he was up on the back of his rising walker. The walker coughed out a short, harsh, grating note and then left with a spray of torn earth.

Alejandro watched them speed across the prairie, impossibly fast, heading toward the dark mass of the Sacred Hills.

"Luis," he said to his aide. "Where is D'Avignon?"

"I'm sorry, Excellency. I do not know."

"Find him," Alejandro said. "Find him at once."

Chapter 10

Plum Moon, Waning
Four Years after the Cloud Fell
In the Sacred Mountains
Alliance Territory

The whistlers swept up the slope, weaving in amongst the rough, black trunks of pine trees. The walker took a more direct route, pushing upward along a deer track, shouldering aside birch and linden saplings on her way through the brush. George lay low along her spine, wincing as low branches scraped across his back.

He had been able to convince the soldiers to leave their sons at home. If these were rogue independents from the Spanish, this would be quite different from a whistler raid filled with more fun than risk. If his suspicions were correct, these would be well-armed soldiers, prepared for an attack. It was a situation that called for experience, not bravado.

They reached the place the boys had spoken of, a tumble of rotten stone near Green Dragonfly Creek, and dismounted. They needed to clamber up a steep hillside and circle around the rim of the camp, in order to scout and attack from above. Whistlers and walkers would only announce their presence to the trespassers.

There were sixteen in the war party—a symbolic number—but this was the first time that George had found
himself as part of the count. In the past, it had always been
"four men for each of the winds, and One Who Flies," or "a
man for each of the six directions, and One Who Flies." For
years, he had been the appendix to any force, tacked on like
an afterthought, but for some unknown reason today he
was no appendage, no addendum to their counting. Today,
when Two Roads set the number and the names, it was
"four fours," plain and simple. Red Arrow had been picked
to lead. Whistling Elk had been chosen sixth, Limps had
been tenth. George had been eleventh; not even the last
named. He did not know why his position in the People's
society had changed, but he noted the shift and felt his
heart respond to the honor.

They scooted toward the cliffside, backs bent to stay low
behind the brush. Red Arrow pointed at the creek as they
passed. The water was cloudy, filled with disturbed silt, not
clear and unsullied as it should have been this deep into
the hills.

Upstream, near the source, men were digging.

In late summer, the forest floor was usually dry and littered with wind-blown duff. Every stride had a twig to step
on and, if that wasn't enough, a man's progress could be
tracked from half a mile just by watching the hip-high
cloud of dust and desiccated pollen that dogged him
through the scrub. But today they found an ally in the recent rains that had dampened the carpet of tinder-dry
needles. The squad kept to the woods, using the evergreen
branches as both cover and a barrier to the little sound
they made in their passage between the silent boles. Within
a hand's time, they were above the *vé'hó'e* camp.

The damage to the creekbed was obvious, even from this
distance. From the spring that bubbled out of the ground, a
bowshot up the hillside, down to the first small pond it
formed along its downward run, trees had been felled and
the earth had been scooped aside.

George recognized the setup at once. A rough sluice
made from split pinewood brought water from the pond
around to a wash-pit where it could flow over screens and
pans, rinse away the silt and leave just stones, gravel,

and—the workers hoped—gold.

Vincent had described the technique at length, back when he was teaching the People how to pan and mine gold, back when he was working *with* them; but never had George imagined it would be so...rapacious. The reality, even on this small a scale, surprised him.

"I do not see them," Red Arrow said.

"Gone?" Limps asked.

George scanned the encampment that lay between them and the sluice-work. Equipment—barrows, spades, and picks—stood in orderly stacks, but nowhere did he see a pot, a pan, or a bag of beans.

"Hard to say," he said. "They may have left last night, or just a moment ago."

"No way to tell from here," Whistling Elk said.

They crept down the slope, spread out in an irregular line. There was no movement from anywhere within the camp or along the creekbank. With signs, Red Arrow called a halt a stone's throw from the clearing. George studied the area but could not see any sign of recent occupation. Chickadees and siskins flitted across the clearing without concern. A fox squirrel bounced through the sunlit clearing, stopping to sniff at a pile of refuse in his quest for food.

From his place behind the thick spruce trunk, Red Arrow rose and signed *Hold.* Slowly, he stepped out into the clearing.

Nothing.

He dashed over to the firepit. *Cold,* he signed, and looked around, listening. The rest of the squad emerged from the treeline.

Gunfire broke the stillness, a volley of rifle fire from the high ground opposite. George heard the thump of bullets hitting soil, hitting wood, hitting flesh. They dashed for cover as more shots were fired, one on the next in quick, rapid rhythm: *tut-tut-tut-tut,* then another burst in a ragged volley. George and Whistling Elk grabbed a fallen comrade and headed to the trees.

"There are so many!" Red Arrow said.

"No," George said. "It is a small group plus one man using a machine rifle. One man can fire as twenty. But where is he?" He searched the slope beyond the camp but could see nothing. "There should be smoke. Lots of smoke."

Gunfire came again, peppering the trees. Bark flew and ricocheted bullets sang past. Some smoke drifted out of the far trees, but not enough to give away their opponents' emplacement. Smokeless powder, George realized. He looked at the men around him. Crooked Creek's leg was badly wounded, and Limps was wrapping a graze to the meat of his upper arm. Red Arrow had blood on his face from a cut to his scalp.

"We need that machine rifle," George said.

Red Arrow grinned. "No one will say that my son put up a better fight than I did," he said.

The others grinned in agreement.

They bound Crooked Creek's wounds and retreated to the safety of the deep wood. Then they split into two groups and headed out to either flank; George went with the first group, creeping low through the brush and downed branches along the far side of the creek, while the others moved high along the ridge. It did not take long to reach their positions, and when George heard the probing gunfire from the high ground, the *vé'hó'e* became an easy target as they struggled to turn the machine rifle in the rugged terrain.

"Mine," Limps said, running up the hillside. He used the point on the base of his war club to spit the first man, pulled it free, and swung the head to crush the ear of the gunner. Then the woods erupted with men and soldiers, *vé'hó'e* and Cheyenne, slicing, stabbing, shouting. Red Arrow hooked a knife behind an Iron Shirt's knee and Whistling Elk shot the man through the heart, while Limps and his fellows brought their fell handiwork down upon the others.

One of the men shouted to his fellows and raised his weapon—a revolver. George grinned. Once an officer, always an officer.

"Mine!" he cried, raised his rifle to high bayonet position, and charged. The revolver found its aim. George ducked low and lunged. The pistol's report was loud above his head, but off its mark. George's shoulder hit the man in the hip, sending him sprawling. Whirling on his knees, he smacked the man's gun with his rifle butt, breaking fingers and grip in one move. He stopped, barrel aimed at the man's head. Quickly, all was still.

George surveyed the ruin around him. Red Arrow's brother grimaced, a hand covering a wound in his side. Limps winced and squinted, the only admission of pain he ever showed. Others bore scrapes and cuts and far more blood than any one of them owned. The Iron Shirts—for that was what they surely were—lay dead except for the officer at the end of George's rifle sight.

But something was missing. He checked the faces of the dead, and did not find what he sought.

"Where is D'Avignon?" he asked the man at his feet.

The man cradled his crushed hand. *"No habla,"* he mumbled.

"Vincent D'Avignon," he said, digging deep for the word he wanted. *"¿Dónde? ¿Dónde está* Vincent D'Avignon?"

"No sé," the man said, shaking his head. *"No sé."*

"¿No sé?" he said. He kicked the man in the ribs and pushed the barrel of his rifle up under his chin. *"¿No sé?"*

"What are you doing?" Whistling Elk asked, coming up behind George.

"He says he doesn't know where Long Teeth is. He doesn't say 'Who?' Not 'What do you mean?' No. He says 'I don't know where he is.'" Whistling Elk's face was impassive. "Don't you see?" George asked. "Long Teeth is behind this."

"We know."

George felt a surmounting anger build within him. "No, you don't understand. It's more than just this. More than just these men, this operation, that machine rifle. He's behind all of this."

"And beating this man? What will that do?"

George looked at Whistling Elk, then noticed that all the others were looking at him as well, their faces hard, eyes steady, observing him.

"Nothing," George said. "Beating this man does nothing."

Red Arrow stepped forward. "Then kill this trespasser and be done with him."

George looked at the Spanish officer, led here by the machinations of Vincent D'Avignon, convinced by promises of gold to risk his life in forbidden territory. The officer's eyes pleaded, but George had no pity.

"Judge, jury, executioner," he said.

The rifle kicked.

Alejandro was staring through cigar smoke at D'Avignon when he heard the walker's roar. He stood from his seat at the field table to look out across the prairie. The sunset lit the rolling grassland with bloody light and the shell of night had begun to darken in the east, but the approaching walker with its phalanx of whistlers was impossible to miss. A cloud of dust followed them, as if they were dragging a set of harrows to plow under the golden grass.

"Explain," he ordered D'Avignon. "They'll be here in two minutes and I want to know what you've gotten us into."

"I just found out myself," D'Avignon said, his voice a thin wheedle. "You know I wouldn't give them a Maxim gun, not after you were so explicit in your instructions to strip the men of any supplies that might point to our involvement."

Alejandro's eyes did not leave the approaching riders. "Nonetheless, they had one, you say."

"Yes, that is what Father Velasquez said."

"Velasquez!" Alejandro said, turning on D'Avignon.

"Mais oui," D'Avignon said, cringing. "I was taking instruction from him this morning and he mentioned—"

"How did he..." Alejandro started, but stopped, returning his gaze to the natives. He waved a hand absently. "No matter. The damage is done. And now we'll have to find out how much this slaughter of our purported allies will cost."

He put the cigar between his teeth and watched as the Cheyenne rode up the last gentle rise. One of Alejandro's bodyguards leaned forward, peering, then pointed. The squad came to immediate alert, rifles ready. Bolts brought ammunition into play.

Alejandro coughed and held up a hand, both to stay his guardsmen and to greet the newcomers.

"Let them through," he ordered.

But the guards did not relax. Suddenly, he saw why.

Several whistlers had ropes tied to their harnesses, and to the end of each rope was tied a body: bloody, mangled, torn, covered with dust-caked gore and stalks of wild, sun-dried junegrass.

One Who Flies halted his walker. The whistlers continued forward, their riders cutting the ropes to deposit the bodies in a tumbled heap. The walker roared again, a sound that made Alejandro's ribs vibrate. One Who Flies tapped the beast down and dismounted.

He was scratched, dusty, and spattered with blood. He walked forward, his gaze unflinching, unwavering, his demeanor every inch the savage warrior he appeared. When he reached the spot where Alejandro stood, he reached into a pouch and pulled out a glittering handful of gold. Alejandro's heart leapt, but then One Who Flies opened his fingers and the gold fell to the ground with a singing of bells. Alejandro looked down and saw that it was not gold, but brass at his feet; empty .303-British cartridge shells from the Maxim gun.

"You are here at our invitation," One Who Flies said, "and are therefore our guests. But guests must not go to places that are interdicted. And, as we told you when you arrived —" He nodded toward the bodies. "—the penalties are severe."

Alejandro's blood surged upward, pulsing though his neck, flooding his ears, his face. The outrage! The temerity! He looked up and down the man he thought he understood, taking in every raw, uncivilized inch of him.

"Just what do you think you are, I wonder?" Alejandro growled. "To come before me and—"

"You wonder what I am?" One Who Flies grinned through smears of dried blood, his blue eyes glinting in the last beams of the dying sun. "I am One Who Flies," he said. "I am the *vé'ho'e* who fell with the cloud! I am the son of Long Hair!" His smile rotted into a sneer. "I am a counted man among the People, and I am currently the only thing standing between your men and total, retributive slaughter. We are not children, Don Alejandro, so do not treat us as such." He turned on his heel and stalked back to his beast.

"Keep your men to the land we have reserved for them. And keep that dog's prick tethered," he shouted, pointing at D'Avignon. "If I see him beyond the limits of this camp, I will bring him back here and make you watch while I feed him his broken teeth, one by one."

The walker opened its mouth, emitted a low, guttural purr, and then shut its jaws with a *thunk*.

"Now bury your men," One Who Flies said.

Alejandro stared, his fury silenced but unabated, his hands trembling as their savage hosts rode into the new-born twilight.

"Sir," ventured one of the guards after a minute.

"Go get Velasquez," he said. "He has rites to perform."

The soldier saluted, realized he shouldn't have, and scuttled off to find the priest.

"And you," Alejandro said, turning to spear D'Avignon with a glare. The rogue had the good grace not to cower, though Alejandro could see that he was visibly shaken and pale. Good, he thought; a little fear will be good for you.

"Yes, Excellency."

"In future, you will approve all prospecting sites with me," he said, looking back at the departing natives. "I don't want you taking our men within a league of these barbarians."

He glanced over at D'Avignon, saw him smile, then saw his smile fade as he, too, looked over the bodies and the distant riders who brought them.

Chapter 11

Plum Moon, Waning
Four Years after the Cloud Fell
Along the Red Paint River
Alliance Territory

Speaks While Leaving sat in the twilight outside the lodge, Mouse Road at her side, singing together as they pounded soaked maize kernels into meal. Her eyes were closed as the song and the rhythm filled her with a sense of peace. She let that serenity seep into her hands, into the stone pestle, into the deep, trunk-wood mortar, and into the pulverized grain that would feed the people she loved.

She saw him coming, even with her eyes closed. The ghosts infected her vision fully now at this hour, and she could see his ghosts walking in formation toward the lodge. She opened her eyes and saw them all; one man and three ghosts, each one wearing the visage of a thundercloud. Mouse Road's voice faltered as she saw him, covered with scratches, dust, and spatters of blood, but Speaks While Leaving encouraged her, kept the song flowing. He put down his saddle and ropes near the doorflap and walked over to where they sat. The two women sang the song through to its end, not allowing bad news to interrupt their task, not allowing evil words to infect the food they prepared. One Who Flies stood and waited.

They finished the song and inspected the condition of the corn meal. One Who Flies remained on his feet, patient, silent.

"You have changed so much," she said to him as they scraped the corn meal out onto a piece of clean hide to dry. "The brash young man I met all those years ago, he was incapable of standing quietly by. To know that young man was to know his mind at once; not like this man standing here now."

"I think you can still see what is on my mind," he said.

"I can see the shape of it," she said, looking up at his clouded face. "But not the story." She cleared the last of the ground meal from her mortar and pestle, put them to the side, and stood. One of his ghosts had an arm in a sling. Another still had his rifle slung on his shoulder. They all had seen violence, done violence, but that was not what troubled them. She searched the faces, spirit and man, and sensed that it was not an act or a deed that concerned them, but a question. "What is it you need, One Who Flies?"

His fixed gaze began to waver. "It doesn't make sense. The Iron Shirts, they...the greed, the death..." He looked back at her, focused again. "I need to know what you know," he said. "I need to know how it all"—his brow furrowed, his mind searching—"how it all fits." His expression softened. The three ghosts of him began to waver and draw together. "It does all fit, doesn't it?"

She watched the ghosts of his possible paths begin to coalesce and realized: this was the moment for him, the axis point on which his futures spun, and as that thought hit her mind his spirit selves snapped into place and One Who Flies stood before her, whole, questioning, ready.

"Mouse Road," she said as her vision began to swim with the light from the spirit world. "I will need your help with this." She reached out as her vision went blind and felt her friends each take an arm to support her. "Take me inside, please. They are coming."

George took her outstretched hand and steadied her with an arm about her shoulder.

"They are coming," she said again as he led her toward the lodge. She stumbled and in another step she pitched toward the ground. He caught her in his arms, and glanced at Mouse Road as she held the doorflap open. Her lack of fear and concern bolstered his confidence.

He had never seen her when a vision came upon her, but now he understood why she had been given her name. Her face was vacant, her sight empty, her voice a monotone. George could see her pulse quick and shallow along the hollow of her neck, and if he had not heard the tales, if his wife had shown one iota of concern, he would have been sure that Speaks While Leaving was preparing to die, was leaving them all for the spirit world, and was describing her journey to them unto her last breath.

He laid her down upon the bedding and felt her cheek—cold and wet—and then lifted her wrist to feel her pulse—weak as twice-used thread. "What do we do?" he asked Mouse Road.

"Do not be afraid," Speaks While Leaving answered. "I am still here. I am safe."

George shook his head to shake away his fear. "What do we do?" he said, asking her this time.

"Wait. This is how they come to me," she said. "*Nevéstanevóo'o,* guardians of the way between the worlds. They are the bringers of my visions."

"Another vision?" he asked. "But what about the last—"

"No, not another. The last one. The same one. The one you asked about."

She grabbed his hand. Her grip was steel, tensed, menacing. Mouse Road rushed closer and the other hand darted out to grab her as well. George looked to his wife and now he saw concern.

"This vision," Speaks While Leaving said, her voice dreamy, "is unlike any other vision."

As she spoke, George's sight began to fade, but not with the growing black of waning consciousness. Everything grew brighter, more luminous, as if the sun was emerging from behind a massive cloud. Mouse Road rubbed her eyes and blinked, seeing the same.

"What is happening?"

"This vision cannot be danced into being," Speaks While

Leaving said. "It cannot be described. It must be seen. I must take you with me, so that you can see it. And then..."

George's body refused his command. His heart raced. He heard a whimper from Mouse Road. His vision went white.

"You will see. And then you will know."

The light grew to an astonishing brightness, filling his mind with a glare devoid of warmth, intensifying beyond mere brilliance into a shimmering, coruscant song of light and power. It consumed him, suffused him, until he could see nothing but the light, hear nothing but the light, think of nothing, ever again, but the light.

And then, with exquisite slowness, it began to ebb.

The light receded, stranding him on a barren plain. Clumps of pale grass studded the powder-dust land around him. The sky continued to dim, its light changing from white to orange, gathering overhead into a swollen orb that sunk down behind him toward the vague horizon. Clouds built, piling up into the ruddy light as the newly-formed sun bled out against their bulk. The setting sun behind him, he looked down from the heavens and saw, beneath this wounded sky, three tracks leading off through the wilderness.

The first, the middle track, led straight away east and before he could think he was flying down its length, speeding through a sere, wasted world. He felt the wind, felt the pelting sand, saw dunes stand up and slough down on either side. The moan of the wind split, became voices, and he saw ghosts along the roadway. He squinted to focus through the grit, and the ghosts became dancers before a Spirit Lodge, became women trekking across the prairie, became soldiers on whistler-back fighting an even ghostlier enemy. He saw only People; no *vé'hó'e*, no Iron Shirts, no bluecoats. The dance became a Vision Dance, the dancers' movements growing ecstatic and fervent; the women on the prairie began to run, looking back over their shoulders as they fled a threat only they could see; the soldiers' paint and equipage shifted from raid to war party, and veteran soldiers fell beneath the spectral slaughter, replaced by more soldiers who also fell and were replaced in turn by the old, the young, until at last they, too, fell and the ground was carpeted with their bodies.

The road ahead reached onward, onward, carrying him forward until it began to diminish, thin out, fade, the ghosts dwindling until he was alone, flying through nothing, through emptiness, toward the end of all things, toward oblivion.

He cried out, was jolted back to the start of the paths, and in a blink sped down the right-hand track, faster than a skyrocket. He swung in a massive southbound curve, skimmed across the sands, flew off the cliff edge of a steep shoreline, and sped out over a broad sea of sapphire waves crested with bloody foam. His course lowered toward the water as he spiraled inward and back around through west, north, and east. He stopped and fell, plunging toward the waves, was dragged back upward by an invisible hand, and sped off again in another retreating, south-bound curve.

On the waters below he saw ghostly ships, pale as death, heading north toward the cliff shore. The path repeated itself, each final drop bringing him closer and closer to the midnight water, and as he neared the surface he saw Iron Shirt soldiers and cassocked priests aboard the ships, saw the Bourbon crest flying from the masts. Another drop, another southward curl, he felt the bloody spray from the red-capped waves, and now it was not soldiers who stood on the decks, but a press of civilians—men, women, families—all heading north toward the prairie.

But the pattern was not complete, and he was pulled onward, inward, downward. He hit the surface and plunged beneath the waves, curving ever deeper. He saw bodies drifting in the water, men in fringed leggings, their hands bound by chains, women in deerskin dresses, all floating, sinking, until the waters closed above, eating the light and swallowing them all.

A gasp and sputter brought him back to the start, and the left-hand path pulled him northward. Walls grew on either side, dark, blurred by velocity, rising to the height of a man, of a house, upward, until he saw only the dark walls, the pale path, and the bloody sky above. The path turned, twisting right, yanked and turned left, sped on, wheeled right, respite, swung left, adding elevation, rising, the dark walls towering, so close above they nearly shut out the sky. The indistinct barriers to either side were just a blur, but he realized he could see past them, through them, into the darkness behind where ghostly figures moved between the pale towers. As he switched back and forth, right to left to right to left, rising, rising, he realized he was in a forest, trees ever taller, the road climbing ever higher, and the figures took shape.

He saw a soldier on whistlerback flanked by a group of Iron Shirts and a group of bluecoats. The road jerked left, and the soldiers fought with the Iron Shirts against the bluecoats. The road wrenched him back to the right and the soldiers fought with the bluecoats against the Iron Shirts. Back and forth the road slammed him, side to side, and with each turn he saw the scenarios play out, the tactics, the strategies, until the truth, the unbelievable and unpleasant truth, developed and became solid, the ghosts became men, features became faces, figures became people he knew. He saw a chief with a grey feather and a bluecoat general with white gloves.

He looked up, and the walls, the treetops, were lowering. Right. Left. Higher. Higher. Until he came through to a rocky mountaintop and circled it, slowing as he spun higher, up to its peak, where he stopped beside two poles, one topped with a fox tail and eagle feathers, the other with a bluecoat cavalry guidon, both tall beneath a sky of orange, red, and purple clouds.

His skin tightened and his breath grew short as he looked out from the height. Below, the three paths glowed across the dark land, each painted with a silver light while the last scarlet rays were doused as the sun's limb slipped over the edge of the world.

He saw them all laid out before him: the straight path to oblivion; the spiraling descent to suffocation; the erratic, tortuous climb to understanding. His mind was crammed with sights and symbols, things he had seen but could not fully describe, but the sense of it all was clear, the meaning of it was clear.

What had to be done was clear.

Light deluged the world, knocking him aside, overwhelming his mind, his sense of self.

He stared up at dark walls of his lodge, back in his own body, covered in sweat and stiff in every joint. It was nearly dark, the sky a circle of indigo through the smokehole above.

He tried to rise, heard Mouse Road's groan echo his own. Speaks While Leaving was already sitting up, reaching over to help them.

"Slowly," she cautioned.

He crawled over to Mouse Road, took her hand and looked into her eyes. She gave his hand a squeeze and signed that she was well. Then they both turned to look at Speaks While Leaving. She had gone to get the tinder bag, and was preparing the flint and tinder to make a fire. George stared at her, unsure of whether she was deranged, or he was.

"What are you doing?"

She raised an eyebrow and chuckled. "What does it look like? I'm making a fire."

Mouse Road struggled to her feet. "Let me help."

George stared at them both. "You must be joking. After what we just saw, you want to make a fire and act as if nothing unusual has happened?"

Speaks While Leaving waggled her free hand at him. "You really should eat something."

"I'm very thirsty," Mouse Road said.

"I thought we could make a quick porridge."

"That would be good. I'll fetch some fresh water." And she grabbed a waterskin on the way out through the doorflap.

George blinked. "You are both insane."

Speaks While Leaving chuckled. "No," she said. "Just practical. That was quite a trial, and without warning, too. Mouse Road has seen me through several visions, and knows what I usually need after the spirits leave."

"But don't you think we should talk about it? Don't you think we should discuss what we just saw?"

She smiled. "Yes. I do. And we will."

His sight blurred suddenly and he put a hand to his head.

"But this was your first vision," she went on, calmly. "And very soon now the exhaustion will hit you. When you awaken, I will have some corn porridge with stewed berries ready for you."

"Mouse Road," he said, his head swimming. "It's her first vision, too. Why isn't she...?"

Speaks While Leaving stood up from the newborn fire, twigs crackling as the flames bit and grew. She came over and made him lie down, a folded blanket beneath his head. "She is a woman. She is stronger than you."

And then he slept.

He woke to the aromas of grilled meat and bubbling corn meal stew and felt his stomach growl.

"He is up," Mouse Road said, and then she was at his side.

He blinked and looked up into her eyes. She was calm, but her small smile was tinged with sadness. "You saw it all?" She nodded. "I am sorry," he said. "I didn't expect I would have to leave you so soon."

"You won't," she said, taking the bowl of food Speaks While Leaving offered and handing it to him.

His stomach snarled again but he ignored it. "Mouse Road, this has to be done."

Her eyes widened and she puffed out a breath of air. "I know," she said. "But do not worry. We will succeed." He took a breath and she countered him with a scowl and a raised hand. "Wait. Let me guess. We both saw it all, but you did not see me there."

"Well, no," he said. "I did not."

"And so you think that means you must do this alone."

He felt cornered, but, "Yes," he admitted.

"Did you happen to think...no, you did not think." Her tone was imperious. "Husband, you did not see me in the vision because you did not look to your side."

The sights of the vision flashed across his mind: the silvered paths, the bloodstained sky, the ghosts of ships, soldiers, and men. She was right; he had only looked ahead, had only seen the vision. But as it replayed, he felt the memory of a pressure, a presence. He looked down at his hand, remembering the warmth, the mutual grip, the tiny fingers clutching his palm.

"You *were* there," he said.

"Good," she said. "Besides, think back on what happened the last time someone told me where I could and could not go."

He laughed. In her last act of rebellion she had run away from several suitors, gone to the *vé'hó'e* border towns, pulled his drunken carcass out of a vomit-slick puddle, dragged him across the Big Salty to the royal courts of Spain, and come back a married woman. He held up a hand, yielding to her superior stubbornness. "As you wish," he said. He took up the carved horn spoon and took a bite of the stew. "But what should we do next?" he asked.

"You two must go where you must go," Speaks While Leaving said, entering with an armful of blankets and travel-sacks. "Do you know where that is?"

"I do," Mouse Road said. "To the Man with the White Gloves. I do not know who he is, but he is the man we must find."

"I know him," George said. "He won't be hard to find. Just hard to reach alive."

"But what of you?" Mouse Road asked. "You will not be with us?"

Speaks While Leaving's smile was grim as she started to put necessaries into the travel-sacks. "No. My tasks take me somewhere else."

"To the Chief with the Grey Feather?" she asked.

"Yes. I must go to the Crow People."

George became very worried. "I do not know which of us has the harder task."

They packed through the night, and as the tardy dawn of autumn bloomed in the east, Speaks While Leaving tied her parcels on her whistler's back. Mouse Road and One Who Flies shouldered their parcels, ready to head out to the field where the walkers nested for the night.

"Please," Mouse Road begged her. "At least bid him goodbye. He is your father."

Speaks While Leaving clenched her jaw and wiped at a tear. "I cannot."

"But why?"

"Because he would stop me," she said, too sharply. She took a breath to calm herself. "It is the only path I still see unfixed. I have told our neighbors that we are going, but not where we go. They will make sure One Bear and.... They will make sure the Council knows that we have gone, and why."

Mouse Road ran forward and hugged her, then retreated to her husband's arm.

So much I see, Speaks While Leaving thought to herself. So much of the little girl is still within you. And yet, the strength of four grandmothers is in you, too.

"I shall see you," she said. She mounted her whistler and clucked at it to rise. The whistler stood and Speaks While Leaving toed it into motion. She turned and raised a hand in farewell. They did likewise, and she had to turn away before the tears blinded her.

Chapter 12

Monday, October 6th, AD 1890
The White House
Washington, District of Columbia

Custer turned away from Jacob and the question before them. He leaned back against his worktable, and looked out through the curved glass panes, past the marble balustrade, to the gardens below. Summer was over; autumn was well underway. Libbie was out among the rose bushes, snipping the last blooms of the season, a light breeze tugging at her hems. Cook prowled the corn rows, selecting the best ears for tonight's corn pudding, while a kitchen maid sought bright red tomatoes amid twisted branches and dark green leaves. Farther out, a groundsman drove a horse-drawn mowing machine across the south lawn, the grass lush, green, and growing again after the recent rains. And finally, beyond the sward of the new Ellipse, Washington's monument stood like a colossal gnomon, built by Man so God could tell what time it was down here on Earth.

He concentrated on this view, letting the serenity of the gardens, the languid pace of strolling tourists, and the silent strength of marble and granite infuse him, calm him. Behind him, he heard Jacob, his Secretary of War, grousing to himself as he penciled notes and totted up figures. Around the library that Custer used as his office, aides and advisors sat on divans reading reports or leaned across side tables in earnest tête-à-têtes. The room was charged with the sounds of quiet activity; the whisper of paper, the murmur of sotto voce conversation, the creak of leather, the clink of melting ice in forgotten glasses of sweet tea.

In times past, the work behind him would have been intoxicating. He would have been infected by the urgency of war, exhilarated by the constant coming and going, the influx of information, the outflow of orders. The tightrope dance between resource and demand would have ignited his imagination and the movement of men and munitions across the stage would have been impossible to ignore.

But now, for the first time, he was deaf to the siren's call. Now, all he wanted to do, the one thing he truly ached to do, was to go down to the garden, take his wife by the hand, and walk with her beneath the maples, smelling the scent of her fresh-cut roses. He was growing tired of it all, something he never thought would happen to him. But the years of conflict, the constant pressure of his office, the crushing demands on time and energy; he was feeling their cost. His body was debilitated, his family torn asunder, his only son caught up in a storm that was about to break upon them all, a storm that Custer felt powerless to avoid and unprepared to face.

There was, however, no alternative. He could not refuse the challenge; the duty was his to perform, was his by oath, and despite his longings for a relief, he was simply incapable of turning it all over to anyone else. He would have to see this through, come what may, so he allowed himself a few more moments of quiet indulgence, watched Cook come in with a basket of corn, green husks and silk shining in the afternoon sun, then turned back to the room and the work at hand.

"So," he said to Jacob. "You agree with him?"

Jacob frowned, put his pencil behind his ear, but did not look up from his papers. The worktable was covered with maps and messages. Jacob paged through a fistful of telegrams, curling back the top corners with a wetted fingertip until he found the one he wanted. Custer waited while his friend double-checked his notes and recalibrated his figures. Jacob had lost weight in the past two years; his hair was thinner, too, and a grimness in his eye replaced the irrepressible optimism that even a decade in the field had never been able to wipe clean. His trusted friend was being worn down, just as was Custer himself, just as they all were.

Had it been worth it? he wondered. Had his actions been worth the costs? He dismissed the feelings of mawkishness the question engendered and considered it seriously. Despite his best efforts and his true intentions, the situation had grown steadily worse. What began, years ago, as a shift in the military strategy used against a clever, adaptive enemy, had brought them now to the brink of war with one of the world's oldest and greatest powers. What would the world have been like, had he—his mind cast back in time—had he died on the field at the Battle of Kansa Bay? Would they still be where they were? Were the United States and Spain destined to face one another in a territorial war? Were they in this fix because of what he had done? Or in spite of his actions? He recalled the day he watched his son sail his gas-filled dirigible off into a cloudy sky, remembered his feelings of pride—national as well as paternal—along with his absolute conviction that he was witness to the birth of a new form of military might. But the dream of that military power died when the dirigible went down beneath heavy weather, and from that day to this, Custer could feel the grip of fate hard on his neck. Had he been wrong? Had he been right? Or was it that his actions made no difference at all and, right or wrong, his nation would be embroiled in a battle with Spain?

"Autie?"

Custer blinked and came back from his reverie. "My apologies, Jacob," he said. "Please, begin again."

"I was just saying that, well, yes, I agree with him."

"You're sure," Custer said, not really phrasing it as a question.

"Yes. Look," Jacob said and turned around a sheet of paper on which were columns of numbers cross-footed to sums and ratios. "It's clear from Meriwether's reports. Each time he engages the Spanish alone, he does quite well, but as soon as the Cheyenne enter the fray..."

"The frame shifts," Custer finished, shaking his head as he looked at the numbers. Action by action, Jacob had noted troops committed, enemy engaged, casualties, fatalities, expenditures. Meriwether had been harrying the Spanish, testing them, drawing them deeper into the Territory, stretching their supply lines. Each time he had been able to pick his ground, pick his moment, manipulating the Spaniards and predicting their textbook responses to each of his tactics. But as soon as the Cheyenne entered the equation, everything went awry. Where the Spanish were slow, the Cheyenne were lightning-quick. Where the Spanish met every attack with practiced chapter-and-verse Napoleonic defense, the Cheyenne met offense with offense, retreat, ambush, skirmish, or whatever other method was sure to cause the greatest chaos. The Spanish had the larger force and greater machinery but did not know how to use them in the open terrain, while the Cheyenne had the tactics but not the decisive superiority of numbers.

"Like he says here," Jacob said, showing Custer one of today's telegrams. "He says that the Cheyenne use arrows to shoot his horses, not their rifles."

"And only shoot them in the rump, I'll wager," Custer said. "A well-placed arrow will turn a horse into a thousand pounds of havoc."

Custer stopped. Around the room, all other conversations had stopped while aides and advisors all eavesdropped on the two most senior military minds in the room. He knew that seniority didn't mean brilliance, but the one thing he had definitely learned during his tenure in the White House was that the presidency required common sense much more than it required brilliance. Brilliance was for the field; that was why he'd put Meriwether out there.

"So," he said, coming back at last to the question that had begun all his rumination. "Double his troop strength, tripling his cavalry?"

Jacob shrugged. "That's his assessment, but I don't know where we're going to get all the troops. Still, the only fault I can see is that it doesn't sound like he's asking for enough men."

Custer grimaced. "He's counting on winter, when the

Cheyenne head to the mountains. But I'm not so sure." He shook his head. "This means it's a proper war, though. No avoiding that."

Jacob rolled his eyes. "Autie, we have Spanish troops in our territory and we're blockading the main ports of Cuba. When was this *not* a proper war?"

"As long as it's undeclared—"

"You can give up on that," said a voice by the door. Samuel Prendergast, Custer's chief attaché, came into the library with a new sheaf of papers and telegrams. He crossed the room, ignoring all the others, and held out the messages.

Custer took them and read each one. The bold, block letters stood out, shouting the crucial words.

FLEET. ARMADA.
BLOCKADE. RELIEF.
WAR.

Custer looked up. The room was silent.

"Spain is sending a fleet to break the blockade."

"Congress will respond as soon as the first volley flies," Jacob said.

"Before then," Samuel said. "They're meeting now."

Custer closed his eyes and sighed. Stray thoughts flew through his mind: how did we get here? And how do we not end up where we are headed?

Chapter 13

Plum Moon, Waning
Four Years after the Cloud Fell
Near the Elk River
Alliance Territory

Speaks While Leaving rode onward beneath the rising mass of darkening clouds. Her whistler breathed easily; she had not pushed the pace very hard and, truthfully told, she might even have held back, hoping to extend her journey for a few extra hours.

The past two days' travel had been a balm to her troubled mind. The solitude of the prairie calmed the anxiety caused by the spectral ghosts that haunted the encampment, and as her distance from home increased, the tension built by the bickering Council factions loosened its grip on her heart. She had guided her mount through the open country, always heading north and west but keeping to the plains instead of forests and hills. She let her whistler's legs eat up the miles, allowing nothing to interfere with the peace she had so long been without.

The wind freshened, and she smelled coming rain. Her whistler scented it, too, turning her head to eye the cloudbank building behind them. The whistler fluted a note of concern but loped on when Speaks While Leaving patted her shoulder. Miles ahead, the land rose and began to rumple. The green grass darkened with scrub-brush, sprouted trees with rising elevation, then climbed up into the shaggy foothills that marked the deep territory of the Crow People. She would be among them tonight, and then the real challenge would have to be faced.

Soon enough, she said to herself. But not now. Not yet.

The sun found a chink in the clouds, and she spotted a hawk's shadow pacing both whistler and rider as they sped through tufts of high prairie grass. She smiled, sensing the hawk's mind above her and she let her own inner eye travel up to it. In a blink she could see with preternatural clarity, saw herself from above, looking down as she rode her whistler through the sun-dappled landscape. She could see each blade of grass that she sped past, saw the wisps of her own hair that had escaped the short tail at the back of her head. When her whistler disturbed a grouse and sent it thundering off across the grassland, her vision reeled as the hawk stooped, spiraling down toward earth, speed stealing the breath from her nostrils, wind streamlining her body, plunging. The grouse drummed its wings in straight-line flight, easily marked as Speaks While Leaving opened her own wings, pulling up from the stoop. The grouse saw the shadow, sensed danger closing, saw sunlight glint from the dark eye as death swept down, stretched her talons, and struck.

Speaks While Leaving blinked again, then looked to her left and saw the puff of feathers, heard the twin-throated shriek as hawk and grouse went down together, bonded in the eternal duet of survival and sacrifice.

Her heart pounded with the memory of the flight and she could almost taste the blood in her mouth, so sharply had she seen it all. She often had dreams of flying, but it was never the flight of a bird. In her dreams she was a feather floating in the sun, struggling toward earth, turned aside by the gentlest breeze, buffeted by whim. The flight she yearned to know was the flight of a bird, with wings to control her every move as master of the air.

But which wings would she choose? Powerful, hunting wings like the hawk that had just given her a glimpse of it all? Or the short, stubby wings of the grouse, used rarely and usually in panicked flight. No, surely not that. Then what of the broad, silent wings of the owl, never heard until it was too late? Or the blurred wings of the hummingbird, zipping up, down, forward and back, hovering to taste each floret on a chestnut tree, sitting on the air as if the world had no hold on her at all?

It was a childish fancy, this sort of dream-gathering, like the game her grandmother, Healing Rock Woman, used to play with the children of their band. "Would you trade your legs," she would ask, coming up behind the first child, "if you could...swim like a fish?" And she would tickle up and down the child's calves. "Would you trade your hands," she would say to the next, hands ready to tickle ribs, "if you could fly like a bird?" She would go all around the circle of children, giggles preceding her, giggles following her, asking what they would trade for the shifting colors of the whistler, the roar of the walker, the sight of the eagle, or the claws of the bear. And dutiful to the game, at the end they all would ask, "What of the buffalo? What can we trade to be a buffalo?" And she would beckon them all close, and they would crowd in, her hands petting their sun-warmed hair as she explained what they all knew quite well. "I am sorry, sweet ones, but you cannot be the buffalo, for you do not have enough to trade. The buffalo is everything to us. He gives us his hide to make our homes, his pelt to keep us warm. He gives us meat to eat; he gives us his bones, his horns, his hooves for our tools and utensils. He has the strength to leap a whistler's back, the courage to face the greatest hunters, and the heart to survive the deepest winter. His hooves make the world tremble like a drum-skin. No, children. We would have to trade away all that we have and all that we would ever have, just to be the buffalo for a single day. That is why we are so grateful, each time a buffalo gives up his life for us."

Speaks While Leaving had not thought of that game for many years. All of her childhood memories, in fact, had been tucked away, hidden from view. And as the warmth of the memory faded into sadness, she remembered why she had stored them all away and never took them out. The path she walked now was very far from those days, as were her dreams of an ordinary life with a husband, a lodge, and children. She was denied that life because of who she was, *what* she was; she was Speaks While Leaving, seeress and vision-maker. She was anything but ordinary, and the simple joys of family, of storytelling, and of happy faces around the lodge-fire were never to be part of her extraordinary life.

But before she put the memories away again, she allowed herself to finish the game, playing all the birds she knew, watching them fly through her dreaming, until she decided on which one would be the one for her.

Blue jay, with his full wings, shiny feathers splayed like the ribs of the fans carried by the women she met in the Land of the Iron Shirts. Yes, blue jay, who would throw himself out of a high tree, arrowing down to a nut or tasty grub, flaring his wings only at the last moment to land with a bounce on the forest floor. Yes, those were the wings she would choose, a dancer's wings that could spiral around trees, twisting from limb to limb, playing chase with all her fellows.

Thunder rolled in, encroaching on her thoughts. She turned, pulled her whistler to a stop, and stared.

The storm that on last glimpse had been building quietly, miles behind, was now upon her. The clouds writhed, rolling as she watched, and even though sunshine still dappled the hills ahead, the storm behind her was dark, thick, and ominous. Lightning flashed. Thunder came on a blast of wind, and out from under the shadow of the storm came another sound: lower, insistent, borne of rushing winds. Dust, grass, and leaves swirled up from the ground, and a dark spiral reached down from the storm.

The wind's moan rose in pitch, and the spiral dropped to the land, an inky finger that dragged a line across the earth, scraping up plants and dirt. It moved, swiftly scouring a trench across the prairie, thickening as it went, hopping up and stabbing down again. The air went opaque with sudden rain, and the panicked trumpeting of her whistler broke through her fascination. She turned northward, toward the hills and the trees, and let her whistler do the rest as the menacing coil spun its way toward them.

Other animals joined them in flight, but many proved too slow and were taken up by an invisible hand, devoured by the storm. The whistler was fast, but the snaking storm was faster, closing the gap as it intensified into something almost solid. The wind buffeted them while debris and hailstones struck her side and her whistler's flank. They could not outrun it, so she yanked on the bridle and sent them off at an angle. The twister leapt across distance as they turned, its towering bulk limned with lightning, thunder crashing and wind roaring like a hundred walkers. She lay low along the whistler's back, aiming for the trees ahead. The twister spun, but did not turn to follow. They ducked in past the line of trees, reaching it along with a pair of does and one terrified coyote. She did not stop, but let her whistler run farther into the wood, following a well-worn deer track that twisted through the trees. She looked back. The branches lashed with the violence of the passing storm and closed behind them. Thunder broke above and the wind howled like a wounded beast. She did not notice when the trail widened.

The whistler sang a rough, high note. She turned and saw the danger. The walker had been hiding at the edge of the clearing, waiting for prey to come in along the trail. The beast lunged and her whistler shrieked, claws tearing into the soft ground. Speaks While Leaving held on as her mount thrust to the side; the walker's lunge went wide, jaws clacked shut on empty space. It pivoted sharply, swinging its heavy tail in counterbalance, snapping tree limbs in the small clearing. From the sheath at her belt, Speaks While Leaving pulled her knife as the walker came at them again. The whistler leapt away, avoiding the teeth, but the walker shoved forward, butting the whistler and sending mount and rider sprawling against nearby tree trunks. Speaks While Leaving's leg was trapped beneath the whistler, tangled in the first rope. She kicked to free herself. The walker set its feet and ran forward again, mouth agape, teeth flashing. Lightning burst in the sky as the jaws came down, teeth sinking into both her arm and the whistler's shoulder. Whistler and rider screamed, their voices lost in the thunderclap. The whistler kicked at the walker's neck with claw-toed feet and Speaks While Leaving stabbed with her knife, aiming for the head that pinned her. The yellow eye saw the blade—too late—as she plunged it deep into the socket. The walker's head jerked to the side, teeth ripping flesh as it recoiled. It reared, twisting, trying to escape the blade and the pain, shaking its head to free the knife. It stumbled backward, breaking more branches as it writhed until, with one terrible swing, it impaled itself, skewering neck and skull on the pointed ends of broken limbs sticking out from the trunk of a spruce. It fell to the ground, thrashed twice, three times, and was still.

Everything was hushed; even the wind had gone quiet, the storm blown out, leaving only the patter of droplets from the leaves above. Sunlight sifted down through the rain-slick branches, dappling the silent clearing. It would have been beautiful, but for the bodies of whistler and walker illuminated by the shafts of light and the thick, nauseous smell of blood that hung in the stillness like a miasma.

Speaks While Leaving moved her injured arm and cried out at the sudden pain. Blood seeped from deep wounds along her biceps and she could feel the grating ends of a broken bone in her forearm. She blinked to focus her mind and worked fast. The walker's teeth had sawn through flesh and bone with equal ease. Her arm was laid open in several places, exposing the twitching muscles beneath. Her hand was useless below the knot made by the broken bone in her forearm. She braced her right foot against the spine of her dead whistler and shoved, rocking it forward just enough to free her pinned leg.

She stopped, tasting metal in her mouth and feeling fire in her lungs. She reached for her side-bag and a length of cloth. Only then did she notice the broken branch that pierced her side. First things first, her teeth had to suffice as she tore off the cloth into strips. She wound the strips of cloth tight about her upper arm to stem the flow of blood.

Then she turned her attention to the length of wood that speared her side. Pain flowed into her like a river, pulsing with every labored breath, every slowing heartbeat. Her vision began to dim, but when she heard the heavy footsteps of an animal, her heart pounded with renewed energy, bringing her back to focus. Through her growing fog of shock, she saw a dark, massive shape lumber into the clearing. She had no weapon, no knife, no tool, not even a stick with which to defend herself. Her only chance lay in stillness, and the hope that the larger bodies nearby would prove more interesting to... Then she saw the glow.

The animal was still in the shadows, but it carried with it a glow. She squeezed shut her eyes, forcing clarity to her vision, but still her vision swam and blurred. The glow atop the animal slipped down to the ground, came forward, and she saw one of her ghosts, one of the spectral figures that followed everyone during twilight hours.

But where those ghosts had always come in threes, this one was alone. She watched as it came closer, curious, her mind detached. The danger of her situation was forgotten, or at least set aside, while she puzzled over this curious arrival. What was this creature, shaped so like a man, broad and tall, but with hair long and unbraided. The ghost came forward quickly, passing from shadow into one of the shafts of light. She smiled.

"It's you," she said.

"Yes," Limps said.

Limps had been a soldier for many years; for as long as Speaks While Leaving could remember, he had been the tall, silent presence on the periphery of anything that had to do with the Kit Fox soldier society. He was never the one expected to become a chief—he never had the gifts—but he was never far away from those who did, including Storm Arriving, for whom he was a constant and dependable advisor. His career was studded with successful raids, skirmishes, and battles. He even faced the father of One Who Flies on the plains along the Kansa River. She wondered if One Who Flies knew that, as she watched Limps dress and bind her wounds.

But Limps had never married, had never even courted a woman. Many of the old grandmothers of her band, gossiping around the beading circle, considered him a Man-Becoming-Woman, but others laughed at that idea.

"He has a heart for women," her aunt, Diving Lizard Woman used to say. "For one woman, at any rate." Others around the circle would nod, agreeing with the obscure proclamation, but when Speaks While Leaving asked what they meant she received only smiles and silence.

Now, as she watched him work, she finally understood. His figure was limned in the glow of his combined purpose; there was no fracturing of possible paths for him. He was unified, a man of single purpose. His brow knitted in concentration. For the most part, he knew what to do—he had seen more than his share of battles and injuries. When there was doubt, she saw it on his face and guided him with a gesture or answered his one-word questions with a word of her own. Occasionally his gaze would meet hers and hold for a moment, just a moment, just the briefest lingering that spoke to her and told her, showed her, cried out to her with the truth that she had never been able to see, the truth that she had never imagined.

"You love me," she said.

He paused in his cleansing of the wound in her side and looked at her. His eyes were black, shadowed by loose hair fallen forward, but they shone, reflecting the light that spilled down through the trees, bathing her. He did not speak, did not acknowledge her statement, but the corner of his mouth lifted in the slightest hint of a smile, just as his eyes grew sad. He returned to his ministrations.

"How long?" she asked.

He froze.

"Forever," he said, and continued his work.

He dressed the wound that had pierced her back to front, layering compresses of tree moss, using brain tissue from the fallen walker as a cleansing salve, binding it all with birch-bark and strips of deerhide, thin and supple. He re-bandaged the wound on her arm, and wrapped her forearm against a splint made from planks he cut from a broken branch. Then he swaddled her in a blanket from her side-bags to keep her warm.

She did not have any illusions about her condition; her injuries were grave and infection almost certain, though the aid Limps had provided had improved her chances greatly.

He brought his whistler near and transferred to it everything he could salvage from her belongings. Exhaustion and shock edged closer to her, fuzzing the edges of her consciousness.

"How did you know where I was?" she asked.

"One Who Flies," he said.

121

"He told you I was going?"

Yes, he signed.

"He told you where I was going?"

Yes.

"Did he tell you why?"

A shrug.

"And now?"

He pointed off into the woods, toward what she did not know. "Now, I bring you the rest of the way." He looked directly at her, eyes bold yet intimate. "You and I. We complete the task. Yes?"

She smiled. "Yes. And thank you."

He nodded again, and she slept.

Chapter 14

Plum Moon, Waning
Four Years after the Cloud Fell
North of the Elk River
Crow Territory

She did not know how long they had been moving, or if the day was young or old. Fog enshrouded them and the sun was hidden, struggling to light the world. Limps cradled her in his arms as they traveled; his hair was bright with droplets of mist, his eyes fixed on the trail ahead, the scars across his bare chest and shoulders pale beneath the light from the leaden sky.

He sensed her consciousness, looked down, his face void of expression. Her vision swam, rocked by the whistler's loping gait. She was still cocooned in the blanket, though now its folds were stifling, not comforting. Her skin was hot against the cool air, though her teeth had started to chatter.

"Fever," she managed to say.

He glanced down at her again. She had not told him anything he didn't know already. Holding her so close, he knew. He had felt her burning in his arms. She realized that he had expected it—with such injuries, it was almost impossible to avoid—and also that he knew what it likely meant. So, she did not press against his reserve, but let him goad the whistler, keep the pace even over level ground, and get them to whatever goal he had set.

The fever increased. She felt like an autumn leaf too close to an evening fire. Her skin blistered, cracked open, peeled back, began to smolder. The fog's moist kiss sizzled against her cheek. Her eyes clouded as they cooked within her boiling blood. She moaned, felt cool water on her lips, and swallowed with a throat seared by her own heat. Her eyelids fluttered and she saw the moon, or was it the cloud-masked sun, swimming in mist? She heard the whistler's fluting call, smelled the spice of its skin, smelled smoke, was she burning again? There were voices, several, shouting, demanding. Whistlers sang, discordant, and a coyote raised a question to the sky. She opened her eyes and stood naked at the edge of a stream-fed pond. It was night and the moon hung low, glistening in a clear sky, but the world around her was lit by the flames that danced on her skin and through her hair. Across the pond, Coyote waited, his eyes bright with her firelight.

"Who are you?" Coyote yipped from across the water.

"I am Speaks While Leaving," she told him.

"No," Coyote said, laughing. "You. Who are *you?*"

"That is who I am," she insisted. "I am Speaks While Leaving."

"No," Coyote said. He laughed again. "You cannot be she."

"Why can I not?"

Coyote rolled on the pond bank, his laughter bouncing off the moon, his pink tongue bright in her firelight. Then he stopped, stood, and looked at her.

"Because Speaks While Leaving is dead."

He turned and loped off into the night, his laughter echoing. A dragonfly flew past, touching the calm water. Ripples reached outward, reflecting moonlight, starlight, firelight. The growing circles bounced back from the pool's edge, and the edge became a rim, became a bowl held in a hand. The moon came down out of the sky, dove into the bowl and came up a pale cloth dripping water. Hands wrung the cloth out and brought it close, laying it gently across her forehead.

The firelight was no longer along her skin and in her hair. It rested nearby, in a firepit, its smoke thick with sage and tobacco and fragrant cedar. As the hands retreated, she saw the rising cone of the lodge above her, and the face of Limps, his features a mask of worry.

"I am better now," she told him, but his face did not brighten with the news. She glanced to the side, and saw several men, dozing around the fire. By their clothing, she could tell that they were of the Crow People. Several were chiefs, and a few seemed to be holy men. She recognized Grey Feather among them, and tried to turn, to rise to greet him, but the pain was too great, her weakness too complete, and she lay back down.

"Grey Feather," she said, and his eyes opened. "I come to you; I come to all of the peoples of the north. You are needed. I have had a vision, and we must all act as one."

The other men had awakened, and though no one spoke, they all sought each other with their eyes. She saw fear within them, and strove to calm them.

"I am Speaks While Leaving," she said, "and I bring this vision to you, to see for yourselves, so that you will know the truth of it."

She reached to the spirit world and began to weave them all together, all the chiefs and grandfathers present, into one mind. Around the edges of the lodge, shadows deepened and stood as the spirit powers stepped into the world of the People, and with a flash of light, the vision began.

She could see their faces as they watched, saw their mouths hang open in silent awe, saw them shout in sudden fright at what played out in their minds.

"Three paths," she told them. "Three choices. At the outset, each one as proper as the next. We can act alone, refusing all alliance with the *vé'hó'e;* we can join with the Iron Shirts against the bluecoats; or, now that we have proven our power to our oldest enemy, we can join with the bluecoats against the foe he fears even more than he fears us."

The chiefs traveled the three paths, seeing each one through to its culmination.

"Solitary action leads to oblivion, as we become nothing beneath the winds of time. Alliance with the Iron Shirts enslaves us, chaining us to their ways. And now, watch, see! See what happens when we join together, first among ourselves, and then with the bluecoats! See!"

She looked at their faces and saw the comprehension dawn, saw the long view come into focus, as the bluecoats suddenly saw them not as hated enemy, but as vital ally. The vision faded, and only the firelight remained. Some chiefs put their heads in their hands, overcome by the experience, while others continued to stare into the distance where the other world had been. Grey Feather rubbed a hand across his face, and looked over at Speaks While Leaving.

"Do you see, now?" she asked him. "Do you understand?"

"Great Daughter, I see," he said, his voice thick. "It shall be done."

Speaks While Leaving looked at Limps. He dipped the cloth into the bowl of cool water. His face was streaked with tears as silently he began to bathe her hands and then her arms. She was too tired to speak any more, and drifted off into oblivion.

Chapter 15

Thursday, October 9th, AD 1890
Advance Camp
Spanish Expeditionary Forces
Near the Red Paint River
Alliance Territory

The tent flap opened and Alejandro looked up from his work as D'Avignon came in, unannounced and unbidden.

"Do you try to be rude?" Alejandro asked, annoyed. "Or is it just a gift you have?"

D'Avignon waved a hand, dismissing the gibe. "They're all gone, Excellency. All of them!"

"Gone?" The man was speaking in riddles. "Who? Gone where? What are you—?"

"From the Indian camp," D'Avignon explained. "All our babysitters are gone. One Who Flies, Storm Arriving, even that spooky Speaks While Leaving. Gone!"

Alejandro leaned elbows on his worktable and steepled his fingers. "Which means what? Exactly?"

D'Avignon looked around theatrically. "It means," he said, "that the hen house is unguarded."

Alejandro rolled his eyes skyward. "I swear to God above, I haven't the vaguest idea what you're talking about."

D'Avignon brandished his fist in exasperation. "We're

free to act!" he said. "We're free to prospect where we will!"

Alejandro shook his head, comprehension dawning. "Haven't you been making progress with your panning in the lowlands?"

"Mere ounces," the rogue said with a wave. He was positively gleeful. He looked around once more, as if there might have been others in the tent beside the two of them. Then he stepped forward, showed the fist he had been flailing about, and slammed it down on the table.

"I'm talking *pounds,*" he said, and lifted his hand to reveal two bean-sized nuggets. Even through the soil that caked them, they gleamed with a honeyed fire.

Alejandro stared. His hand reached forward of its own volition, needing to touch the nuggets and prove that they were real.

Despite the dirt that clung to their crevices, the metal was smooth and still warm from D'Avignon's clutch. With a finger and thumb, Alejandro picked up one of them. It was the size of a broad-bean.

So heavy! he thought, and realized that he was grinning.

"You see?" D'Avignon said.

"Where did you find them?"

"Up there." D'Avignon pointed in a generally northward direction.

"Damn it," Alejandro said, feeling the jubilant mood sour. "You know what happened last time."

D'Avignon crossed his arms over his chest and rocked back on his heels.

"I picked those up off the ground."

Alejandro blinked. He looked at the nuggets, then back at D'Avignon.

"This site is too rich to ignore," D'Avignon said.

Alejandro thought about it. The Cheyenne, with One Who Flies as their spokesman, had been perfectly clear: no mining in their holy hills. But D'Avignon was right. This was too rich an opportunity to ignore. And now, with their overseers gone and the tribes already starting to leave the main camp for their winter grounds, who would know? If Storm Arriving, One Who Flies, and most of the soldiers were busy with shoring up Pereira's incompetence, who would be here to check on what they were doing? Who would be here to object?

"What about men? Who would we get? I'm still dealing with the problems the last group created."

D'Avignon smiled. "I have that completely under control. A small group. Hand-picked from our panners. I had to promise a bit more, but with what I've seen already, that won't be a problem. And that earlier trouble? It will only help keep this group in line."

Alejandro thought about it. Hard. It was risky, but the reward! He looked at the nugget again, felt its heavy warmth in his palm. He'd been playing it too safe with these savages.

"Why not?" he said. "The Crown will get their lands; the priests will get their souls. Why shouldn't I get their gold?" He laughed. "Bring your men here. Tonight, when the priests are at compline."

D'Avignon rubbed his hands together. "We'll be here with bells on."

After D'Avignon left, Alejandro toyed with the two nuggets of gold. He pressed on one of them with the edge of his thumbnail, leaving a dent in the soft metal.

He shook his head in disbelief, grinning.

When the priests were occupied with their late night devotions, D'Avignon brought his squad to Alejandro's tent. They were eight in number, rough men already used to the work D'Avignon had set for them at the lowland sluices. They smelled of sweat and soil, but had an easy manner around each other. Alejandro saw smiles and lots of eye contact.

Good, he said to himself. He knew that if they were already comfortable working as a team, there would be less friction. He stood and saw them all square up and give him their attention. Another good sign.

He looked at D'Avignon and motioned toward the tent flap. The prospector took a quick look outside, drew the flaps closed, and nodded.

Alejandro looked at the men, let them see him assaying each of them in turn. "You have been chosen for a very special project," he began. "This job is risky, and it has dangers. To minimize these, there are strict rules to which you must adhere. It is also a project that is of the utmost secrecy."

He went to his desk and picked up his Bible. He held it out toward the men.

"Hands on the Book."

The men gathered forward and all touched the book. Alejandro could feel their heat, sensed their readiness, like a pack of wolves ready for the hunt.

"You will all take a solemn oath. Before God, you will swear to say nothing of this project, tell no one of our activities or our goals, and to follow all my specific rules to the letter." One by one, he looked each man in the eye.

"Before God, do you swear it?"

"I do," they all said.

He smiled at them and saw his smile returned.

"Now, to business."

Chapter 16

Plum Moon, Waning
Four Years after the Cloud Fell
North of the Sudden River
Alliance Territory

George urged his walker up toward the crest of the low rise. From her position behind him on the wicker saddle, Mouse Road clambered up to stand on the walker's haunches. She peered cautiously over the rise.

"A blind man could find them," she said. "But they are still ahead of us."

It was true. It had not been hard to track the Spanish army. They left a trail as plain as a herd of bison. As they crossed over the top of the rise, George could see the swath of dark, torn earth, the ruts through uprooted grass, the trampled brush, all wending and winding across the prairie like the path of a staggering drunkard. As they had been tracking the army, twice each day they discovered the refuse of a night's encampment. The Spaniards did not travel fast, nor were they fastidious.

"We should sight them soon," he said. He pointed out a similar trail a half-mile distant. "That must be the blue-coats. A smaller force, but less than a day ahead. We will probably meet them at the Black Rocks."

At midday they stopped at a creek to let the walker drink her fill. Mouse Road was filling waterskins and George was rubbing the walker's flanks with sagebrush when a faint *boom* echoed over the rim of a rolling hill. The three of them froze, heads high, listening. Another *boom,* then *boom-boom-boom.*

"At the Black Rocks, just as you said," George said. In a few moments, he and Mouse Road had stowed their belongings, mounted the walker, and were on their way.

The walker loped over the folds in the rolling landscape, pushing up the gentle slopes, chuffing with each step, thudding downhill on the far side, until they came to the top of a low, flat rise and she slowed, sensing her rider's desire.

Steel-grey clouds were piled up above a hard line in the sky, their bellies dark with shadow, their towering heads blinding white with crisp sunlight. Beneath the clouds, dappled with acres of shadow and light, lay a broad plain studded with hummocks of amber grass and pools of bronze blanketflowers. George scanned the landscape and assessed the situation.

The Spaniards were nearest to them, attacking from the right as George looked out across the battlefield. Their artillery was on the slope of a rise, fire blazing from muzzles in flashes that lit the bellies of the clouds and spewed founts of smoke. The cannonshots were answered by bursts a mile distant, pockmarking the land where the bluecoat forces scurried in seemingly haphazard frenzy. Across the land between, beneath the arc of cannonfire, the Spanish infantry advanced in precise squares, moving in blocks, shifting by ranks and files, wheeling at shouted commands. The Spanish cavalry stood on the right flank, waiting for the artillery to finish before committing themselves to the fight.

The bluecoats, by contrast, were all mounted, riding helter-skelter over the field beneath the huge dark mass of exposed rock that gave the place its name. George saw the flash of yellow lining as US Cavalry capes fluttered. The bluecoat riders flowed over the land, commanding nothing, but occupying every extent of their chosen territory. The Spanish artillery would just dial in the distance for a volley when, like a flock of starlings, the US riders would double-back, steer into, or veer away from the infantry. And at every turn, every halt, every pause, the American carbines would raise, level, fire, and drop a handful of infantry or even wound one of the Spanish horses. The bluecoats were outnumbered at least five to one, but they were like fish in a stream, the Spanish tactics too clumsy to touch, much less catch them.

Puffs of smoke from the left caught George's eye, and off to that flank he spied soldiers from the People. Their whistlers were bedded down, camouflage skins matching the amber of the dried grass. Behind these living ramparts, soldiers leveled rifles and took long shots at the bluecoat riders. The distance was so great that few of the shots found any mark at all. George estimated their number at a hundred, only half of the still-unused Spanish cavalry that stood on the right flank, but a force that, used correctly, could easily turn this battle around.

He shook his head. "Schoolboy tactics," he muttered.

Mouse Road tapped him on the shoulder and signed a question against the din of cannon-roar and gun-fire.

George gestured to the Spanish forces. "The Iron Shirt war chief is not very experienced," he shouted over his shoulder.

Good, she signed, and George laughed at her succinct appraisal.

He nudged the walker into motion and guided her toward the whistler riders. They were spotted quickly, but a rider on a walker had to be a friend, so they approached without challenge. George led his walker to the rear, a bit away from the main group, and they dismounted. When they turned, Storm Arriving was there, fists on hips, his expression as dark as the clouds overhead.

"What are *you* doing here?" he demanded.

George hadn't thought of how to broach the subject, so he sidestepped. "It can wait," he said as he walked around Storm Arriving and his glower to view the battlefield. "Why aren't you out there? What is that idiot waiting for?"

Storm Arriving barked a laugh and George knew he'd struck the right note. "His name is Pereira, and he is as green as springtime. We could not understand a word he said until two days ago, when Little Fox arrived to interpret the Iron Shirt's tongue." He came up beside George to view the field. "Now I wish his words were still unknown to us."

Mouse Road came up between them, and George felt her hand slip into his. "You do not like what he says?" she asked.

Storm Arriving grunted in disgust. "He tells us to wait, like his own riders wait, until the field is prepared and ready for us. But the field is never ready."

"What do you mean?" Mouse Road asked.

"Watch," Storm Arriving said. "It will happen any moment."

George knew what was meant; he could see it on the field, as clear as if it were a diagram on a chalkboard. The artillery was to pound the enemy position while the infantry moved into the mid-range and set up in defensible squares. Then the infantry would advance at the quick-step, moving directly against the softened enemy fortifications, while the cavalry units would range wide, taking the enemy from the flank or rear.

Down on the field, the cannonade had been useless—there were no fortifications to soften—but the infantry had dutifully performed its slow, ponderous dance. A bugle call went up from the artillery lines.

"There it is," Storm Arriving said. Shouts drifted through the sudden quiet. Infantrymen readied bayonets. Spanish horses whinnied as riders prepared. The whistler riders, George noted, did not bother to ready themselves.

As if taking orders from the Spanish bugle, the bluecoat cavalry turned as one and simply, almost casually, departed the field, disappearing around the bulk of the Black Rocks.

"And there they go," Storm Arriving said.

The Spanish cavalrymen were ready to spur their mounts in pursuit, but another bugle call was given, and the entire army halted. Infantry turned and headed back to friendly lines. Artillery squads began to sort their equipment and stow it for travel. The cavalry remained unused on the flank, brides at an empty altar.

"Every time," Storm Arriving said.

"What do your patrols report?" George asked.

Storm Arriving shrugged. "The Iron Shirt general instructed us not to send out patrols. He did not want us to get shot by his pickets."

"Still," George said. "What do they tell you?"

Storm Arriving glanced across at him. "Do you think you know me so well?"

George kept his gaze on the battleground. "Do you think I know you so little?"

Storm Arriving humphed and let a moment of silence linger between them. "My scouts tell me that the bluecoats are not retreating from our advance, but leading us onward. They report that the bluecoat foot soldiers and cannon-men approach from the north." He gestured to the right, where the main support force of the Spanish army spread across the plain like a disturbed anthill. "And they report that the Iron Shirt pickets are more interested in the schedule of supply wagons from the west than they are in bluecoat scouting parties to the east."

"The bluecoats shorten their supply lines, while the Iron Shirts lengthen theirs," George said. "Where are the rest of your riders?"

"Why do you think—" He was cut short by a sisterly thump to the arm from Mouse Road.

"Stop it," she said. "I see only Kit Fox. Where are Red Shields? The Little Bowstrings? The war chiefs sent you many others."

Storm Arriving glared at her from the corner of his eye. Then a smile crept across his lips, the first one George had seen on his face in a very long time.

"They range far ahead of us," he said, and George could hear the pride in his voice. "While the Iron Shirts worry about provisions, we worry about the enemy." His smile broadened into a grin. "The bluecoat supply wagons keep us well fed. Tragically, some also catch fire and burn."

For the first time, George wished that Storm Arriving was less adept as a military leader. His expertise and experience were not helping to bring Speaks While Leaving's vision into reality.

"And now I would ask again why you are here," Storm Arriving said, "but we will only be interrupted." He nodded toward an approaching squad of riders. "Your arrival has been noted."

Five Spanish riders on horseback pushed up the rise toward them. George saw at once that two were officers—a captain and his aide—while the other three were for appearance of strength and, possibly, judging from the wary look in their eyes, for protection. The two factions were not on the best of terms, it seemed. That was good.

Storm Arriving motioned to his men, calling over his interpreter, but before he could finish the command the captain arrived and spoke.

"Do I address the son of American President Custer?" he said, speaking in thickly-accented English.

Judging by the captain's tone, he wasn't sure if he was about to be welcomed or arrested. Nevertheless, he answered, "Yes. I am the son of President Custer. Among the Cheyenne, I am known as One Who Flies. Who, may I ask, are—"

"I bring you greetings from our commander, General Francisco Antonio Perez Almeida Pereira, and an invitation to dine with him and his officers, this evening."

Storm Arriving looked over at George, wanting to be included in the conversation.

"He invites me to dinner with the Iron Shirts," George explained.

Storm Arriving rolled his eyes.

"Do you accept?" the captain asked impatiently.

George wasn't sure what he'd stepped into. "Captain, I am not here in any official capacity," he began.

"Do you accept?" the captain repeated.

George considered his options. A refusal, no matter how diplomatically stated, would lose all grace in the delivery and translation from this messenger. Acceptance was the wisest course, despite the annoyance it would cause Storm Arriving.

"Graciously," George replied with a bow of the head, doubting that either his words or his sarcasm would be accurately conveyed to the general.

"You will be called for," the captain said, then turned and departed.

Storm Arriving laughed bitterly. "We have ridden with these...soldiers...for half a moon. We have saved their skins in battle, and yet they keep us separate and will only speak to us in their own tongue or with gestures from a child's game. You arrive and before the sun moves not only do they have someone who speaks your Horse Nations tongue, but they invite you to eat at their fire." He walked a slow circle and lifted his hands to the heavens. "These are the allies we are given?"

George looked to Mouse Road. She nodded.

"Let me tell you why we are here," he said.

Storm Arriving looked at them both, having noted their silent exchange. "The Council did not send you."

"No," George admitted.

"I am not going to like this, am I?"

George squinted one eye into a half-grimace. "I do not think so."

Storm Arriving grunted. "We will return to the camp. The Iron Shirts never march on a battle day."

George and Mouse Road went back to the walker and fell in parallel to the other riders, keeping a prudent distance between his mount and the whistlers. Behind them, the Iron Shirts trudged back to their own encampment, urged onward by drumbeat and shouted command. George looked to the east, to the Black Rocks beyond which the bluecoats had ridden. It was easy to see that the Spanish were not the allies they had hoped, but... He shook his head.

"What is it?" Mouse Road asked.

George shrugged. "It is just hard to believe," he said.

She put her hands over his eyes. "Remember," she said, and the vision filled him, as clear as if he was staring at it with open eyes: the paths, the journeys, the choices, the outcomes. The conviction filled his heart, but his mind refused to give in, resisting what felt so true.

"But the bluecoats," he muttered. "Allies?"

He heard his wife's breath in his ear, heard her smile. "After all the things you have seen, you balk at this?"

And then he understood: he doubted it *could* be simply because it *hadn't* been; with that thought, it was gone, the doubt gone in a puff of wind like a dandelion's seed-head.

The soldiers' camp was separated from the Iron Shirts', primarily to keep the whistlers away from the Spanish horses but George knew there were other, uglier reasons, just as the Council had instructed Alejandro's force to camp downstream from the People. The two cultures were opposite in nearly every way, though no different than the People and the bluecoats might be. Each side thought little of the other, deemed them filthy and backward, judged their people mad or savage or demented or monstrous. George was probably the only person alive who had truly experienced both cultures. The People were not all good; he knew that, just as he knew that the Iron Shirts were not all bad. Reconciling the two cultures would not be a task of years. With either the Iron Shirts or the bluecoats, it would be the work of decades.

He looked over at the whistler riders. The soldiers complained, joked, laughed, trading jeers and barbs as men will to keep their spirits up after a disappointment. Storm Arriving rode in their midst, shrouded in silence, a man apart. Convincing him would be difficult—George wondered if it was even possible. "Contingencies," his father used to say, over and over, to George, to his command staff, to whomever would listen. "Plan for what you want, and then plan for what will work." George knew what he wanted; he just needed to figure out what would work.

At camp, Storm Arriving set his soldiers about their duties while George made his walker comfortable, taking off the rope and wicker riding gear, and rubbing her down with a rough piece of hide to clean away the dust of their journey. As she was soothed by his ministrations, her calmness fed back to George, an echo of an echo. His mind was emptied of questions as he worked, leaving a blank slate upon which answers could be written. By the time he turned away from his walker to go and find Storm Arriving, contingencies had begun to form.

Storm Arriving sat on a spread hide, cleaning the disassembled pieces of his rifle. Mouse Road stood nearby, scratching his resting whistler's spine. She was telling him about Alejandro as George walked up, and of how his Ravens had been unfairly doling out their assistance to the poor.

Storm Arriving glanced up at George. "You two did not come all this way to complain about the Iron Shirts' Ravens," he said as he began to reassemble his weapon.

"No," George replied. "We came to tell you about Speaks While Leaving."

Storm Arriving's face went cold, his look dismissive beneath a raised eyebrow.

"She has shown us her vision."

A flicker crossed his features. "Shown?" he said, putting the last pieces of his weapon in place. "You mean she told you of it."

"No," George said. "She showed it to us."

He sat down across from his old friend and told him of their experience. Mouse Road joined in the telling, the story spilling out of them. George held nothing back, hoping his zeal would be infectious. He told of his own reluctance, his own doubts, and of the feeling of truth that had filled him whenever he recalled the vision. But as they spoke to him, a fire began to smolder within Storm Arriving, and the more fervor they put into the tale, the more that fire grew. Finally, they stopped, their words petering out, the outburst imminent.

"The bluecoats," he said, barely controlled. "After all the visions of the Iron Shirts, after she went across the waters to bring them back here, now she says that *they* are the true danger, and our hope lies with the *bluecoats?*"

"I had the same thoughts," George said quickly.

"The spirits only told her part of the tale," Mouse Road said.

"You know the visions are sometimes unclear," George added.

"Unclear?" he shouted, his hand flashing out to grab George by the shirtfront. "My daughter died because of her vision, and you say it was because it was unclear?" He released George and stood. "How much do we risk, while she searches for clarity? How many will die this time, because she is not clear?"

George raised his hands, his gaze lowered deferentially. "To survive, we must build an alliance with the *vé'hó'e*," he said. "The Iron Shirts are the leverage we need to bring the bluecoats to our side. I know you see that."

He glared at George. "I see only a mess, made by her visions. I see only the lives it has cost us, and the lives it *will* cost us to put things right." He turned and George stood to

139

follow, but Mouse Road rose and put a hand on his arm.

"Let him go," she said. "For now."

The sun was ready to set, and George and Mouse Road were leaning against his walker, waiting for Storm Arriving to return when two riders came up from the Spanish camp, a third horse in tow. They stopped, and one of the riders dismounted. He came forward, stopping some yards away, unwilling to approach the walker. He gave a shallow nod in greeting.

"Your presence is expected at our commander's tent," he said. He indicated the third horse. "If you will accompany us?"

George turned to Mouse Road and gave her a smile of farewell.

Eyes open, she signed.

He swung up onto the horse—it felt small and spindly compared to riding on the back of whistlers and walkers—and followed his escorts back to the Spanish camp.

The general's tent was a large, square affair, with a peaked roof, crenelated fringe, and striped awning over the entrance flap. It reminded George of the pavilions of old, and he fairly expected to see conquistadors in chain mail and crested metal helmets stationed at guard rather than the riflemen who stood on either side.

Ushered within, he saw at once that the general was new to command. A small group of officers stood talking and laughing, smoke from their cigars heavy in the air. The trappings of power and privilege had been placed around the interior: a rack with three swords stood atop a heavy sideboard, a tray with crystal decanter and snifters to one side. Next to the sideboard was a stand with the chain mail and helm George had expected to see outside. Strung taut along one side of the tent was a hide, painted with a map of the states of Nueva España. In the center of the room, a long, narrow table with three chairs on either side and one at the head, all with places set before them in china, linen, and silver-plate. George had seen the tent of many a field commander, from the brilliant to the able to the comical, and this one betrayed a serious lack of self-confidence.

140

During his evaluation, conversation had halted. George noted the slack-jawed expressions. He didn't know what these men had expected—after all, he had lived with the People for over four years—but they obviously had expected something other than a blond-haired native in deerskins and breechclout. He saw their surprise and, from a few, disgust, and did his best not to react in kind.

An officer—the general himself, by his uniform—disengaged from the group of stunned gawkers and came over to George, hand extended.

"Mister Custer," the general said in English with only a hint of an accent. "Welcome. I am General Francisco Pereira."

George smiled. The general was young, just a handful of years older than George himself; some high-ranking relative had likely brevetted him to the rank. He shook the offered hand. "A pleasure to meet you, General" he said.

"I remember seeing you during your visit to San Francisco, some years past. At the *corrida?*" He turned to his other guests. "He and his men had come at the invitation of my uncle, the Viceroy. You should have seen them, gentlemen. It was a remarkable exhibition of riding skills."

The ice broken, the tone set, the other men followed suit. The officers, all hand-picked for the occasion, spoke enough English to carry on a polite conversation, and this they did, over drinks, over dinner, over cigars and brandy afterward. The conversations were innocuous and without substance, despite George's attempts to steer the talk to more meaningful discussions. He had not been invited as a representative of the People; he was here as the son of President Custer, as a curiosity, an interesting spice to enliven their mundane society.

Only once, during the fish course, did he manage to garner any useful information. Complimenting on the sauce, George asked how the general managed his butter stores in such a long supply line. The answer, accompanied with a nonchalant wave of the general's hand, told much more than the general intended.

Following the meal, George returned to Mouse Road and immediately sought Storm Arriving. They found him sharpening his knife, sitting near the story fire where some of the men tied tales one to the next, laughing at stories of one another's missteps, smiling at each other's valor.

"Back from supper with your friends, I see," Storm Arriving said.

George ignored the taunt. "Time is shorter than we thought," he told him.

"Short? For what?"

"For defeating the Iron Shirts. We must break with them and ally ourselves with the bluecoats, and soon."

Mouse Road nudged George's arm. "You have learned something," she said. "What?"

Storm Arriving snickered. "Learned something? From that squirrel-head? Impossible."

George shrugged. "He said it as a brag, but it told me much."

"What?" Mouse Road urged, more interested than her brother.

"I asked how he managed to get fresh butter, with his supply lines so long, and he told me it was impossible now. Then he said that it was no matter, because they'd be getting more soon enough, plus some fresh fruit for his table."

Storm Arriving stopped honing his blade. "Fresh milk fat *and* fresh fruit?"

"Yes," George said, glad that Storm Arriving had come to the same conclusion.

"What?" Mouse Road said. "I don't understand."

Storm Arriving was still staring at his blade, turning it this way and that, studying the edge in reflected firelight. "Milk fat would turn, and fruit would surely spoil, if they came here from the Tejano Coast. So, he must be traveling toward a new supply line, a shorter one."

George leaned forward. "And there's only one place for that," he said.

Storm Arriving pressed his lips into a thin line and frowned. "The Bay of Kansa. The Iron Shirts will be landing a new force somewhere on the northern shore, east of the Sand Hills."

"There is nothing out there but ghost towns, abandoned when the railroads failed. The nearest opposition would be from Fort Whitley, and truthfully, I don't think they're up to facing Iron Shirts." He hooked a thumb toward the Spanish encampment. "Even this group would give them a nasty time."

"When do you think they will arrive?" Mouse Road asked.

George shrugged. "A week, perhaps two. Pereira did not seem to think he would be without butter for very long." He turned back to Storm Arriving. "So you see, we don't have much time before things change dramatically. We *must* broker a deal with the bluecoats. Now."

Storm Arriving finally looked up from the study of his blade. "You think this news changes my mind? With more Iron Shirts, and hopefully some smarter ones, we will have no problem beating the bluecoats."

George slumped, rubbing his forehead. "That is not the point," he said. "Whatever side you ally with, that side will win this conflict."

Storm Arriving pointed at George with his knife. "And you say it should be the bluecoats."

"Yes."

"Because my former wife said so."

"Yes!"

"The woman who you said is not clear about what her visions are telling her."

George grimaced. "You are twisting it all up. We, Mouse Road and I, we have seen this vision. It could not have been clearer."

"In your great experience with visions," Storm Arriving said derisively. He turned his palm upward, signifying his disagreement. "I will not create a new enemy by aligning myself with an old one." He spat on his whetstone and began honing the knife once more.

"Brother..." Mouse Road began.

"No," he said, cutting her short. Then he glared at both of them in turn. "I say no."

Mouse Road looked at George, distress written across her brow. He motioned and they stood and walked away.

"What will we do now?" she asked. "If we cannot convince my brother, how can we avoid the other paths of the vision?"

George put his arm around her shoulder and she put hers around his waist. They stood for a time in silence, and

George kissed the top of her head, the scent of her calming his whirling mind.

Contingencies. Contingencies.

Then a smile began to grow on his lips.

"I have an idea," he said to his wife. "When the time is right, we will need to be ready to move."

Chapter 17

Saturday, October 11th, AD 1890
North of the Niobrara River
Unorganized Territory

Meriwether stood outside his tent, surrounded by activity. Men and horses were gearing up, readying tack and harness. His elite sharpshooters were checking their weapons and supplies. Infantrymen looked on, still displeased that they were being left out of today's fight.

Soon, he said to himself. Soon enough.

He reached into his white glove and pulled out the quarter-folded slip that contained the President's wire. He unfolded it and reread the message. It was a personal wire, not a message relayed through handlers or a coded message from Jacob's War Department. This was from the President himself, and its cryptic tone worried Meriwether all the more.

JOHN,

PUT THE KETTLE ON.
COMING FOR A CHAT.
WESTGATE. WEDNESDAY NEXT.

AUTIE

It didn't make sense or, to be more accurate, it made sense only if Meriwether was missing some important fact. Custer was known for many things, but not making sense wasn't one of them. He was shrewd, and he knew Meriwether well enough to know he'd puzzle over the wire's hidden meaning.

Developments, then. And big ones. Something that could change everything.

The Spanish were nearly in the jaws of his vise. In a week's time they would be within easy range of his foot soldiers and artillery teams, both of which were itching to take their shot at the invaders. The Spanish had been very accommodating, following his strike forces like sheep back to a point where his own supply lines were short enough to be defensible—he had to give the Cheyenne credit for causing that particular headache—and from which he would be able to hit them with a blow that would break their backs, their spirit, and their capacity to do any more harm. When he was done, their only choice would be retreat, and he would make them pay for every bloody step.

What was it, then? What could change everything?

Custer had promised him everything he needed, but Meriwether wasn't so naïve to believe that Custer the commanding officer didn't share a face with Custer the politician. Promises were hopes, and hopes sometimes went unfulfilled. So, either Custer needed some of the men he'd given to Meriwether or....

Spanish reinforcements.

That had the ring of truth to it. And not reinforcements from the west; Meriwether's scouts would have spotted movement of that type. From nearer, then.

From Kansa Bay.

It made sense. The cliffs along the gulf's northern shore were nearly unscalable, and the jungles at the base were home to all sorts of nasty creatures that would tear a landing force to bits overnight. Kansa Bay, however, was lined with sandy beaches all around, none of which were fortified to any extent, especially along the northern side. Meriwether closed his eyes and let the map of the region float in his mind's eye.

He had struggled to pull the Spanish forces across the Niobrara, but in that one thing they had been reluctant to comply. They had followed him eastward like sheep, but it had taken him a fortnight to get them across the Niobrara. Meriwether now saw that rather than him leading the Spaniards into a trap, they had been slowly marching him closer to their own rally point.

"Put an idiot in charge, and make me believe they're all idiots," he said and then cursed himself for an idiot, too. He re-folded the message and stuffed it back under the cuff of his glove.

"McGettigan!" he shouted. His adjutant appeared at his side with a crisp salute. "Change in plan, Captain" he said. "Everyone comes on this trip. Gather the command staff."

"Sir!" McGettigan said, and hurried off to spread the word.

It didn't take long before cheers were heard among the infantry. Meriwether hoped those cheers would keep their spirits up through a forced march.

The men were ready in record time and, to their credit, did not complain at all as they marched through the day and most of the following night. They had outpaced the light artillery Meriwether had selected for the fight, but with double teams of men and horses, the cannon were able to spell each other and catch up while the infantry prepared the stage.

It would not be the stage he had hoped for. There had been many sites from which to choose—the gentle hills that rolled through this part of the territory provided ample combinations of high ground surrounding a level battlefield—but he had been timing things so that it would all come together at the perfect place. Now, though, he was being rushed into a choice, and neither the ground nor the condition of his men would be perfect. But Meriwether had learned long ago that insisting on perfection was the hobgoblin of little minds; it didn't exist, and thus had no place in military thinking.

So, his men would be tired, and the heavy artillery would not be present. But he would have surprise, and more than enough men to handle this simpleton Spaniard. Now, to lay the trap, and let the fool walk into it.

Scouts thundered up to the command group, horses shiny with sweat in the dim light of the waning crescent moon. Urgent words were exchanged and the scouts were let through to speak to Meriwether.

"Sir," said the squad's lieutenant. "They moved up during the night. And you can guess where they are now."

Meriwether closed his eyes and took a deep breath. "Camped?"

"No, sir. Prepared and ready. Heavy rifles and light artillery already emplaced. They own the high ground, sir."

He shook his head. Not good, not good. How they knew was a question for future discussion. The important question right now was whether or not to commit to the changed conditions. He had lost surprise, but he still had better men and better tactics. He looked back to his scout leader.

"Well done. See to your men." The lieutenant saluted and rode off. Then to McGettigan, he said, "Bring me the command staff. We need to talk."

The scouts Storm Arriving had sent out to watch the bluecoat camp had come back as soon as the foot soldiers had joined up with the main body. He knew the land here very well, having patrolled it for years in his younger days, and he could see the path along which the bluecoats were leading them. The battleground would be in one of two spots, and judging by how fast the bluecoats could push their foot soldiers, it was going to be the one nearest the Iron Shirts.

Convincing the fool Pereira was easier than expected. The bluecoats would be at the ground in a day, but the Iron Shirts could be there overnight, if they hurried. The advantages of being there first were obvious, even to Pereira, and so they moved.

They had moved quickly, and now, they waited. Storm Arriving sat with his men in their usual place along the left flank. His sister and One Who Flies waited a stone's throw away, putting a little distance between the lone walker and the whistlers. Pereira, still unable to imagine anything other than what he had already seen, had arranged his forces in nearly the same manner as before: infantry waiting in the center, Iron Shirt cavalry on the right, whistlers on the left. The only deviation was that, since he had sufficient time, he brought his big guns to the high ground. Storm Arriving knew the bluecoat general would do something altogether different from before, and wondered how much he would unbalance Pereira's expectations.

He glanced over to his sister and, now, brother-in-law. They sat close, in deep conversation. One Who Flies pointed out to the field, then drew on the ground before them, explaining something about the coming battle. Mouse Road questioned something on the sketch and One Who Flies signaled agreement. Pleased, they both smiled.

Two emotions flooded through Storm Arriving. He felt a surge of happiness, seeing his sister so happy in a mate. His little sister, so often a thorn in his side, was always the questioner, the challenger, the rebel of the family. He had despaired of ever finding a satisfactory mate for her, and had given up on her ever falling in love. But on her own, she had found a mate perfectly matched to her every aspect, a man with whom Storm Arriving, if he were honest, could find little fault.

Balancing that happiness, though, was a bitter, sharp-edged envy, for he knew he would never know that happiness. His heart had been lost to the wrong woman. Speaks While Leaving was both more and less than a woman; the spirits had given her a power that set her apart. Straddling the divide between this world and the other, that power came at a cost, and the price was very high. He often thought back on their short, happy time together and, in truth, he missed his former wife.

Looking over at his sister's happiness and love, he thought that perhaps his pride and grief had done more damage than had Speaks While Leaving. Babies die, all over the world, for no other reason than because sometimes babies die. Little Blue Shell Woman could just as easily have taken ill at home as she did in the Land of the Iron Shirts. Striking the drum and casting Speaks While Leaving aside had only created more damage, tearing apart their damaged love rather than working through their shared grief to strengthen it.

What, then, of this vision? As his mind turned back to that question, he felt his heart go hard once more. Visions. Had they not seen enough of them? And yet, over the years, her visions had almost always borne fruit. Was it possible that all the backtracks and all the recent missteps, that the problems among the bands and among the allied tribes were all just preparing the ground for this last action? Mouse Road and One Who Flies claimed to have seen the vision and felt the truth of it. But Iron Shirts had come from the southlands to fight *for* the People, not against them. And now more were coming across the Big Salty to join them. This could not be ignored. They had not even been able to get the Crow People to join them for a single season. No, it was not to be believed. She had been mistaken before; she was mistaken now.

His thoughts had taken his attention away, but movement at the far end of the vale brought him back. The battlefield was a long stretch of firm ground flanked by low folds of land on either side. The sound of drums and the high piping notes of bluecoat flutes carried into the vale. Then they saw the flags and the ranks of foot soldiers, all marching into view.

Why wasn't the artillery starting to fire? He looked over at the high ground and saw the artillery teams in disarray, men scrambling for cover, others pulling wounded toward safety. He looked across the field to the high ground opposite and saw small puffs of smoke from the scrub that dotted the slope.

"Snipers!" he shouted, and ordered his men. "Up! Ready!" But before they could mount, the bluecoat cavalry appeared, charging their rear, carbines firing.

His soldiers met them on foot, firing rifles as they tried to mount up. Separated from the main group, One Who Flies got his walker up and in motion. One roar from the great beast set the bluecoat horses skittering to the side in fear, giving their soldiers the moment they needed.

The bluecoats moved downhill in an ordered retreat, trying to draw the riders off, but Storm Arriving refused the bait. "The snipers!" he ordered, and his riders sped off toward the scrub where sharpshooters were making good use of their long rifles.

Meriwether peered through his binoculars and would have chuckled if it hadn't been so sad. The Spanish commander had set it up just as he had every time before. Predictability meant death in their business, and Meriwether was going to prove the point. Instead of pushing into the center with his riders, he split his cavalry and sent them to take the flanks by the rear. The Spanish cavalry was in dire trouble, decimated in the ambush and now foolishly following the Union riders out of the view of their command structure. The Indian riders had fared better, reacted faster, and refused the chase in favor of going after the snipers. Meriwether gave a hand signal and heard his orders relayed to the flagmen. His light artillery opened up on the slope between the Indians and his snipers, stopping the assault before it happened.

Artillery nullified, cavalry scattered, it was now a matter of who could out-tactic whom down on the field. Everything was in place. Time to bring it home.

"General!" McGettigan was pointing off to the right.

Meriwether looked and saw it. One of the Indians was riding out onto the field, alone. He brought the binoculars up again, found, focused.

"It's one of those big walkers," he said, "and the rider has a white flag on his rifle. He's—oh, for Christ's sake!"

"What is it?" McGettigan asked.

"It's the President's son. Of all the hare-brained, reckless, arrogant..." He didn't finish his sentence, but remembered his words to his commander-in-chief.

I treat him just like any other combatant.

If it were any other tribesman, riding out onto the field under a white flag, what would he do? Except it wasn't just any other tribesman.

He sighed.

"Call it off," he told McGettigan.

"Sir?"

"Call it off," he said again. "Let's hear what he has to say."

Bugles trumpeted and flags waved. Troops halted,

turned, and headed off the field. Riders went out to recall the cavalry, artillery teams packed up their caissons, and the long rifles snuck back up and over the hill. The Spaniards stood like waxworks, confounded by the sudden reprieve, and the Indian riders pulled back as soon as the Union soldiers broke off.

Meriwether headed off the field with his command staff, moving back to the staging ground, fearing all today's action had done was to give the Spanish general a preview of future tactics. He just hoped the man proved to be as dense as he was unimaginative.

As soon as George heard the drum and fifes, he recognized the tune of "The Girl I Left behind Me," and knew that John Meriwether was on the field. The song was his marching song, just as "Garryowen" had belonged to George's father.

"Now," he told Mouse Road, and instead of following Storm Arriving against the sharpshooters on the hillside, they rode out onto the field, flying a stolen piece of General Pereira's table linen as a white flag.

"Parley!" George shouted to any and all who might hear him. "Parley!" He kept it up, riding across the empty field between the two forces until, when the signal flags were raised and the bugles sounded the recall, he knew they were safe. From up the hill behind them, he heard his name.

"One Who Flies!" Storm Arriving shouted. "What are you doing?"

"Planning for contingencies!" he shouted in reply. And then the bluecoat rider came up, struggled to control his mount, and accepted their offer of parley.

As they were escorted back behind the lines, the army parted like the Red Sea before Moses, but not out of respect or deference. Many of these men had barely heard of walkers, much less seen one ridden through their ranks. Veterans and green-stick privates alike drew back in fear; some just plain ran, falling over their own feet in instinctive haste to distance themselves from the towering monster. As for his own effect on the soldiers, George knew that he and

Mouse Road were nigh on invisible. Recalling the day he first saw mounted walker, he knew that, even if he were Lady Godiva, these men would never see him. They would only see legs as tall as a man, teeth long as their fingers, a mouth that could swallow a sheep in a gulp, and a living, intelligent, hunter's eye the color of golden wheat and the size of a saucerplate. They would remember the thud of its footsteps, the rumble of its breath, and the sound of their own fear-thick blood pounding in their ears. Such was the awe George's walker inspired in the uninitiated.

They left the battlefield, the infantry at their back, and rounded the bend to where the bluecoats had established their staging ground. The place was controlled chaos, to which George's walker added no order. Ahead, George spied the general in the center of it all; one man in a swirl of motion as reports came in and commands were issued. He spied the walker and visibly mastered himself. All movement shrank back from the general as George rode closer. At a respectful distance he bade his walker halt and coaxed her quietly to the ground. He helped Mouse Road descend, and then stepped down himself. Together, they walked up to the general.

"General Meriwether," George said in English. "Thank you, sir, for honoring our request to parley."

Meriwether nodded. "George," he said in greeting. "You're looking...healthy. And who is this with you?"

"This is Mouse Road," he said. "Of the Tree People Band, sister to Storm Arriving, the man who leads our soldiers. She is also my wife."

That got a reaction. Meriwether's brow knitted but his lips ticked upward the tiniest bit.

"I see," Meriwether said evenly. Then he turned to face Mouse Road and gave a shallow bow. "A pleasure, ma'am."

George told her what he had said, and she replied, "Also for me," which George translated in turn.

"You came here at no small danger to yourselves," Meriwether said, arms folded across his brass-buttoned chest. "You have asked for parley, and I am here to listen. What is it you wished to say?"

George knew this man. Resolute but fair, he would not be swayed by flattery or obfuscation. The general's principles had cost George a few scars, the small joint off his little finger, and several friends during that first year. The debt had been levied back and forth many times since then, paid for tenfold in blood and treasure, by both sides. George hoped the general felt the same way.

"I am here to propose an alliance between the tribes of the Unorganized Territory and the United States of America."

Meriwether's hand rose slowly to cover his mouth. Then George saw his shoulders lift in a tiny shrug. Then another. Then he saw the crinkle at the corner of the general's eye. And then he heard the general's quiet chuckle. Meriwether raised his hand to forestall a complaint.

"My apologies, young man," he said as he regained his composure. "It's just that, well, you do know how to surprise a man."

George nodded; the action felt unnatural after so many years among the People. "I hope that means you will consider the proposal."

"I'm not the man you need to talk to," Meriwether said. "You know that. I'm a soldier, not a politician. My diplomacy is of a more...distinct nature. I can't provide the sort of answer you need." He motioned to his adjutant, took a pencil from the captain's ear and scribbled three short lines. Then he handed the paper to the adjutant. "Send this. Quickly," he said, and then turned back to George.

"Are you rested enough to ride?" he asked.

"To where, general?"

"To talk with the person who can give you an answer."

Chapter 18

Moon When Ice Starts to Form, New
Four Years after the Cloud Fell
North of the Elk River
Crow Territory

They needed to return home, but Speaks While Leaving simply did not have the strength. She had lain in the medicine lodge for three days, and while the fever seemed to have broken, it had stolen all of her vitality.

Every time she roused from her fevered sleep, Limps had been there, his spirit glowing, his face haggard and sad. She tried to speak to him, tried to reach out and touch his gentle, caring hand, but she could not. She felt like a child's doll, limp and unable to move on her own. Soon, even opening her eyes was too much for her to do, so each day, each hour, she relied more on her "other" sight, than on her human eyes.

It was morning, and there was a dense fog across the camp of the Crow. Limps was near her, bundled in blankets against the cold.

Limps, she said, speaking to his spirit, hoping she could reach him. She saw his head lift, as if he had heard a distant noise. She tried again.

Limps.

Slowly, he turned to look at her.

Yes, she said. *You can hear me.*

A look of startlement crept over his features but he did not move.

It is fine, she told him, trying to reassure him. *Do not worry. I just do not have the strength to speak.*

"Yes," he said. "I understand."

Limps, please, find Grey Feather. I think it is time to return home.

"Yes," he said. "I will."

He left and she drifted through the spirit world. The people of the camp had their ghostly companions, just as she had seen at home, but these apparitions were close to their hosts. The world was humming with tension, as if all the possible futures were being drawn into one. The path was being chosen, but the world still needed to be guided, coaxed into the proper choice.

Then she found her mind above the land, flying toward the rising sun, heading home except there was no wind, no sense of movement. She was weightless and motionless, and the earth was drawn past beneath her, blurred by unknowable speed until it stopped and she looked down to see the camp of the People below her. The circle of the great summer gathering was broken; bands had left for their winter camps, soldier societies had been dispatched, allies had gone home. Only a few bands still tarried, while downstream, the camp of the Iron Shirts had grown larger.

At the center were the square tents the *vé'hó'e* preferred to use, but around it had grown a circle of lodges. As she drew closer, she saw that these were all families who had adopted the new *vé'hó'e* god. They had cut their braids and wore clothing made of Trader's cloth like the *vé'hó'e*. She saw them praying with the Ravens, receiving their benedictions, eating their bread.

As she watched, a faint sound distracted her: a scraping, thudding sound. She turned, searching for it, and flew north to track it down. She skimmed over the trees and up the rising land until she found them. Men, *vé'hó'e*, digging in the earth, scarring the body of the Sacred Hills, tearing the yellow metal from the ground and packing it away.

Anger pulsed through her and she was back in the medicine lodge. It was evening, and Limps was sitting nearby with Grey Feather. Heads bowed, they looked as if they had been waiting for some time.

Limps, she said.

Limps touched Grey Feather to rouse him. "She speaks."

Limps, we must return. We cannot wait any longer.

"We do not have to wait," he said, coming closer. He turned to Grey Feather. "Tell her."

Grey Feather looked at Speaks While Leaving, a wary look in his eye.

"Tell her," Limps said. "She hears."

"Our riders, they have returned," he said. "The word has been spoken, and it has been heard."

Limps, she said. *We leave in the morning. I cannot ride. You must prepare me for travel.*

"I will," he said.

Chapter 19

Thursday, October 16th, AD 1890
Westgate
Yankton

Custer sipped his steaming tea, tasted the floral, citrus, and bitter leaves, and tried to ignore the soft discussions located around the hotel's lounge. Samuel and Jacob were leaning on a table, looking at maps and coordinating telegraph messages, while Hancock was discussing perimeters and entry points with his security team. Custer took another sip and then concentrated on steadying his hand. The cup was over the table before his arm began to waver, tremble, shake; the china cup chattered against the rose-bordered saucer as he brought it to rest. Nothing was spilt, but his forehead was beaded with sudden sweat.

The train trip west had exhausted him, which angered him immensely. Why, after so many months of struggle, after subjecting himself to the quackery of surgeons and medical "innovators" alike, was he still so easily made infirm? Why, after just a few hours activity, was he still so susceptible to tremors and instability? Why did he still need a twenty-minute nap in the afternoon to avoid the fatigue that slurred his speech by evening? And why, oh, why was it that he could not consistently master his sibilants, no matter how many times he repeated the elocutionist's exercises?

Two ghosts sat on posts drinking toasts to their hosts.

He hated it, hated it all, and—no, he refused that next thought, for despair was the cracked door, the little death whereby all was lost. His only solace reached out and put her hand on his. His Sunshine, his one love.

"Thank you," he said.

"For what?" Libbie asked with a smile. It was an old dialogue, one that they had shared a thousand times.

"For everything," he said, truly meaning it. He pulled at his watch chain, and popped open the case. The blue-steel moon hands angled outward over the scripted Waltham name.

"Don't fret," Libbie said. "He'll be here soon enough."

Custer shook his head. "It's times like this that I wonder at the wisdom of being a teetotaler."

Libbie slapped the back of his hand and stood. "Walk with me," she said.

He grabbed the bone handle of his cane and levered himself upward. Hancock, the ginger-haired chief of his protective detail, rose but Custer waved him away. "We're just going to the gardens," he said. But Hancock did not retake his seat, and Custer knew he would follow them, regardless. He sighed.

The common room at the Persistence Hotel was well-appointed, with brass fittings on doors of golden oak and thick carpets with intricate designs woven in deep reds, dark purples, and bright yellows. The walls, paneled in pale poplar, bore framed photographs that told the story of the town, its triumphs as well as its tragedies. As they walked to the front door, Custer glanced at the pair of photographs situated prominently on either side.

The photograph on the left showed a row of stately gentlemen, all standing in a row, chests out, hands on lapels to keep still for the exposure. Behind them rose the cabled arches and iron trestlework of the soon-to-be-finished bridge they had built across the great river. Custer had studied their faces before and recognized in their features the pride they all felt, but in them he also saw something else: arrogance. These men—dignitaries, engineers, soldiers, and businessmen—considered themselves invincible, untouchable by any danger, incapable of failure. What they dreamed, they could do, and there was no obstacle that could not be swept out of the way. It was beyond their capacity to imagine what would befall the grand and impressive structure that rose behind them. Their assumed omnipotence did not allow for what the other photograph would show.

On the right was a photograph of the same bridge, taken a few short days after the first. The view was taken a little to one side, to show the length of the span. Here, in contrast to the first image, the men who stood in the foreground had their backs to the camera, all staring at what had become of the structure. The heavy stone footings on either side of the main span were cracked, two were broken, and between them where once had risen two graceful arches with a deck was suspended from cables of woven steel, there now was empty space, twisted girders, and wiry tangles. The whole of the central span lay in ruin, destroyed by explosives set by the Cheyenne. Pieces of the structure reached up out of the river like skeletal fingers, bones of metal, broken and bent. In a midnight flash, the pinnacle of their skills had been brought down by those they considered less than human. Viewing the photograph, Custer was unable to see the faces of the men who stood staring at the wreckage, but still he could tell what they were feeling. Their arms hung limp at their sides, hats no longer at cocky angles but now either in loose-fingered hands, on the ground, or missing altogether. Their shoulders sagged. One man had squatted down, his head in his hands, his world turned in on itself. These men, gods on earth just a few days before, had been transformed overnight into wretched, disconsolate men; stunned mortals, their mouths filled with the ashes of yesterday's fruit.

Custer and Libbie walked through the open doors—Hancock at a respectful distance behind them—and stepped out onto the hotel's wide porch. The Persistence Hotel stood on high ground inside a bend in the river. It had a commanding view of the growing town of Westgate, and from its porch the couple could see the lower section of town, its streets lined with sturdy, square buildings all whitewashed and clean. Down at the end of the main street were the riverside docks where ships from afar and ferries from across the river exchanged their cargoes. And there, in midstream of the river, were the pylons of the new bridge that was being constructed. This bridge would be much less elegant than its predecessor, with trestles spanning the short distance between each of the bulwarks built up from the riverbed. No long arches, no cable suspensions; nothing but the same simple, sturdy, reliable design that had been used for a hundred years. Custer loved innovation, but the frontier was rarely the best place to test something new.

The midday sun was refreshing, warming Custer's face and melting the tension from his shoulders and arms. The front garden was filled with the creepers and huge leaves of squash and the yellowing leaves of bush beans. Robins ran about, stopping to eye the ground or overturn a fallen leaf in search of a grub or worm. He patted Libbie's arm in thanks for her suggestion of a walk. They had just begun to descend the front steps when they heard a carriage coming around the bend in the road.

"There," Libbie said. "That must be him."

"In a carriage?" Custer said. "That's not like John at all."

But it was true. The carriage—a low-slung, covered landau drawn by a pair of chestnut mares—was driven by a uniformed teamster, with one soldier at shotgun and one more at the rear. It jounced on its long springs, rocking along the rough road and creaking as it was brought to a none-too-gentle halt at the gate before the hotel's small garden. The private at the back jumped down, opened the door and dropped the step for the occupant.

Meriwether emerged, stepping down but, instead of greeting his President and First Lady, he turned and extended his hand. From within the carriage came a small female hand, a thin wrist wrapped with leather and beads, a well-toned arm, and a deerskin-clad shoulder.

"What the...?" Custer said.

The woman inside took Meriwether's hand and gently, steadily, stepped out of the carriage. She was small-boned, quite young, with dark almond-shaped eyes, cheekbones high and broad above a gracile jaw. Her hair was dark as a

161

raven's wing, almost purple-black in the sunlight, done in two plaits that wound from nape to crown and back, decorated at the back with tufts of grouse and owl feathers. She wore the tunic-like dress of her people, the ties loose at one shoulder, a wide girdle of beads and shells tight around her small waist. On her feet were hand-wrought boots of supple leather, with beaded strips down each side and fringed hide decorating the tops.

She said not a word as she descended, nor did she look at Meriwether. On the ground, she stepped to the side and turned back to the carriage.

Custer looked to Libbie and found her as puzzled as he was.

Then another hand emerged from the landau's interior and grasped the jamb. Custer immediately noticed the missing joint on the little finger. Libbie gasped, and he knew she had seen it, too.

"It can't be," she said.

Their son—thin, haggard, skin as brown as a wheat-berry, his hair sun-bleached to flax—stepped down from the carriage, took the young woman's hand, and looked up. His eyes, the same piercing blue as Custer's own, crinkled at the edges as he gave a small, meek smile.

Libbie's breath broke. "Oh, Heavenly Father," she said, running forward. George reached out to accept his mother's embrace, and for a time her sobs and George's quiet words of comfort were all that could be heard in the garden.

Meriwether discreetly stepped away and walked up toward the hotel. Custer reached out for his arm as he passed. Meriwether halted.

"What is this?" Custer whispered.

Meriwether looked back at the trio near the carriage, then back at Custer. "For the moment, it is a reunion; nothing more. Later? We shall see."

Meriwether continued up to the hotel, explaining the situation to Hancock. George, Libbie, and the young Indian woman walked up the path. Libbie's eyes were red but there was a smile on her lips. George stopped a few steps away. He held out his hand.

"Hello, Father," he said.

Custer, still stunned, reached out dumbly for the handshake.

"I know," George said. "Bit of a surprise."

Custer expelled a "ha" of agreement. "Quite," he finally managed.

"One of many, I'm afraid," George said. He took the hand of the young woman at his side. "Mother. Father. Please allow me to introduce you to Mouse Road. My wife."

Custer forgot to breathe. He saw his own gaping expression mirrored on Libbie's face. Then her features went slack, her eyes rolled up, and George turned to catch his mother as she swooned. Hancock was there in an instant, and together he and George carried Libbie up into the hotel. Custer stood there, staring at the empty doorway. Then he felt a small hand take his arm. He turned and found the woman, Mouse Road, his daughter-in-law, standing at his side, looking up at the hotel, waiting for him.

"Parlez-vous français?" he asked her

A shy smile as she looked down. *"Un peu,"* she said.

He did not know what to make of this woman; her demure aspect did not match his expectations of the kind of woman his son would eventually take to wife. Then again, here she was, holding the arm of one of her people's most hated enemies.

"Aidez-moi s'il vous plaît?" he asked, indicating the stairs ahead.

"Oui. Bien sûr."

Slowly, leaning on her arm, they walked back up into the hotel to see how Libbie was recovering from the shock.

Their entry to the hotel lounge put every man in motion. George was able to nod a greeting to both Jacob and Samuel as he and the general carried his mother and laid her down on the divan. Others went for cold water, for a fan to cool her skin. Samuel waved a sheaf of telegrams over her head while some man with red-hair and a muscular build took her wrist in a two-fingered hold and checked her pulse against his pocket watch's second hand.

George had never known his mother to faint, and he seriously regretted being the cause of it. Providing a surprise was one thing, but to stun your mother insensible, well, that was just mortifying. Once she was settled on the divan, he just stood there. "What should I do?" he asked of no one in particular. Meriwether shouldered him aside and undid the top button of her high collar. Then he undid the buttons on her wrists.

"That's the extent of it," the general said. "Usually there's a cluster of women to take over, but here..."

"Let me through."

George stepped back to let his father pass. Heavily, clumsily, his father knelt at her side. He took her hand, patted it, then reached up and pinched her cheek. George's mother blinked once, fluttered her eyelids, and then shook her head a little. An audible sigh passed through the room.

"There now, Sunshine," George's father said. He looked up and motioned to the serving maid for the glass of water she had brought. With trembling hands, he dipped his handkerchief into the cool liquid and dabbed it against his wife's temples and forehead.

George watched this tableau of tenderness, seeing the side of his father that was rarely shown to anyone, family and outsiders alike. He glanced around the room and noted as the other men—soldiers, statesmen, administrators; all men of action and purpose—looked away or busied themselves with messages or reports, all somewhat embarrassed to witness such a gentle moment from a man who was, to many, a legend. Only Meriwether looked upon the scene frankly, with a warm smile of his own. The general patted the President's shoulder.

"Back with us?" he asked George's mother.

She took a deep breath and lifted her eyebrows above widened eyes, looking around, wondering. "Yes," she said, and then remembered. "Autie," she said. "I saw George."

"He's here," Custer said, nodding back toward their son.

She looked past her husband's shoulder, saw her son, and smiled. Mouse Road stepped to his side and the smile faded.

"Yes," she said. "That's right." Then, before the menfolk could stop her, she shifted to a sitting position and rose, hand out. "Forgive me, my dear, but I think I missed your name."

George muttered a quick translation and Mouse Road

replied.

"*Je m'appelle* Hohkeekemeona'e," she said, reaching out and clasping his mother by the wrist.

George smiled. "She says her name is Mouse Road."

His mother's reciprocal smile was slow in coming. Eventually, it arrived, dimly at first, but as her gaze moved around the trio, from son to husband to unexpected daughter-in-law, her confusion and disbelief receded, and soon she pulled George into another embrace.

"All right, all right," Custer said. "Time enough for that later. John, I presume there's more reason for this than a family reunion?"

"Indeed," Meriwether said.

George's mother recognized the implication and rose with regal dignity. She spoke to the serving maid. "Emily, will you please bring some tea into the sun room?" Then she turned to Mouse Road. "Would you care to join me, dear?"

George spoke to his wife. "She asks if you would join her for some hot tea. You can stay, if you prefer."

Mouse Road looked at George's mother and considered the invitation. "I will go," she said. "She is someone I must know better."

George spoke to his mother. "She is learning French, but she has no English."

"*Je comprends,*" his mother said, and with a gesture led the way, leaving the affairs of state to the men.

With the departure of the women, the atmosphere in the room abruptly changed. All eyes turned to George, though no longer with expressions of welcome for the surprise return of a wayward son. Eyes had narrowed, eyebrows quirked. All papers were put down, all other interests put aside. It was back to the business of diplomacy: argument without anger, suspicion without insult.

"What is this all about, John?" Custer asked. "There are things we need to discuss. Alone."

Meriwether nodded. "And I believe I know what they are. But this man—your son—came to me under a flag of parley, just as I was about to engage the Spanish. What he told me...what he offered...was important enough that I brought him immediately to you, as I believe it bears directly upon the items you wanted to discuss."

Meriwether was trying to speak without letting any hints fall, and if the Spanish general hadn't clumsily let his own news slip during his self-aggrandizing dinner, George would have been in the dark as to Meriwether's meaning. But the only thing that would have brought his father here, personally, to discuss strategy with his commander in the field was a major change in the status quo, and George was already well aware of what that change was. It was time to prove he was here to participate.

"You needn't tiptoe around the subject," George said. "The Spanish are about to sail into Kansa Bay, probably with reinforcements, definitely to establish a new supply line for their existing forces." George did his best not to enjoy the open-mouthed stares from both his father and Meriwether. All around the room, stunned expressions ruled on every face.

"I had guessed," Meriwether said. "But—"

"You guessed?" Custer blurted.

"Well, naturally," the general replied. "You wouldn't come all this way just to—"

"I'm glad to know my motives are so transparent."

"More importantly," Meriwether said, deflecting the topic, turning to George, "is how you found out."

George shrugged. "I can draw inferences, too."

His father took a step closer and leaned on his cane. "I want to know why you are telling us."

"To prove my earnest intentions," he said.

Meriwether cleared his throat. "It is why he's here in the first place, sir."

Custer squinted and looked at his son. The room was silent, waiting. "Why *are* you here?" he asked George.

"To propose an alliance between the United States and the Allied Tribes, so that we might act together to repel the Spanish forces."

Jacob Greene laughed out loud. "Repel the Spanish forces? You are the ones who brought them here in the first place!" he said. "And now you're ready to turn on them? If you would turn on them, why not turn on us? What makes you think we would ever trust you?"

Discontented murmurs rumbled through the room, and

George understood their mistrust. It was there, strong and unforgiving on both sides; mistrust born of a century's hate and strife, nourished by the blood of generations. Whereas he might be able to convince the People with his description of a vision from Speaks While Leaving, these men would react to such talk with derision and scorn. He closed his eyes for a brief moment and recalled the view from atop that mountain, beneath that wounded, blood-soaked sky. Yes, regardless of whether he spoke in realities or metaphor, the calculus remained the same. Now he just had to trust in the vision itself, and speak to these men in a language they could understand.

"You are right, Jacob. We brought them here. Have you ever wondered why?"

"Why?" Jacob said, puzzled at the question. "Why, to get rid of us, of course."

"Wrong."

Be delicate, George cautioned himself. Do not make them feel stupid.

"We brought them here to prove to you that we could." He let the words sink in. "How could we prove to you that we were serious about our goals? How could we prove to you that we deserved the respect due a sovereign nation?" George stepped to the table where the map of the Unorganized Territory had been spread out. "How could we convince you," he said, gently placing a hand over the spot where the Sacred Mountains stood, "that we were willing to protect this by any means necessary?"

George looked up from the map and saw his father's smile.

"You were dining with the devil," Custer said, "even at the risk of your very soul."

"A ploy?" Jacob said, aghast. "You brought invaders to our shores as a ploy?"

"A ploy. A tactic. A stratagem. A...vision?" He smiled at Jacob. "Call it what you will, Mr. Secretary. I believe it worked. I believe we got your attention."

"This is outrageous!" Jacob shouted.

But Meriwether was shaking his head. "No," he said. "It is merely 'politics by other means.'"

"Indeed," Custer said.

George kept it rolling. "With us, the Spanish can defeat you. With us, you can defeat the Spanish. We, to put it bluntly, are the key."

Custer sat down on the divan and rested both hands on the head of his cane. "And if they defeat us, what do you foresee?"

"I see the Spanish holding the territory between the Mississippi and the Missouri, a buffer between our angry nations, an enemy on your border."

"And if reversed?"

"I see you holding those same lands, as we had discussed during our last...visit together."

Custer studied his son, and George knew he was remembering the outcome of that visit; the violence, the blood, the death, the dishonor. But his father was shrewd, too, and not one to let emotion or past pain ruin a chance at victory. They had been about to announce an agreement that day, on the White House steps, just before the assassin's gun went off. "*Just* as we had discussed?" he asked.

George raised an eyebrow. "With one exception."

His father squinted. "What exception?"

"As to territory, we hold to the agreed-upon plan," George said. "The Alliance would cede everything east of the Missouri downstream of the Trader River. It would also cede all lands between Kansa Bay and the Niobrara."

"And the sting?"

"The Alliance offers thirty million dollars."

"What?" Jacob blurted. "It was fifty million!"

"Conditions have changed," George said.

"In gold?" Custer asked.

"Autie!" Jacob said.

"Quiet," he ordered. Back to George, "In gold?"

"In gold," George replied.

"Do it," Custer said with a glance at Jacob.

"You can't mean it!" Jacob said.

"No argument," Custer said, pounding his cane on the floor. He stood and looked at every man in the room. "I'm selling two-thirds of the land for three times the price. *And* I'm getting us out of this damned war! Do it."

Samuel, the president's aide, cleared his throat, reluctant to disagree. "Sir," he said. "Only Congress has the power to—"

"Damn Congress," Custer said. "If they can't see the sense in this, we'll find another way to make it so. We've been pouring blood and gold into this Territory for a hundred years, and in all that time, what have we gained? Have we gained one square mile of governable land? Have we established one town that hasn't been lost or that exists under constant threat?"

"But sir," Samuel said, his voice all patience and understanding. "How can we cede sovereign control to a group of insurrectionists?"

Custer leveled a steely-eye at his aide. "In case you hadn't noticed, we have been superseded. The Cheyenne and their alliance have already been recognized by the Spanish Crown as a sovereign nation. Besides, we're not ceding anything. We're selling it. We bought it from the French. We're selling it to the Alliance. Simple as that. Now you men," he said, waving an arm at the suit-coats around the room. "Start setting things in motion. We need to act quickly."

George hadn't spoken a word during this last exchange; he'd barely breathed through it all. His father was agreeing! It was going to happen! He could barely believe it and was afraid that any word he said might destroy it all. His mind whirled with thoughts, with ideas. He wanted to run into the other room and shout the news to Mouse Road, to hug her and swing her around! It was happening!

"Mr. President."

It was Meriwether, and his baritone was like a knell. Motion stopped as every man sensed the coming of an objection that might change the President's mind. Custer pivoted on his cane and gave his general a gimlet eye.

"Yes?"

The scrutiny unsettled Meriwether. George saw him glance around and find neither friend nor foe; he was on his own and he would receive either acclamation or denigration, depending on how his words were received.

Meriwether took a breath and settled himself before speaking. "Sir, we have no guarantees." He nodded to George. "I intend no offense, but it is only prudent to point out that we have only your assurance that this offer of alliance is genuine."

George's father looked from general to son through narrowed eyes. George knew his father well enough to see that the general's complaint had struck home, and to be honest, it was accurate. Accurate, but not deniable.

"I have acted as translator, as interpreter, and as liaison for the People for many years now," he said, taking the reins away from the general. "And I challenge the general..." He extended an arm and turned to point to every man. "I challenge anyone in this room to name a moment, or cite an instance, where what I said was not backed by the full authority of the Great Council." It did not matter to George that this was the first time he had done exactly that; he wanted these men to consider his past credentials. He watched as his father, Meriwether, Jacob, and several others exchanged glances.

Eventually, consensus was reached. "No," his father said. "You have always been a trustworthy messenger."

George tried not to feel any sting at the characterization, but he also felt the pressure of their trust. It hurt to twist it in this way, but if he was wrong, then all was lost anyway.

"Then I tell you," George said, "as a messenger from the Cheyenne's most trusted speaker, that this is a true and genuine offer. If you accept it, we will return to the People and ratify the agreement."

Meriwether scowled, untrusting, as did others, but it was George's father who made the decision.

"Do it," he instructed.

Men moved to obey.

"Now," Custer said to George, "let's go see your mother."

Chapter 20

Thursday, October 16th, AD 1890
North of the Red Paint River
Unorganized Territory

The horses' hooves made hollow drumbeats as Alejandro and D'Avignon rode across the stony creekbed. The prospector had led them on a circuitous course, going well out of their way before doubling back toward the Sacred Hills. There were other places, he said, where mining was possible, but nothing to match the promise of these dark, foreboding heights.

"Look," D'Avignon said, pointing. He jumped down from his dun-colored criollo and tossed the reins to Alejandro. He knelt down at the water's edge, dipped a hand into the running edge of the creek, and scooped up a small handful of gravelly sand. "Hee-hee!" he laughed as he picked at the grains. Then he leapt up and ran over to Alejandro, thumb and forefinger pinched. "Your hand, your hand," he said, and Alejandro held out his palm to receive the treasure.

"There," D'Avignon said.

Alejandro stared. In his hand was a globular nugget the size of a split pea. "*¡Dios mío!*" he swore. "It is just as you said."

"Just lying there, waiting to be picked up and taken away," D'Avignon said, grinning. "Worth the risk?"

Alejandro nodded. "Without a doubt."

D'Avignon took back his reins, mounted, and led off again. Alejandro tucked the nugget of buttery gold into his shirtfront pocket for safekeeping and followed, gently guiding with knees and reins.

He had surprised himself by how quickly he had become re-accustomed to living it rough. The aches of the first weeks had quickly disappeared, and the increased activity and lean rations had slimmed his belly and lightened his step. He had put away his finer clothes and requisitioned more durable garb from stores, so now he rode in dungarees and a shirt of cotton twill, with an overcoat of wool-lined oilcloth that shrugged off rain and thorny snags alike. He felt fifteen years younger, relished the slap of cold air on his face each morning, drank burned coffee like a veteran, and stuck to the saddle as if born to it. To be honest, he felt a little guilty, enjoying any part of this ordeal when he knew his wife was worrying about him, and when he thought of how much was really at stake, both personally and politically. But he *was* enjoying it, or parts of it at any rate, especially this part, riding across the streams and hills of a magical landscape.

From the moss-clad rocks they rode upslope beneath the spreading branches of age-old trees. These were not dark, slope-shouldered spruce or tall, pillared ponderosa. They rode instead beneath the bright russet of bur oak and the flaming yellows of fading aspen. The sun, snared by the autumnal colors, was diffused by a million leaves, surrounding them with a rich, heavy light that hung in the air like fine silk. Chickadees chased each other, angry sprites that argued from branch to branch. The air was thick with moisture and the smell of dew-fed mushrooms growing in the humus of the forest floor. The horses' hooves were quiet now, treading the soft, spongy earth, and their misted breath went in and out like air through a smith's bellows. The sound was comforting, filled with strength and life, and for a time both men rode in silence.

They climbed upward along a twisting, crook-back trail, the creek running joyfully to their right, the higher ground on their left. The trail wove between trees, around boulders, growing thinner with each switchback, until Alejandro could not tell where the path lay at all.

"You know where you are going?" he asked.

"*Naturellement,*" D'Avignon replied. "I have been up here too often to go astray."

As if to prove his point, the sound of voices drifted through the wood; angry voices.

"*Merde!*" D'Avignon put heels to his horse's flank and sped up the slope. Alejandro did the same, and his paint leapt forward to follow D'Avignon's criollo.

Alejandro leaned forward, held up an arm to ward off low branches, kept his knees tight against his gelding's sides, and twisted his torso to maintain an even balance while his horse pushed up the tortuous path. Then the ground leveled out, the path straightened, and D'Avignon lashed his reins in urgent command. The horses sped forward and Alejandro heard more voices shouting in anger and alarm. Ahead, a sun-filled clearing appeared in which two men grappled, raising dust. D'Avignon rode through the brush and dismounted, jumping into the midst of the fray, arms out in an attempt to separate the combatants. Alejandro rode into the clearing and saw a knife blade flash in the sunlight.

"What is going on here?" he demanded in his best military-command voice. The fight became a frieze.

Two men stood at odds, D'Avignon between them. One man held a knife, its long, fixed blade clean and sharp. Ringed around the trio were the other men of the camp, clothing soiled with dirt and sweat, faces grimed and hair greased by weeks of living rough.

"What is going on here?" he asked again. He pointed to the man with the blade. "You. Speak."

Faced with authority, the fight drained out of the men. The man holding the knife drooped, waved the blade in the direction of his opponent, and the explanation worked its way to the surface.

"Emilio," he said. "He stole—"

"You lying son of a whore!" Emilio lunged, but D'Avignon kept him back.

The gunshot made men jump in alarm. They looked and

saw Alejandro, pistol pointed at the sky. He nodded at the man with the knife. "Stole what?"

The knife hit the dirt and the man straightened up, a glimmer of the soldier within returning. "He has been pocketing some of the gold."

"I—" Emilio began but checked himself.

"And you," Alejandro said to Emilio. "You deny this allegation?"

Emilio nodded. "I deny it."

"Search him," Alejandro said to D'Avignon.

D'Avignon did so, searching the man's pockets, even his boot tops.

"He keeps it in his pants," the accuser said. "I saw him by accident, down at the privy hole."

Alejandro looked back at Emilio. There was a twinge of fear—a slight wideness, a heightened activity—in his eye. "Take it out."

"But—"

"Take it out or I'll have you stripped and then we'll find it anyway."

Emilio considered his position, dropped his façade of indignation, and instead opted for pitiable justification. "It's my mother, sir" he said, his face suddenly all sadness and sentiment. "My aged mother, a widow. She is ill, and only has my youngest sister to care for her."

"Take it out," Alejandro repeated.

Reluctantly, slowly, Emilio undid a button on his shirt, did the same to his undergarment, and reached in below his belt. After a moment he pulled out a leather pouch that had been suspended from his naked waist by a length of twine.

"Take it."

D'Avignon grimaced as he reached out and took the sweat-stained pouch.

"Open it."

D'Avignon complied, spilling some of the contents out into his hand. Tiny nuggets glinted in the sunlight.

"How much?"

"Several ounces, at least."

The second gunshot produced much the same reaction as the first, and men ducked their heads amid shouts of

174

surprise. As the echo rocketed through the hills, Emilio hit the ground, the back of his head blown out. Alejandro holstered his sidearm.

"What is your name?" he said to the dead man's accuser.

"Bernardo Gomez Contreras di Marianas," he said.

"You will be our overseer," Alejandro said, and he looked around the group. "You are all receiving a handsome wage," he said, then pointed to the dead Emilio.

"He took an oath. You all took an oath. Before God Himself, you swore. This is the punishment for betrayal. Bernardo is our overseer, and will report to me directly. Keep him safe, if you value your own skins, for men like you are two-a-penny, and I can replace you all in a single afternoon. You are in the middle of a strange, vast, dangerous land, and D'Avignon and I—and now Bernardo—are the only ones who can provide you a way out of it, a way home, with enough riches to last you years. Do not think you can leave here with more than your fair share. But work well, work hard, and you will be amply rewarded." He looked again around the ring of men.

"Am I understood?"

"Yes, sir," they responded as one.

"Good. Now bury that man."

He saw D'Avignon staring up at him, one eyebrow lifted in unspoken question.

"What?" he asked as the other men carried the dead man off into the woods. "You didn't think me capable?"

D'Avignon cocked his head. "To be honest, no, I did not."

Alejandro dismounted and tied his reins to a tree branch. He held his hand out for the pouch of gold. With an oily smile, D'Avignon handed it over. "If I learned one thing only, in my years of command, it is that without strong leadership, men like this will degenerate into howling apes within a month. Add women or strong drink—"

"Or gold," D'Avignon supplied.

"—or gold," Alejandro agreed, "and it can happen overnight." He tucked the pouch into his vest pocket and gestured to the camp around them. "Now, if you would show me how well these men have done?"

The camp was rudimentary; the crew had been chosen

with such privations in mind, and they had not made many improvements over the basics needed for survival. Stacked stones formed a windbreak on two sides of the firepit, and a heavy kettle hung from tripod astride the ashes of last night's fire. Deadwood was piled nearby, but had not been sectioned or split. Even the tents Alejandro had provided had not been erected as such, having been repurposed instead as tarpaulins and coverings for crude lean-tos. Downslope—and presumably downwind—Alejandro saw the bloody remnants of a butchered deer amid a midden of other refuse. The conditions were far too brutal for his liking, but then he was not the one living here. These were base, uncouth men, well-fit for the conditions. The promise of gold consumed all else in the fires of avarice, purging them of all civilized needs.

D'Avignon led him through the camp to the only tent that was set up according to its original purpose. Auburn leaves and rust-colored pine needles littered its conical roof, but Alejandro noted that all the guy lines were still taut and trimmed. The land around it had been cleared of brush and woodfall.

"Yours?"

D'Avignon snorted. "You have to ask?" he said. "These others, they live like wild dogs. I'm surprised they don't sniff each other's asses to say 'Good morning.'"

He stopped at the flap to his tent, crouching to inspect the opening. He undid the laces with care, and then inspected the threshold. Alejandro saw him pull up a pair of small twigs that had been tied with a length of thread. "No one has been in," he said, and then entered himself. Alejandro followed.

Within, there was little more than a horsehair pallet and a crate on which was a metal cup, bowl, and spoon. The only other item was a strongbox, all oak planks and steel fittings. A lock was fitted to the hasp, and D'Avignon produced a key to open it. The lock snicked, and the strongbox lid creaked open, revealing the product of the crew's labors.

All Alejandro could see was the brassy tops of pickle jars, but then D'Avignon reached in and grabbed one. Using two hands to support the weight, he pulled it up and out of the box. The quart jar was full of glittering gold, in dust and small nuggets like the one D'Avignon had found at the creekbed. He brought the jar over and held it out to Alejandro.

So heavy! Alejandro could not keep the grin from spreading across his face. It was a fortune!

"How many have you filled?" he asked, staring at the dozens of jars in the box.

"Most," D'Avignon replied. "It's more weight than the box can hold, actually. We'll have to separate them into manageable groups to get them back to main camp."

Alejandro was giddy, and he had to work to keep from laughing like an idiot. His dreams, his plans, it was all coming together. After so much time and so much heartache, the years of humiliation, the shame of demotion, the long, slow climb back to relevance and position; now he was bringing his name, his family, all back to their proper place. This gold would assure his family's return to their rightful echelon of society, while the army out on the prairie would fulfill his promise to the Queen Regent. The possibilities before him were innumerable, the heights he could achieve as reward for these actions, unguessable.

"Is there more to glean from this site?"

D'Avignon smiled. "To be sure," he said. "Every spadeful upturns a fortune."

"We will start moving this out tonight," Alejandro said. "Just you and I, in small, discreet packages."

"As you command," D'Avignon said with a grin and a bow.

The men were returning, voices raised again in arguing tones. D'Avignon frowned. "They cannot have dug a decent grave already," he said as he and Alejandro stepped out of the tent.

The men had indeed returned, but they were not alone. They crouched in a tight group. Alejandro heard the creak of bowstring and leather and realized that they were surrounded by tribesmen. They looked different, somehow foreign; their headgear was of fur and pelts instead of feathers, their facepaint was stark and disturbing, their clothing heavier and less ornate. He saw few rifles among them but many bows, spears, and warclubs. All the bows were bent, steel arrowheads pointing at the cowering miners. Alejandro took a step and the bows creaked tighter. One of the natives stepped forward. He pointed to the pistol at Alejandro's hip, opened his hand, and with a twitch of his fingers wordlessly commanded its surrender. Slowly, Alejandro did so. The Indian took his pistol and stepped back among the others.

Alejandro waited, but none of the Indians said a word.

"What do they—" a miner began, but got a spear butt shoved into his back as an answer.

The Indians had the upper hand, but for some reason they did not move, did not speak. The miner's unfinished question echoed through Alejandro's mind.

What do they want?

He studied these strange men, trying to discern which one was their leader. They were at least twenty in number, but Alejandro saw others in the woods beyond the camp's clearing, moving furtively behind the trees, and he could not guess their full number. But neither could he guess which man was in command, and that told him their leader was the one for whom they all waited.

Finally he heard movement in the thicket at the edge of the clearing. The guardian archers took a step back. One of the miners whispered a Hail Mary, eyes glancing fearfully toward the approaching footsteps. The branches parted and a tall native stepped through the gap, followed by several others. The man was powerfully built, his hair loose and long about his shoulders. He wore the light deerskin of a Cheyenne warrior and carried a rifle in his massive hand. Alejandro recognized him; he was the silent brute who often accompanied young Custer; the man they called Limps. His visage, devoid of war paint, was more fearsome than any other of his party; his gaze burned with an intensity forged by rage, and when its focus fell on him, Alejandro truly feared for his life.

"Please," Alejandro began, his French slow and deliberate so Limps could understand and the mining crew could not. "We tracked these men to this place, D'Avignon and I."

"Yes," D'Avignon chimed in, also in French, quick to turn any situation to his own advantage. "It is true. They are deserters. They disobeyed our orders."

Limps swept his hand to the side to silence them, then

closed his eyes and cocked his head. When his eyes opened, he stared at Alejandro. "Speaks While Leaving says that you lie."

Alejandro bristled at the affront, despite its veracity. "She calls me a liar?" he said, hoping bluster would help them play for time. "I will not stand here and be insulted, not even by a chief's daughter. I will return to the camp. I will see her face to face and see if she still calls me a liar!" He took a step toward his horse, but a raised hand stopped him once more.

"No need," Limps said, and beckoned over his shoulder. Two other warriors came forward, then four more, bearing a litter on their shoulders. As they came near, the men lowered the litter and Alejandro saw upon it a figure, covered head to toe in heavy buffalo and pale deerskin. Limps walked over to the body and drew back the flap from over its face. It was Speaks While Leaving, her skin ashen, her lips dark with death.

"Speaks While Leaving travels with us," Limps said. "She says that you lie."

"*¡Dios mío!*" Alejandro said. "He is mad."

Limps walked toward Alejandro, his step measured, balanced, his black-eyed gaze riveted to Alejandro's own.

"She is dead!" Alejandro shouted. He looked at the other warriors, pointing to the corpse of Speaks While Leaving. "She is dead!"

Limps walked closer, until Alejandro could smell him, a mixture of sweat, leather, the spice of whistlers, and the distinctive scent of decomposition.

Alejandro's voice trembled as he tried to reason with the warrior before him. "Limps," he said. "I know she was important to you, to all the People. But she is dead. Speaks While Leaving is dead."

Eyes still staring, Limps reached out and plucked the pouch of gold from Alejandro's vest pocket. "Speaks While Leaving says that you lie. She says that you have betrayed us."

He ran. He turned and he ran. Sure that he would be struck by a dozen arrows, he ran all the same. He stumbled, sprawled, got up, and finally reached his horse. Tearing the reins from the branch, he struggled to get his foot up into the stirrup, the horse skittering in a circle as he tried. He stopped. He looked back at the clearing.

Limps and all the men—miners, warriors, and D'Avignon alike—stood stock-still, staring at Alejandro. The miners' faces were wide with surprise; D'Avignon's eyes were narrow with calculation. The warriors stared down their aimed arrows, waiting for the command. And Limps...the long-haired warrior looked at Alejandro.

And smiled.

Alejandro got his foot in the stirrup and spurred his mount down the mountain path, heedless of the danger. Better a broken neck than the vengeance he saw in Limps' eye.

Chapter 21

Moon When Ice Starts to Form, New
Four Years after the Cloud Fell
Sacred Hills
Alliance Territory

Speaks While Leaving stared as Alejandro tore off down the path, lashing his reins side to side. The smile Limps wore turned feral and vicious. The soldiers with them—Crow, Cradle People, and Blackfoot alike—stood immobile, faces stony and grim. The Iron Shirt miners cowered, shivering beneath their captors' icy glares. Above her, birds sung in the sunlit boughs, oblivious to the change in the world beneath them, deaf to the thunder that still echoed through her mind.

Speaks While Leaving is dead.

The words were an explosion, a blast that ripped the sky and shook the ground. She lifted her spirit-self off the litter and, for the first time, turned and looked at the body she left behind.

The soft, pale deerskin that had covered her face—Had it always been there? She did not remember it.—was pulled back to reveal her face, only it was not her face. She did not see the warm skin or the shine of sweat that always accompanied her vision-fever. Her skin was ashen, dry, both dark and pale in the same moment. Her cheeks were sunken, slack, the bones around and beneath her eyes pronounced, skeletal. Her lips were swollen, dark, cracked, and her closed eyes deeply set, unnaturally flat. But her hair was dark, glossy; parted in the middle, someone had braided it back from her hairline, working strips of red cloth into the plaits, winding the ends tightly with elkskin and otter fur. About her neck was a collar of long shells and bright beads of silver, not a thing she ever owned, but fine and beautiful, a gift from an unknown hand. On her ears were small cuffs of silver from which hung chains of shells and an eagle's downfeathers. On one cheek someone had painted a long, upward pointing triangle, white, an icy tear falling from her shrunken eye.

There was no breath in her nostrils, no pulse beneath her skin. There was no blood to warm her silver adornments. There was only stillness and the chill of a waiting grave.

There was only death. And decay.

She was dead.

Speaks While Leaving was dead.

And yet... How long had she been so? She looked at her body and guessed it must have been days since she had taken her last breath. But Limps had spoken with her in that time. The chiefs had listened to her, taken her counsel. So, was she? Was she dead?

Yes. Dead. Or dreaming.

Or both.

Motion distracted her, drawing her from her fascination. She heard a shrill whistle, faint but distinct, and a figure rushed toward her, rushed through her, a blur that dispelled her like a pebble in a still pond, rippling her but not destroying her. She coalesced and turned, saw a whistler running toward Limps. He held out his hand, grabbed the first rope as his mount ran past him, and leapt up along her spine, his feet deftly finding the loops, his hand brandishing the cold steel of his bone-handled knife. His toes dug into the whistler's sides and the pair sped down the path after Alejandro.

No, she thought. And *No,* she said.

Limps did not falter, either deaf to or heedless of her

admonition. He raced down the straightaway and disappeared into the trees at the first bend in the mountain trail. She wanted to follow. She leaned forward to run, and then was at his shoulder, following his twisting, plunging path down the mountainside.

Do not do this, she told him.

He grimaced and bared his teeth.

Do not, she repeated.

"Ah!" he cried, and slashed the knife blade through the air. "Leave me alone!"

No.

Stop.

Limps yanked on the reins and the whistler fluted in exertion as it left the path and half-ran, half-fell down the incline.

Stop.

"Aah!"

The whistler twisted away from reins made suddenly taut and began to slide down the steep slope. Clawed toes tore at the earth, lofting a spray of needles and dirt. Low boughs lashed and snapped. The beast's foot caught on a root and for a sickly moment mount and rider hung in poise, balanced yet imperiled, before gravity demanded tribute, sending both tumbling. The whistler trumpeted. Limps grunted as he hit the ground, rolled, spun, slid. He grabbed a tree trunk and was on his feet in a moment, knife still in his hand.

"He is the cause!" he shouted. "He makes our pain!"

No. He is the spark, she told him. She reached out, but could not touch him, so she willed her calm upon his mind. *He is the fulcrum of our future.*

Tears shone on his cheeks as he sought her in the forest gloom. His rage broke, and a terrible grief filled his features.

Calm radiated from her. *Go. Find him. But take him to the Council. We will follow.*

"Aaah!" he cried as he sank to his knees, weeping. One hand touched the earth, then the other, as he slowly folded in upon himself. His anger bled out into the ground, leaving him with only sadness. "As you wish," he said quietly, sheathing his knife. Then he stood, walked to his whistler, mounted, and rode off to find his quarry.

She retreated, back to her body, back to the others. The soldiers stood alert, listening to the woods for sounds of approach. Crow, Cradle People, and Blackfoot—just a handful of years past she would have called them enemies, but not now.

She moved close to one of the elders, a man they called Badger. He was short and wiry, bearing scars along his arms and chest that told of rough encounters with man and beast. He wore a badger's pelt atop his head, the creature's head peering over his own, shading his eyes, seeing what he might miss. He carried a bow of wood and sinew, short and strong like its owner, and at his hip was an axe, head black, honed edge winking in the sunlight. When Badger spoke, bigger men listened; Grey Feather and the other Crow leaders had told her to trust him, and so, she did.

Badger, she said softly.

The man did not move.

BADGER!

He jumped, spun in the air, and landed facing the other direction. His cadre of soldiers stared at him as at a snake that talked. Badger looked one way, then the other, spun again, became still, and cocked his head to listen.

Badger, she said again, and saw his eyes widen.

"Who speaks?"

She smiled—or did she? She could not say, but she felt as though she did, and that was enough for now.

I am she who travels with you, she said, and saw the pulse quicken along his neck. *And you are the man Grey Feather told me to trust. Was he mistaken?*

Badger clenched his teeth and closed his eyes.

"No," he said.

Peace. Calm. Gratitude.

My thanks.

The cords on Badger's neck relaxed and she saw his chest lift in a deep breath.

The men around him grew anxious with his odd behavior.

Tell them, Badger. Tell them that I am with you. Then take these men to the Great Council. I will guide you.

Badger glanced at the trees that surrounded them, saw nothing.

184

"Yes," he said.

The sun was bloated, a shimmering coal burning between the ceiling of bloody clouds and the undulating curves of golden, wind-blown grass. Speaks While Leaving sat, sharing the litter with her ashen corpse, its face covered once more by the shroud of pale deerskin. Her litter lay across a travois, pulled by a whistler, and her entourage of warriors flanked her on either side.

Limps had obviously come before them, for the entire tribe was waiting as they approached the camp. Even from this distance, dying sunlight gleamed from a thousand knives. Badger called a halt, fearing the worst.

Do not worry, she told him. *They know. You are bringing me home.*

Badger glanced from side to side, seeking support. Finding none, reluctantly, he faced forward and toed his whistler into motion. He kept to a stately pace and, as they approached, above the whistle of the wind could be heard the keening of women. As they neared the throng, the knife blades were raised, edges sawing through braids grown decades-long in ancient expression of loss. Men and women alike knelt, dousing themselves with handfuls of dry, sunscorched earth. As the travois and its shrouded body came near, wails rose and tears tracked down through dusty cheeks.

Speaks While Leaving felt their pain, felt each tear as a blade-touch, a thousand cuts across her soul. Even the return of Three Trees Together had not seen such a display, and it humbled her, anguishing her, reaving her from top to bottom. Faces of friends, relations, and neighbors were lined up before her, features contorted, faces twisted by grief, mouths open in circles of anguish, begging for solace.

I am here, she said to them, trying what she might. *Be at peace. I am with you.*

But her words went unheard, leaving her engulfed by the mourning of thousands and by wave upon wave of anguish, fear, and uncertainty. She turned to the men who bore her toward the Council Lodge and saw that they, too, wept, overwhelmed by the emotions around them, each soldier grieving for a woman he did not know.

The multitude parted before them, closed in behind them, enclosing them in a bubble of sorrow. Speaks While Leaving said no more, wished her spirit blind, until she saw Limps standing ahead of them, tall and stony in the last light of the dying day, hair loose in the breeze, cheeks shining with renewed misery.

It was too much. She fled, striving upward, outward, inward, aching for the stars and the darkness of death, finding neither, finding only that as the world contracted beneath her, her pain expanded, filling her every aspect, encompassing her, defining her. She recoiled from flight and fell back, dragged down from singular anguish to face the broader distress of her tribe. Sinking earthward, she looked down and saw their glowing, life-filled spirits encircling the dark spot of her corpse, surging and ebbing around its procession, and did not know if she had the strength for this last task. This last vision, this final dream of what should be, was too vast, too ravenous.

But as the sun set, a ghostly light rose on her left, followed by another on her right. She turned and saw two more rise behind her. The mourners below her were unmoved, unfazed by the four swirling pillars of brilliance that rose from the corners of the encampment. She recognized them: the *nevé-stanevóo'o;* the four Sacred Persons, created by Ma'heo'o to guard the corners of the world. They had been plaguing her sight since the day they brought her this vision. That day, the earth had trembled and brought fear to every heart, but this evening they radiated only calm, their serene power giving Speaks While Leaving the strength to continue.

And so she returned, taking once more her seat on the travois, and rode beside her body to the Council Lodge.

The lodge of the Great Council glowed with light from the hearth at its center. The lodgeskin's painted designs— spirits of power like eagles, dragonflies, and the Thunder Beings—shimmered with burning light. Outside, waiting, were chiefs of the bands and chiefs of the societies; men of peace and men of war, the grandfathers of the People. As the funereal troupe approached, the elders moved inside. The soldiers picked the litter up from the travois and brought Speaks While Leaving within the lodge, setting her down near the flickering fire.

On the other side of the fire knelt Alejandro, his hands tied behind his back. Limps brought in D'Avignon and shoved him to the ground beside the ambassador. The other prisoners were kept near the doorflap.

At the *vá'ôhtáma,* the position of honor at the rear of the lodge, Speaks While Leaving spied a familiar figure, his hair salted with silver, his face lined, his mouth grim.

Father, she said.

One Bear startled, eyes wide, and took an involuntary step forward.

"Daughter?" she heard him say.

Father, she said again. *You can hear me.*

Gasps and murmurs told her that others could hear her as well. Even Alejandro looked about him in confusion and fear.

I am here, she said. *I am with you. And there is much I want to tell you.*

One Bear rushed to the litter and pulled back the deerskin that covered her corpse's face. Everyone saw, and everyone now knew.

I am dead, Father.

He looked around, up toward the smokehole, all around the lodge, seeking her.

She went up to him and wished she was flesh again, to feel once more the warmth of his embrace, to touch his tear-stained cheek. Regret filled her, for her stubbornness, for her headstrong nature.

I am sorry, Father.

"No," he said softly. "Do not be so."

"Madness," said a voice, and as one the Council turned to look at Alejandro. "Sheer madness," he said.

Limps lunged and struck a blow that sent the ambassador to the ground. Alejandro lay there, nose bloodied, chuckling quietly. Beside him, D'Avignon said nothing, did nothing, observing all with his coyote eyes.

The Iron Shirts have betrayed our trust, she said to them all.

"It is true," Limps said over the rumblings of disbelief. "We found them in the Sacred Mountains. Mining, for this."

He motioned to the soldiers at the back, and they carried forth the crate that held the glass jars of powdered gold.

"This is too much," said Two Roads, chief of the Kit Fox soldiers. He walked over to Alejandro, reached down and grabbed him by the hair. He hauled him up and took out his knife.

Wait! she said.

"Why?" One Bear asked her. "How many times must we be taken as fools by these *vé'hó'e?*"

They have broken their promises to us, Speaks While Leaving said. *Our agreements are void. We are free to act. But not just against this one.*

"What?" the chief of the Ridge People band blurted. "You expect us to turn against all of the Iron Shirts?"

"Daughter," One Bear said, "I know you. You never speak without a plan. But you have kept too much hidden from us."

No more, she said. *Look around you. I have brought the Crow People here. I have brought the Cradle People. The Blackfoot. Their chiefs have seen the vision I kept from you. They have seen it and they believe it to be true. Riders have been sent. Many are coming.*

Her father closed his eyes and clenched his fists. "You tell our oldest enemies of this vision, but do not tell your own people?"

She hesitated, and then admitted her guilt. *I did not think you would believe me. As you said, I was arrogant.*

"Will you show it to us now?" her father asked.

Yes, she said. *Now.*

She opened her mind, and let the vision flow. It burst from the world of spirits into the world of men, flooding everyone in the Council Lodge with the sights, the sounds, the import of what she had kept from them. And as the elders of her tribe lived the vision of the three paths, as they grasped the whole of it, as they absorbed its meaning, Speaks While Leaving felt a surge of power from outside. Four lights, the guardians of the world, grew brighter and brighter, infusing everything with a glow of ethereal power until, when the vision played out to its end, the lights shot up into the night, dimming, and took their place among the stars.

Around the lodge, men gaped and looked to one another for confirmation that they had, indeed, just seen what they had seen.

"You were right," One Bear said. "I would not have believed you."

Speaks While Leaving felt tenuous, as if she was draining away, like water through cupped fingers.

And now?

One Bear addressed his fellows. "Any dissent?" he asked.

None spoke. The path was clear.

Chapter 22

Moon When Ice Starts to Form, Waxing
Four Years after the Cloud Fell
North of the Sudden River
Alliance Territory

The morning mist swirled in the lazy air. Sheets of it rose from the ground, grey tendrils reaching out with ghostly hands, caressing the flanks of the passing horses. George rode a grey mare, borrowed from one of the general's aides, and Mouse Road was perched atop the broad back of a sorrel gelding, hands twined in the poor beast's mane, her face pinched by discomfort and the fear of tumbling off. Meriwether and his men accompanied, ranging near or far as their duties dictated, their misty forms vacillating between suggestion and reality, their horse's hooves squelching across the rain-soaked grassland.

The sun was just an idea in the east and the wind of last night's storm was just a memory. The day lay quiet, sullen and expectant, or so it felt to George. He tried to dampen his hopeful spirit, his experience counseling caution while superstition warned him of jinxes. But even so, there was a giddiness within his breast, a puppyish exuberance he could not keep entirely quiet.

"Must be getting close, now," Meriwether offered.

Meriwether had been a cipher during their return from Westgate. Aloof and patently suspicious on their outward journey, on the trip back he had stayed closer, at times even riding alongside George and Mouse Road. As a conversationalist, he was not verbose, but neither was he the pillar of silence he'd been before.

"Indeed," George replied. He noted the copse of poplars in the curve of the creekbed. "We're nearly there, in fact. Just a mile or so more." He glanced over, noted the general's furrowed brow, and saw the muscles of his jaw working under the unshaven stubble.

"Something on your mind, General?"

Meriwether glanced over and George saw the man's jaw clench once more.

"I misjudged you," he said.

George did not reply, but let the old soldier find his own words in his own time.

"I thought you were..." he began. "I thought you were just..."

He took a breath and held it for a moment before releasing his words. "I thought you were a dilettante."

George could not help but chuckle. "A dilettante, eh?"

Meriwether's shy smile expressed some of his embarrassment. "Yes," he said. "A dilettante, a dabbler. A gadfly bent on making his name at the expense of others." He turned and leveled his gaze at George. "At the expense of your father."

George took that in, mulled it, and nodded. "And now?"

Meriwether looked forward again, peering out into the thinning mist.

"I watched you two, you and your father. You weren't out to hurt him or to shame him, but you weren't a pushover, either. You were..." Again, he paused to seek the proper word. "You were professional. A firm negotiator, but respectful." He shrugged. "It surprised me, is all. You were both working for peace. That's not something I usually get to see."

George nodded. "You're thinking of the Spanish."

The general squinted into the distance. "Yes," he said. "The Spanish." He nodded his head to the west. "Those soldiers out there, your 'Iron Shirts,' they are all I usually get to see. They want to make war and, with skill or without it, they succeed. Making war is easy; any idiot with ten thousand men can do it for a fair spate of time. But making peace, well, now. That's where the true skill comes in. And it's not something a general gets to see on the battlefield."

Mouse Road guided her mount closer, questioning George with a few deft gestures.

He talks, she signed. *All good?*

Yes, George responded. *All good.*

All good, but still, a question had been nagging at him.

"General," George said. "My father trusts you completely and I know you will follow his orders to the best of your abilities. But what I need to know is if *we* can trust you, not as a soldier, but as a man. Is your heart in this?"

Meriwether looked neither right nor left, stared straight ahead, betraying nothing. George, fearing he had trespassed on the general's conversational mood, spoke quickly lest he offend a new ally.

"My apologies," he said. "I did not mean to imply—"

"No," Meriwether said with an absent wave of his hand. "I was just considering. It is an honest question, and you deserve an honest answer."

George let him ruminate in silence, fairly sure that he had already been given the answer. When Meriwether did speak, his words were measured, his tone almost avuncular.

"As you said, first and foremost I am a soldier, and as a soldier, your trust would not be misplaced. I will not waver in my commitment to my commander's orders.

"But as to my heart, well, let us say that there the situation is much less clear-cut."

He paused and they all rode in silence, with only the sounds of hooves, tack, and harness around them.

"In my heart," he went on, "I believe our race is superior to your native friends, and I believe that placing the great prairies of this continent in the hands of a tribe of hide-wearing savages goes against God's plan." He held up a hand. "I know, that's not what you wanted to hear, but that is what I feel. However..." He twisted in his saddle, put a hand on his hip, and looked George square in the eye.

"You and your friends have been very clever. You have

us over a barrel and, truth be told, I would rather have your hide-wearing savages on my back doorstep than those cursed Spaniards. And so, yes, as far as that goes, my heart *is* in this fight." He pointed at George. "But if you or they so much as hint at betraying this agreement, I'll bring down God's own wrath upon you all."

He straightened in his saddle and gazed forward again. "I hope that answers your question."

George blinked, taken aback by the general's unvarnished honesty. "Indeed, sir, it does."

They rode onward, pushing into a canter as the morning brightened and the terrain smoothed out. Soon, Mouse Road pointed out the tall, lone sycamore that was their landmark. George relayed the news.

"It's just up ahead," he told the general. "Best we part ways here and go on foot the rest of the way. No sense spooking your horses."

Meriwether nodded and called a halt. George dismounted and Mouse Road gratefully did likewise. They turned the reins over to their escort and George regarded the general once more.

"Thank you, sir."

"Don't be discouraged, son," he said. "I'm just an old Southern boy at heart. There are plenty who would side with you. This war with the allied tribes has gone on for far too long, and many are weary of it." He leaned forward and extended his hand. "The natives have earned an honorable settlement."

George reached up and shook the general's hand. Then Meriwether touched the brim of his hat and nodded to Mouse Road.

"A pleasure making your acquaintance, ma'am," he said, then turned and spurred his horse into a trot.

George and Mouse Road watched them disappear into the thinning mist. George shouldered their bundle and set off for the sycamore tree. The sun was a smoky ball of dim fire, but grew brighter as the mist burned away. Mouse Road walked quietly by his side, the tall, dew-heavy blades of prairie grass whispering as she passed. She slipped her hand into his and he could not help but smile.

"He said something you did not like," she said.

George sighed. "No. He just spoke honestly."

"But it made you sad."

He shrugged. "A little."

She stopped and gripped his hand to halt him, too. "I do not want you to be sad. Not today. Not when we have everything so close. Not so close to victory." She stepped up to him, reached forward and sought him beneath his breechclout. George's eyes went wide and she laughed, grinning.

"Not today," she said. "No one is allowed to be sad today."

George found his tongue tied in knots by her uncharacteristic brashness. "But, can we," he started, trying to calculate if this was the right time of month. "Your moontime, isn't it due soon?"

She caressed him and lifted her eyebrows. "Past it."

"But, then..." He couldn't think with her doing that with her hand. "You mean that you are...?"

Her smile became knowing and her hand stroked him, up and down. "Yes," she said, her voice little more than a whisper. "The child will be born in springtime." She took his hand and placed it on her breast.

"Wait," he said.

She took a step back, hands on hips. "One Who Flies, I did not think I would have so much trouble getting you to lay with me."

"No," he said, shaking his head to clear it, to deny her accusation, to bring him back from the dream he had stepped into. "I just, I mean...if you are...can we?"

She walked back to him, took him once again in hand, and looked up at him with smiling eyes.

"We most certainly can."

They loved, then and there under the brightening sky. His skin thrilled at the cold of the dew-moist grass, the warmth of her touch, the heat of her enveloping sex. They loved, silently and with urging words, laughing and crying out. She guided his touch and he complied happily, finding pleasure in hers, before she reciprocated in kind. They loved and after, lying in the crushed grass beneath the open day, he had to admit that he was no longer sad at all.

She lay beside him, her body stretched out, an arm and one leg draped across him, her breath warm on his neck, her breasts a pleasant pressure against his ribs. He watched sunlight glimmer along her waist-long braids and gleam from the sheen of sweat at the small of her back. Her scent, made of musk and smoke and the scent of fallen leaves, intoxicated him. He breathed it in slowly, held it, and released it in a sigh. She snuggled closer against him; he closed his eyes and, lulled by the drone of bees and the sun's renewed warmth, drifted toward sleep.

Then the ground beneath him trembled with a pulse—*thrum*—like a raindrop on a drumhead, and he knew their brief idyll was near an end. Mouse Road felt it too, her body stirring as the pulse in the earth grew stronger. They could hear it, now—deep, sonorous, at the limit of the ear. George stroked his wife's cheek, kissed her eyes, and reached for his clothes just as he heard the great footsteps close in on them.

"Hello, chick," he said.

His walker halted, tense and still a few yards away. She eyed them and snuffled at the air, smelling new scents. George laughed and his walker blinked, put at ease by his radiated mood. She rumbled, deep in her throat, satisfied at their reunion.

The sun was climbing toward its zenith when they headed off, veering south away from Meriwether's trail. The general told them that the bluecoats would draw the Spanish forces slowly to the north, and George figured that a long hook around the southwest should bring them in on the Spanish right flank.

They traveled at an easy pace, giving the walker ample rest. They ate from their stores of dried meat and biscuit as they rode, and George scanned the terrain idly. On their left was a line of trees, leaves rustling, and ahead a low rise, but his mind was on other things.

"What?" Mouse Road asked when her arms around his waist detected his quiet chuckle.

"I was thinking of my father," he said as they rode over the top of the rise. "This is not what he expected when he dreamed of being a grandfa—"

Shouts.

George saw soldiers, Spanish uniforms. One of the soldiers screamed, gaping at the walker. The beast chuffed and all of the Spaniards grabbed their rifles. George waved a hand to ward them off, stop them, to show them that it wasn't just a rogue walker, but they did not see him. All they saw was the beast, the teeth, the size of her.

Gunsmoke and muzzle fire. Bullets sang past. The walker twisted, veteran of battles, knowing when to retreat. Mouse Road's grip failed. George turned, saw her falling as the walker turned to run. He reached for her, caught her sleeve, but couldn't hold her up, wouldn't release her, and then he fell, too. The walker pushed off toward the trees. George hit the ground, hard. His head swam.

The soldiers rushed in. He heard words, an argument. Someone grabbed him and rolled him over. He reached out, tried to defend himself and pain struck him in the face. Thrust back onto his stomach, they set upon his back like a barrowload of bricks, their hard-boned knees pinning him to the earth, their hands binding his arms and hands.

"Mouse Road!" he cried. He writhed, trying to catch sight of her, but his view was obscured by men and knee-high grass.

Orders were given in hissing, lisp-filled Spanish. George craned to see his captors. Their uniforms were dark blue, not the sky blue of Pereira's forces. Marines, then, and from Spain; not the Creole-manned ranks from Cuba or the Tejano Coast.

These were the reinforcements, the armada sent by the Spanish Crown, here and already in the field.

The soldiers argued with their leader, but the louder voice prevailed. They lifted him to his feet. He fought, butting the soldier in front of him. Unbalanced, he fell, and earned a kick to the ribs for his attempt.

"Mouse Road," he cried again, for she had not answered his first call. The soldiers, holding his arms from behind, lifted him again, and he saw why his wife had been silent.

Mouse Road lay on the golden grass, blood staining the breast of her deerskin dress. Her eyes fluttered as she lay senseless.

Desperate anger filled George's brain. He shouted—an incoherent, rage-born roar—as they dragged him toward the woods, leaving Mouse Road behind.

Horses whickered as they approached, nervous and

fidgety at the smell of gunsmoke and blood. George counted four horses, one for each soldier, tethered near the remnants of an overnight camp.

One man gave orders to the others. They set George down against a tree and began to break camp.

"No!" he shouted at them. "You have to go get her!" He tried English and French, then his pidgin Spanish. "You idiots! She is wounded. You...*tu cabrón! ¡Tu pendejo!*"

The sergeant stormed over. George jerked to the side and the butt of the sergeant's rifle hit the trunk of the tree. George let the image of Mouse Road, bloody and unconscious, fill his mind. He let his anger bloom, let obscenity spew from his mouth.

It was all that was needed.

The sergeant hauled back for another blow, but it never came. The low branches behind him shook and the walker exploded into the clearing.

She took the nearest soldier in her jaws and tossed him into the second man. The horses reared, pulled free and fled, trampling the third soldier in their panic. The sergeant was taking aim at her and George surged upward, shoulder to the sergeant's ribs, bowling him over. The walker stepped in and snatched the sergeant headless. Then she turned to finish off the others.

George searched the body for a knife, found one, and cut his bonds. Free, he ran out from under the trees, into the sunlight.

Mouse Road moaned and he fell to his knees at her side. He cut the shoulder-lace of her dress and exposed the wound. A wave of relief swept through him when he saw it. The bullet had run a gash across her collarbone and cut across the inside of her upper arm. Blood pumped out of the wound, soaking her clothing and the grass around her. Her eyes opened. She smiled at seeing him, then winced at the pain.

"I...I fell," she said, still disoriented. "I hit my head." She moved her arm and cried out, more in surprise than in pain.

"Hush," he told her, laying the hand of her wounded arm across her belly. "You were shot, too."

"Shot?" she asked in alarm. "Oh, yes," she said, remembering. "Yes, I was."

With the Spaniard's knife he cut the sleeve from her dress and folded it into a compress. He put it on the bleeding wound and then put her good hand on top of it.

"Pressure. Tight," he said, and then, "Don't move."

He raided the soldiers' camp, avoiding the sight of his walker and her current meal. He found what he needed and returned to Mouse Road. He worked silently and Mouse Road did not offer any conversation. Rum was his disinfectant and strips of clothing made both a serviceable compress and the means of keeping it tightly bound. A pair of kerchiefs for a sling, and he hoped she was strong enough to travel.

Finally, when they were on the move once more, he spoke.

"I am sorry," he said. "I should have been more careful."

She squeezed him with her uninjured arm.

"No one is allowed to be sad today," she said, and he laughed.

But he kept a sharp eye out, nonetheless.

They went farther to the south to avoid more encounters with new arrivals from Spain who couldn't tell ally from foe. Though George knew he had officially turned coat, he hoped to play the friendly liaison as long as he could. Before long, it was clear that the Queen Regent's marines had indeed landed, and in force. George and Mouse Road skirted patrols, keeping close to trees for cover, and soon crossed the trail of torn earth and flattened grass made as the marines had moved north to join Pereira.

"How many?" Mouse Road asked as George stared at the swath the Spanish left behind.

"Hard to tell," he said, studying the lanes of overtrodden ground. "Foot soldiers. Many. Plus at least a hundred horse. And supply wagons." He pointed to ruts, off to the side; deep cuts in the pale grass. "And artillery. Five guns, probably. That won't help. These men likely know how to use their artillery."

"What can we do?"

He frowned and nudged the walker into motion.

"We will think of something. Right now, we need to keep out of sight."

They did so, cutting a long, wide curve around the rear of both contingents, rounding up to the western flank where, George hoped, they would find Storm Arriving and his patrols before the Spaniards found them.

Mouse Road bore up, stoic despite her weakness and the pain of her wounds. George insisted they stop to inspect the dressing regularly. Despite his efforts, the wound kept reopening, and each day she bled through the dressings.

He put her before him along the walker's spine and lashed her torso to his, so he could hold her up and keep her from falling. By the time they came upon a Kit Fox patrol, she was limp and insensible, her skin cold and pallid.

"Help her," he cried to the approaching soldiers.

The patron rode in at once.

"She is wounded," he explained. "And has lost a lot of blood."

Sun Rising was the leader of the patrol. "Blue Feather has the fastest whistler," he said.

The others agreed and in moments Blue Feather sped off, Mouse Road in his arms. The rest mounted and followed, but at a slower pace to accommodate George's tired walker.

"We met a new group of Iron Shirts," George explained. "They did not know who we were."

Sun Rising, a thin, hook-nosed man with pock-marked cheeks, grinned.

"They arrived two nights ago. Many Iron Shirts. The bluecoats have been running before our greater numbers." He raised two fists. "This hand is the Land Iron Shirts, and this one is the Iron Shirts from across the Big Salty. First one hits the bluecoats, then the other." He moved his fists in slow, punching jabs. "And the bluecoats retreat. They have no time to rest from the first blow before a second blow comes in."

George could appreciate the tactic. The marines' commander was undoubtedly a more experienced man than the greenhorn Pereira. But he hoped this "retreat" was all part of Meriwether's plan, and not because Pereira truly had them on the ropes.

"And you?" he asked Sun Rising. "Where are the soldiers of the People?"

"Ha!" Sun Rising beamed. "We are the wolf that lunges in from the side to bite. We are the hawk that swoops in from the sky to slash at their eyes. When the Iron Shirts push the bluecoats, we steer their retreat. It will not be long, now."

George heard the pride in the soldier's voice. "Not long before what?"

Sun Rising's smile was peaceful, serene, assured. "They will have the White Water at their back, and no time to cross."

"You seem confident," George said.

Sun Rising signed his agreement. "We have a good war chief."

George's walker had caught her second wind and they picked up the pace. The land was gentle, but George's mind was a-stir with fretful worry. He recalled to his mind's eye old maps of the region and, with an imaginary finger, traced the courses of the great rivers and their tortuous paths— the Sudden River, the White Water, and a half dozen others that fed into the Big Greasy.

Meriwether was a master tactician, but he had been away from the field for a handful of days. Could his adjutants have boxed him in along un-fordable banks? Could they put him in such a grave situation in so short a time?

He was also disturbed by the utter faith and gleeful anticipation that Sun Rising held for Storm Arriving and the impending battle. Speaks While Leaving's vision was clear as summer's sun to George. Hopefully, he would be able to convince Storm Arriving. That in itself was a big enough task, but George had definitely *not* thought that he would also have to convince every soldier the People had in the field.

These worries piled themselves atop his fear for Mouse Road's health. He swirled the questions and possible answers around in his head, not watching where they were going, just letting his walker follow while he struggled to see his way through to what needed to be done.

And so, he was brought up short when they rode around a grove of trees and he saw the battle groups arrayed on a great plain.

George guessed the view stretched for nearly ten miles

across a vista as flat as a table. The sky above was brilliant blue and, for once, without a cloud. Prairie grass carpeted the plain in a nap of taupe and gold.

Two encampments lay like dark patches on the prairie's otherwise seamless fabric. The nearest, but a mile distant, was alive with movement and sound. Canvas billowed, wheels turned and creaked, horse-drawn carts grew heavy as pots and equipment were tossed aboard. Men dashed about, striking tents and loading supplies. Pereira's forces were preparing to depart.

Miles ahead, dimmed by the haze of dust and distance, the other patch of land seethed with similar activity, but there the obscuring clouds were not dust but smoke from cookfires as the marines settled in for a rest.

George peered into the distance, squinting to the north, looking for sign of Meriwether and his bluecoats. His eye scanned the plain, side to side, all the way to the horizon. At one spot, he thought he could make out a line of greenery against the deepening gold, perhaps the edge of scrub or the limit of some trees. At another, he thought he saw the glint of sunlight on a distant river. But these were phantoms, dreams of his waking mind. Even a West Point cadet knew better than to rest within sight of the enemy.

If only we'd acted sooner, he thought. *Before the marines arrived. Mouse Road would still be...*

The idea fell apart as he formed it. They had needed an agreement with his father. Without it, there was never any hope of convincing Storm Arriving to switch sides.

But now? With greater numbers and high morale, how could he convince them to betray their alliance with the Iron Shirts? How could he prove to Storm Arriving that the crooked path was the straightest route to peace? With so much more to dream on, he felt hope slipping through his fingers.

His walker stopped and turned her head. She stared at him with her great, golden eye, and for a moment—a brief, crystalline moment—he felt *her* emotions, *her* strength, felt them flow into *him.* The hair on his neck stood up. His heart lurched, then began to pound, hard. He felt strength, he felt power. He felt that there was no challenge he could not master.

He felt invincible.

Yes, he said to her.

She held his gaze a moment longer, then turned and stepped off to catch up with the others.

Chapter 23

Moon When Ice Starts to Form, Waxing
Four Years after the Cloud Fell
North of the Sudden River
Alliance Territory

George followed his guides down toward the camp. As before, the soldiers of the People were encamped a short distance away from the Iron Shirts. As they approached, George noted that the number of soldiers had remained constant in the camp of the People.

Good and bad, he judged it, for while it meant no major defections had occurred, it also meant there had been no increase to their forces. And, considering the insight he had just gained into the company's morale, it also meant that Storm Arriving was surrounded by true believers.

Storm Arriving was waiting, hands loose at his side, face a scowl, eyes locked on George as he rode up.

George unhooked his leg and slid down his walker's flank.

"How is she?" he asked as he touched down. Storm Arriving stepped forward and wheeled a backhanded blow at George's face. The assault took George off guard, as did the next, full-fisted punch. He saw dark stars and stumbled sideways, but recovered quickly enough to see Storm Arriving's advance.

George held up a warning hand and his walker shifted her stance, legs tensed, neck back, head ready to strike.

Everyone froze.

George took the moment to feel the side of his face and blink away the pain. Then he looked around.

Storm Arriving was a statue of fury while the soldiers around him were pictures of shock and surprise. George walked up to Storm Arriving, his own anger echoed by his walker's menacing rumble. The war chief's eyes had lost none of their rage.

George stared at him, meeting the challenge.

Storm Arriving seethed.

Sun Rising took a tentative step. Without breaking his gaze, George raised a finger and Sun Rising halted.

"One Who Flies," the soldier said, his tone pleading entreaty. "Do not."

"A chief should show more control," George said.

Storm Arriving shivered with unspent rage. "First, you endanger my wife, then my daughter, and now my sister," he said.

George shrugged. "You think they would listen to me, when they will not listen to you?" He touched his face again, feeling the bruise beginning to rise.

"That is the last time you strike me," George said to him. Then he looked at his walker.

"Watch him," he told her, and stepped around the stunned war chief.

"Sun Rising, take me to my wife."

Sun Rising gave George a worried, sidelong glance as he led him toward the center of the camp. George measured his gait as they walked, calming his own anger. He knew it had not been wise to humiliate the man he most needed on his side, and only hoped that his show of strength would counter the sting of shame he had inflicted.

He halted, then, and closed his eyes. He thought of a quiet stream and the *chee-rik* of diving lizards calling from the banks above. His blood subsided, his muscles unclenched, and deep within, he felt a taut string loosen. The echo of raised voices behind him confirmed that his walker broke stance and settled down to rest, releasing Storm Arriving and his men. George motioned to Sun Rising, and they continued onward.

"There," Sun Rising said, pointing to a huge chestnut tree. George hurried onward and saw beneath its yellow-leaved boughs a woman crouching down, weaving smoke from a smudge stick over a patient laid out on a mat of furs.

George moved to his wife and knelt at her side. He felt her brow, found it damp but warm once more. He checked her wound. The old dressing had been removed and replaced with a poultice. The air smelled of the healing smoke of smoldering sage.

"She will be fine," the woman said.

George looked up and realized that his wife's healer was no woman after all.

"Whistling Elk!" George said. "Thank you for tending to her. She will be well?"

"Yes," Whistling Elk said. "You did well with the wound, but she is weak from the bleeding. She drank a good deal of water, which is good, but she needs all her strength to recover. She will be much better by morning."

George touched the swelling along his cheekbone. "Too bad you did not inform Storm Arriving."

He heard his friend sigh. "That man has enough anger to burn the sun," Whistling Elk said. "He was furious when you took her and rode off to parley with the bluecoats, but when she came back, wounded by a bluecoat bullet—"

"What?" George said. "No. It wasn't the bluecoats. It was the Iron Shirts that shot at us."

Whistling Elk set down the smudge stick and rose, brushing dust from his dress and leggings.

"I will tell him that," he said as he walked over to put a hand on George's shoulder. "But I do not think it will cool him. He blames you for much."

"I know," George said, looking down at Mouse Road. He thought of all the trouble and sorrow Storm Arriving had met in recent years—one sister dead, a wife with a stubbornness to match his own, a daughter dead of red fever contracted in a foreign land, the People divided, the Alliance crumbling, and now Mouse Road, the one remaining member of his family, wounded and brought down on what he saw as a fool's errand.

"He blames me for everything," George said, "but I do not know why."

Whistling Elk gave George's shoulder a gentle squeeze. "Because it is easier," he said, and then left.

Mouse Road moaned, and George forgot about everything else. Her eyes fluttered and then George saw nothing but her ink-black pupils.

"I am thirsty," she said.

"Of course," he said, and went for a waterskin near the tree's trunk. He poured some water into a horn cup and brought it to her lips. She sipped and fell back upon the furs that blanketed the wicker headrest.

"How do you feel?" he asked.

She pondered, her brow wrinkled as she estimated.

"Better," she said, and George believed her.

"Your brother will be glad to hear it," he said.

She squinted, looking at his face. She reached up and touched the swelling bruise along his cheekbone, and winced in sympathy.

"He was displeased," she said.

"A little," he answered.

She closed her eyes and took a deep breath. "He is such a tangle," she said. "It is not as if he thinks you are responsible for..." She gave George's chuckle a quizzical look.

"That is exactly his thinking," he said with a smirk.

She blinked up at him. "But that...that is not..." She clenched her fists and shut her eyes again. "*Oooh!* He makes me so angry!"

George patted her arm. "Hush," he said. "Save your strength. Besides, getting angry will not help."

"It *does* help!" she said, trying to sit up. "Why, I have a mind to go to him and say just what I—" Her strength faded and she fell back against the headrest.

"And say what?" Storm Arriving said, walking up with Grey Bear, Whistling Elk, and a small group of his command staff. He looked from Mouse Road to George and back. "You were talking about me, no?" He walked to his sister's side opposite George and knelt beside her.

"What is it you would say to me?" he asked, his voice almost gentle.

"I would say," she began, and then paused. Her breath was labored, her energy burned up, but she had enough in reserve to point a finger and poke her brother with it, punctuating her words. "I would say...no one...tells me...what to do. Not him. Not you. No one."

Storm Arriving took her hand in his. "I can see that, now," he said. "I do not know how I could have thought otherwise."

She pursed her lips and closed her eyes. "Good," she said. "Now, we have news to tell you. We met with...husband...you must...I need to..."

"Sleep," George said. "I will tell them."

"Yes," she mumbled. "Tell them." And she slept.

They stayed there, the two men, silently watching the woman sleep. George looked out across the plain. Dust rose from the army camps, and the sky above had collected clouds to paint with the evening sunset, but George could care about little more than that she was resting and that she would recover.

She, and their child.

"One Who Flies."

Storm Arriving had a furrow in his brow. He straightened his back but kept his gaze lowered. When he spoke, it was loud enough for those nearby to hear him.

"I—" he began, his voice rough. "I should not have struck you. You showed great restraint." He paused, his jaw clenching as if chewing his words. "A chief should show such restraint. I have shamed myself. I promise that I will do better."

It was not an apology, but it was an admission of wrong, made before others. It was the kind of abasement a chief makes when he fails in his responsibility, and George knew it had cost his proud brother dearly.

George held out his hand.

"We will say no more of it," he offered.

Storm Arriving clasped George's wrist, sealing the bond. Then he stood. George stood as well.

"I need to speak with you," he said. "About this war."

"Later," Storm Arriving said. "My council and I will meet you here."

George stayed with Mouse Road through the afternoon

and into the evening. As she slept, he watched the two commanders—Storm Arriving and Pereira—set about preparing their men for the coming action. It was obvious who had the easier job, for while he could see Pereira's staff scuttling from wagon to wagon, overseeing the proper stowage of all the paraphernalia associated with sheltering and feeding an army, Storm Arriving merely walked among his cohort, chatting amiably, gesturing to a loose tie-down or an overlooked item. Where Pereira had to ensure his men decamped in proper order, Storm Arriving simply understood that they would do so on their own. On the other hand, the People's soldiers knew that anything left behind was lost. A man who went back in search of a forgotten knife or cartridge belt would be heaped with ridicule upon his lonely return.

As night set in, George heard nothing but quiet conversation from the soldiers nearby, while from Pereira's camp came a constant clatter of banging lanterns, the neighing of fractious horses, and the raised voices of displeased men.

Mouse Road drifted in and out of her dreams, at times recognizing George, but at other times mistaking him for her deceased mother.

"You are too hard on him," she said at one point. George tried to rouse her, but she persisted. "Yes, Mother. I know he's skinny. Yes, and hairy, too."

"Mouse Road," George entreated, not wanting to hear this long lost echo of an old conversation.

"Hush, Mother," she said. "My mind is made up." She smiled in her sleep. "I like his eyes."

She slept soundly then, and spoke no more on the topic, for which George was very grateful. After a while, she stirred, waking fully as Storm Arriving returned with his counselors, Grey Bear and Whistling Elk.

Storm Arriving went to his sister's side while the others sat nearby, forming a loose circle.

"How are you feeling now?" he asked.

"Stronger," she said. "The sleep helped."

"It is what you need most," Whistling Elk said. "Especially with a young one on the way."

Storm Arriving looked at Whistling Elk.

Whistling Elk blinked and asked simply. "You did not

know?"

Storm Arriving stared at Whistling Elk, then looked at Mouse Road, and finally turned to George, who held up his hands to ward off a renewed tirade.

"I only learned of it this morning," he said, and then to Whistling Elk he asked, "How did *you* know?"

Whistling Elk tsked and laughed. "I have known this one since she was five summers old. We women, we know these things."

Grey Bear cleared his throat, bringing Storm Arriving back to the reason for their visit.

"Yes," Storm Arriving said. "One Who Flies, we are here to listen. What is it you wanted to tell us?"

George glanced at Grey Bear and Whistling Elk. "How much has he told you?"

Grey Bear shrugged. "That you think we should break with the Iron Shirts and ally the People with the bluecoats instead."

"That *I* think...?" He gaped at Storm Arriving. "You did not tell them of the vision?"

"Vision?" Whistling Elk said, surprised. "*The* vision?"

"Yes," George said. "The one Speaks While Leaving had and would not share."

Grey Bear frowned.

"It was not important," Storm Arriving said firmly.

"Not important?" Whistling Elk was incredulous.

Grey Bear gestured his dissent. "Storm Arriving is correct. It is not important." He waved an arm toward the forces on the prairie. "That is important. Visions can be misread. That is truth."

Whistling Elk would not be put off. "I think that it is *very* important. Tell us, One Who Flies. Tell us everything."

George did so, giving them every detail of the vision and of how it had been shown to him. Mouse Road supported his story, making sure the soldiers knew that she had seen and felt its power just as her husband had.

Whistling Elk listened, eyes wide with astonishment, but Grey Bear's expression remained closed, his eyelids narrowed in skeptical disbelief.

"But now," George said, when he had told them all, "Now it is more than just the vision. Now we have the promise of the bluecoats, the promise of Long Hair himself."

Storm Arriving and Grey Bear both stiffened at the name.

"You have spoken to Long Hair?" Grey Bear asked.

Mouse Road spoke quietly but with resolve. "That is where we went. We met with the bluecoat war chief and with Long Hair himself."

George leaned forward, anxious to enhance the importance of his words. "He has agreed to fight the Iron Shirts with us as an ally. He has agreed to leave us the lands this side of the Big Greasy. He has agreed to a lasting peace."

Whistling Elk grinned broadly. Storm Arriving dismissed it all with a sneer. Grey Bear's brow was furrowed once more, consternation plain on his face.

"More empty promises," Storm Arriving said.

Whistling Elk thumped his thigh in exasperation. "You discount all this?"

"Of course I do," Storm Arriving said. He stood and pointed out at the field. "Do you think Long Hair does not see the size of this enemy? Do you think he does not fear our numbers? Our strength?"

Whistling Elk leapt to his feet. "But he has agreed to everything we wanted. And the vision—"

"The *vision,*" Storm Arriving spat. "Always the *vision.* The vision is blind. The vision does not count men on the battlefield. I *do.* And I say that Long Hair would promise us the moon and the stars to save his soldiers. Even if we could save them."

Grey Bear held up a hand for attention and the other two fell quiet.

"You do not believe we can win, if we ally with the bluecoats against the Iron Shirts?"

Storm Arriving was calm but earnest. "Our soldiers are brave, and we have made Pereira mighty against the bluecoat war chief's greater skill. With him, against Pereira alone, victory is sure, but with the new soldiers from across the Big Salty? Their commander is skilled and wary. Can we win against both forces combined?" He folded his arms across his chest. "No. Not with the numbers we have."

"But with the spirits on our side," Whistling Elk began.

210

Grey Bear stood, joining the others. "For years the spirits have guided us to this alliance with the Iron Shirts. Now they guide us away, but do not give us the numbers to succeed?" He scowled at the ground as he wrestled with the dilemma. "Ma'heo'o is powerful. But Vé'hó'e, the Trickster, he is also a powerful spirit. And we can be as easily guided by the one as we can be tricked by the other." He looked out over the plain, at the thousands of men, horses, and machines making ready for war. "We near the end of this. We cannot risk defeat." He faced the group once more.

"I stand with Storm Arriving."

George's heart sank, not because Grey Bear had sided with Storm Arriving, but because his logic was irrefutable. And then he realized that logic was the whole problem.

"You are right," he said.

Mouse Road gaped at him and Whistling Elk sputtered, at a loss for words.

"No," George said to them, "they are right. To switch alliances now, and with these numbers? It makes no sense."

Storm Arriving and Grey Bear were attentive while the other two kept a stunned silence.

"But let me ask you one simple question," he said, purposefully gazing at each man before he raised his eyebrows and said, "When has Speaks While Leaving ever been wrong?"

He saw the question hit them, saw their unique responses—dismissal from Storm Arriving, agitated concern from Grey Bear, delight from Whistling Elk—and continued.

"For over a decade, this woman, this *seer,* has guided you with visions. She has guided the People to plenty and to prominence. She foretold our trip to the City of White Stone, and of our success against the bluecoats. She even foretold this alliance with the Iron Shirts, though none of you believed it would happen."

"She *made* that alliance happen," Storm Arriving argued. "Against the will of the Council, and against *my* will, she *made* that happen."

"Does that make her vision false?" George asked. "Does that mean you are *not* allied with the Iron Shirts?" He stood and pointed to the plain that had been the focus of their calculations. "Yet now, because her vision points you in the opposite direction, you disbelieve her. Despite the fact that she has been proven true all these years—" He shook his head. "—No, it is *because* she has been proven true for so long, you decide to ignore her. You decide to forget all the past and look only at that field and the forces upon it."

Mouse Road sat up. "It is worse than that," she said. Her words were to her husband, but all of them turned to listen. "Not only do they forget the past, they are blind. They see only men and soldiers. They do not see what is right before their eyes."

George was puzzled. He did not know what Mouse Road meant. Neither, it seemed, did her brother.

"I see more than you think I do," he chided his little sister. "I see men down there, I see soldiers, but I also see their war chiefs. I see the land on which they march. I see the paths they have taken to get here and the tactics they have used. I see the dead they made yesterday and the dead they are likely to make tomorrow."

"And yet you are blind," she said.

"To what?" Storm Arriving said, temper flaring. "What do I fail to see?"

She pointed.

"One Who Flies," she said. "The man who fell from the cloud. The man foretold by the first vision Speaks While Leaving ever had. The man who will free us from all *vé'hó'e.*"

It was Storm Arriving's turn to gape.

"See *him,*" Mouse Road said. "Hear *him.* Then decide."

The tumult of thoughts colliding in Storm Arriving's mind was plain to see on his face. Slowly, he brought a hand up to cover his eyes and stood there, as blind in fact as Mouse Road accused him to be, seeing only his own thoughts, hearing only his own inner voice.

George looked out beyond the circle of their council, saw men gathered by lantern-light, preparing for the morning's battle. He watched them and worried, knowing full well what even ill-led troops could do in such numbers. They were *thousands,* perhaps four-to-one compared to Meriwether's troops. Back in classes at West Point, such odds would be described with words like "overwhelming" or "insurmountable," and yet here he was, begging commanders to commit their forces to the disadvantaged side. Faced with such reality, how could anyone side with faith and visions?

"I cannot," Storm Arriving said, looking at them all once more, and within George's soul a small voice shouted in relief while another cried out in despair. Grey Bear's face was sorrowful as he signed his concurrence, and Whistling Elk sank down to the ground, fists against his temples.

They remained like that, none of them able to break past the conflict of their own thoughts, until the fluting of whistlers forced them all back to face the world.

Sounds gathered in the darkness. Questions were answered, and urgent voices were ushered toward the council meeting beneath the cloak of the chestnut tree.

"Storm Arriving?"

"Here," he said.

Three men joined their circle. In the dim light, George could only see pale shapes in deerskin tunics and caught the glint of moonlight along rifle barrels. Scouts, back from patrol.

"What is it?" Storm Arriving asked.

"Riders," said one of the men. "From the west."

"And from the northwest," said a second scout.

"And the north, crossing the river," the third scout said.

Storm Arriving stiffened at the news. "Bluecoats?" he asked.

"No," the scouts said, almost as one.

"Then who?"

"Riders from the Greasy Wood People and from the Cut Hair People," one said.

"No. They were from the Inviters. And the Little Star People."

"No," the third said. "They are Crow People, plus our own soldiers, Elkhorn Scrapers and Dog Soldiers, by their shields."

They all stood, dumbfounded, until Whistling Elk's high-pitched giggle broke the silence. His laughter built, deepening as it grew, until he was rolling on his back, beating his thighs, laughing so hard his cheeks shone with moonlit tears.

Chapter 24

Moon When Ice Starts to Form, Waxing
Four Years after the Cloud Fell
North of the Sudden River
Alliance Territory

A small, distant segment of Storm Arriving's attention grew annoyed at Whistling Elk's hysterics, but the main force of his mind, including the portion that governed his ability to speak, was utterly paralyzed by confusion.

Soldiers. From the Crow People. From the Greasy Wood People, the Little Star People, the Inviters, the Cut-Hair People. Not to mention soldiers from the People themselves. All riding this way? All coming here? Why? And how many?

He forced his voice into action. "How many?" he managed.

"I could not be sure in the dark," the first scout said. "Sixteen, perhaps twenty." The other scouts told of similar numbers.

Whistling Elk's laughter began to ebb as the truth sank in. Storm Arriving blinked twice and shook his head to clear it.

Riders, he thought, concentrating on what they knew. *Small groups. News? But from so many places?* The meaning of it escaped him.

"You," he said, pointing to Grey Bear, "and you," he said, nudging Whistling Elk with a toe. "Gather squads. We must meet these riders."

"What about One Who Flies?" It was his sister, sitting up, now.

Storm Arriving considered it. "He can come," he decided. "But borrow a whistler. We must ride quickly."

One Who Flies signed acknowledgment.

The men moved to fulfill his orders and he went to his sister's side.

"And you," he said to his sister. "You rest."

She smiled the broad, infectious smile he loved so well, and his heart eased at the sight. Then he pressed down on the emotion, squelching it. The time was too serious, and the situation unknown.

He put a hand to her cheek. Her skin was warm and her pulse stronger. "I did not believe him," he said, "but he was right. You are better already."

"You need to trust more," she said, pressing his hand close.

He frowned, knowing that to trust was the one thing he found hardest to do.

"Stay quiet," he said. "We will return before the sun."

The two squads formed up at the edge of camp. Whistling Elk and Grey Bear had each chosen three men, but with One Who Flies and Storm Arriving himself, it was not an auspicious number. He did not know if the spirits truly cared about such things, and in his own heart he doubted if they cared about anything at all, but it did not feel right, leaving with such a number. He pointed at Heron in Treetops.

"You and your brother," he said. "Prepare to ride with us. I...I need your sharp eyes." The young soldier tipped his hat and sprinted off, returning with his brother and their mounts.

There, he thought. *Now we are three sets of four. Good enough for absent spirits.*

The sky was a patchwork of dark and light. Soot-black clouds obscured the glinting stars and broke up the glowing sky-river to Séáno. The air that had begun to move at sunset was now a steady breeze, hissing through the dry grass and tugging parched leaves from the trees.

The camps of the Iron Shirts were dark, all their fires put out, all their men ready for the sunrise and their march to meet the bluecoats.

The bluecoats.

Off in the darkness, miles ahead, the bluecoats waited. And Storm Arriving knew where they were going.

The bluecoat war chief had proven his knowledge of the land at every turn. The Iron Shirts still thought they were chasing the bluecoats, but Storm Arriving knew otherwise. From their first encounter, the bluecoat war chief had led them, drawing the Iron Shirts along like a puppy after a bone. He'd led them from battle site to battle site, testing them at every turn. He had tried their infantry at Crazy Woman Creek, assessed their artillery skills at the Black Rocks. He led them to stony ground near Whistler's Spring to see how their cavalry fared, and every night, all along the way, he tested their picket lines and their sentries.

Storm Arriving had seen the weaknesses, had seen the heavy guns fail to find a moving target, saw the large horses struggle across broken ground, and saw the infantry paralyzed by the Iron Shirt commander's inability to respond and adapt. So he knew where the meeting would take place, could see it all in his mind. The field below the White Cliffs had every advantage nature could provide the bluecoats, and a few other things as well.

The men were ready. They waited patiently, clicking tongues when their whistlers began to grumble.

"We go," he said, and they headed out into the cool, wind-blown night.

They rode west, away from the camps, not wanting to risk being seen by the Iron Shirt pickets. Then they headed north toward the White Water, to the place where the scouts reported having seen the incoming riders. The wind was cold and kept them fresh as they rode. The waxing moon had set, but soon the clouds separated and silvered starlight helped to show the way.

Storm Arriving watched One Who Flies.

Could he be right? he wondered.

The visions. All the visions. The years and *years* of visions. He wanted to believe in them, to trust in the power

216

he had felt on that day, just a few moons past, when the sky darkened and the ground shook. Mouse Road said she had seen the guardians rise from the earth that day, and he believed her. It wasn't a question of whether the spirits existed; it was whether or not they cared, and if Speaks While Leaving had correctly understood their meaning.

One Who Flies was convinced; that much was clear. But Storm Arriving simply could not deny the numbers on the field. The bluecoats had chosen their ground with cunning, but that had only bettered their chances, not evened them.

Believe, my heart.

Storm Arriving yanked the halter so hard his whistler fluted as he jerked to a stop.

"Hold," Grey Bear ordered, and the group reined to a halt. "Storm Arriving," he said. "What is it?"

Trust, my love.

Storm Arriving could not stifle the moan that escaped him. He had not heard her voice for a moon, had not touched the silk of her hair, or smelled the luscious scent of her skin, and now all his memories of her flew through his mind.

See, he heard her say, and the night exploded, swirling around him. Colors flooded in, light bloomed, and he *saw.*

All that One Who Flies had described appeared before his eyes. All that Mouse Road had told, now repeated itself to him. It was more than mere sight and sound. He experienced it, he felt it, he *knew* it. And when the vision bled out and night returned, when the voices of men and the fluting of his mount reached his ears, he bit back stinging tears.

Come, she said. *I wait.*

He sat astride his fractious drake, holding him steady through sheer habit, his mind stunned by the power that had completely overtaken him. He had always known that her power was great, but to speak to him, to *show* him her vision—he was astounded. It was more power than he thought humans could possess, and yet he had seen it as clear as if he had lived it. His mind shied but he forced himself to see, to truly see what it was she had shown him.

A hand touched his arm, and he found One Who Flies at his side, visage serious. Storm Arriving gazed at him, no challenge in his eyes. He put a hand atop his friend's.

"How could I have been so very wrong?" he asked.

Surprise widened his friend's eyes, and then his smile gleamed through the dark. He said nothing, but only gave him a pat of encouragement.

Storm Arriving pulled his drake's head around and slapped his flank, heading off toward their rendezvous.

His mind was ablaze. The vision was real! Its meaning was undeniable. The world had changed in a heartbeat and no matter what they met in the night ahead, he had to understand it in a completely different way.

The scouts led them along the banks of the White Water, back to the area where the riders had been seen. Ahead, a whistler's trumpeting called to them and Heron in Treetops pointed.

"There," he said.

Atop a treeless arm of land overlooking a bend in the river, riders had gathered, their whistlers signaling with shifting patterns along their chameleon skin. Storm Arriving led the party that way, and as they drew near, he saw that his scouts had told the truth.

Riders waited atop the rise, and even from a distance he could see the garb of different tribes. He saw the feathered headpieces of the Inviters, the badger-fur topknot on a chief of the Crow People. The shell and bead work of the Cloud People shone in the moonlight, and he could see the shields of the Elkhorn Scrapers, the Dog Soldiers, and other societies of the People. But he could also see that there were only a hundred or so men gathered atop the ridge. Many, but not nearly enough.

One Who Flies divined his thoughts. "Perhaps they will tip the balance," he said.

"They are too few," Storm Arriving said as they started up the slope.

"You have said that one of your soldiers is worth ten bluecoats. How many Iron Shirts are they worth?"

"They are too few," Storm Arriving repeated, his voice raspy with emotion. "I wish that it were not so; as much as you, I wish it, but it *is* so." He looked up at the soldiers waiting on the ridge. "I cannot think of what this means. Having seen..." His feelings—frustration, remorse, hope, anger, desperation—all welled up, throttling his words. A soldier rode forward from the group. When Storm Arriving saw the large frame and loose hair of Limps, he felt his heart would burst.

He toed his whistler ahead and clasped the arm of his longtime friend, a smile on his face and tears streaming from his eyes.

"Speaks While Leaving," Limps began.

"I know," Storm Arriving said. "She spoke to me—I do not know how, but she did, and she showed me. Her vision, she *showed* it to me."

Limps nodded up at the riders on the ridge behind him. "She has shown all these chiefs. All who see it, believe. All who see, understand."

Two other riders came down from the ridge. It was Two Roads and One Bear, father to Speaks While Leaving, chief of the Great Council; an unexpected presence among these soldiers.

Storm Arriving greeted his chief with deference. "My heart is glad to see you," he said.

One Bear signed his own greeting, but there was no joy in his face. "We have come to join with you. My daughter..." He paused. "We have all seen the power of her vision."

Storm Arriving looked once more at the troop of men on the ridge. He would not show disrespect to his chief for the men he had brought, but silently he wished it had been many more. Perhaps Speaks While Leaving could explain it.

"Your daughter showed her vision to me as well. She said that she would be waiting for me." He scanned the ridgetop again. "Where is she?"

Limps turned his whistler upslope. "She rides with us," he said, and urged his whistler into a jog.

Storm Arriving followed, perplexed. His men fell in behind him, and as a group they rode up the ridge. Limps did not stop, but rode through the gathering of tribesmen. The soldiers spun and rode alongside them as they crossed over the narrow arm of land. Limps slowed as they reached the far side and the land fell away, sloping down into a broad curve of land embraced by the river.

The pale starlight found no grass there, or any graveled banks along the shore, for the ground from hillside to the shining water was filled, covered by mounts and men.

Storm Arriving gaped. He heard One Who Flies say something in his own language, his voice filled with awe, and Storm Arriving echoed the sentiment.

There were thousands, soldiers from every tribe, pale as spirits in white war paint, all here because of one woman and her vision of the future. And Storm Arriving knew where she was: in the middle of them all, at the heart of her creation.

Yes, he heard her say. *I am here.*

He kicked his drake and the beast leapt forward. They juddered down the slope and Storm Arriving whooped in delight. He regretted his every action against his wife, cursing his own stubbornness and mistrust. He knew with his deepest thought that he could never doubt her again. The love that he had twisted, denied for so long, he now let free, and it filled him, sending his soul to flight. He whooped again and the multitude began to move, opening a path as if his devotion had bid them all part to aid his passage to his one true heart, his wife, his love.

He rode past them, rode past the thousands, heading to their center, and there he found a circle of open ground. His drake skidded to a halt, tail smacking the earth, his whistling call echoing from the hillside. But the circle was empty, the starry light touching only trampled earth, with one dark shape lying at the center.

Storm Arriving jumped down from his mount and ran to it, then stopped, and fell to his knees.

It was a travois; two pale lodgepoles braced and bound with rope. Across the travois was a litter, and upon it, a precious cargo. Pale elkhide lay beneath and a massive buffalo robe was draped over its top. Storm Arriving heard other riders enter the circle, heard one man dismount. Footsteps approached him, but Storm Arriving could not look away from the fur-draped bundle.

"So small," he said, his words distant in his own ear. "In my heart, she was always so tall, so..." He sunk down, palms on the ground, and touched his forehead to the cool earth. His fingers dug into the turf and his shout was no longer one of elation. With a keening howl of loss, he tore the earth, raised his fists to the sky, and screamed again, tortured and feral. There was no other sound. All was silence, save for the ragged breath that burned his lungs.

Then, with trembling hands, he reached for his knife. Tears blurred his sight, and the glint of stars along his blade filled his vision with a glow that seemed to limn the shrouded body of his one and only wife.

He reached back and took hold of his braid. With two slow, brutal cuts, he severed it.

He did not move for a time, but knelt there, hands clenching his knife and his sacrifice, his breath shuddering in and out, in and out. Then, slowly, he got to his feet. He placed the braid atop the buffalo robe, and turned.

Limps, One Who Flies, Grey Bear, and Whistling Elk stood before him, somber and bleak, faces wet with new-spilled grief. Behind them were One Bear, Two Roads, and the others from the ridge. And standing, surrounding them all was the assembled might of a dozen tribes; thousands of men, their ghostly war-paint glowing in the starlight, all of them kneeling, all facing the body of the woman who had filled them with this single purpose.

When he spoke, it was with a calm, steady voice. He did not have to shout. His words would pass outward from him like ripples in a still pond, from the first man to the last.

"I am Storm Arriving," he said. "And this is Speaks While Leaving, my wife. She has brought us here. She would have us all work together. Like the bluecoats, like the Iron Shirts, she would have us all be one, a nation undivided." He turned as he spoke. "We have tried before, and we failed. We cannot fail this time, for if we do, if we cannot fight together—if we cannot *live* together—we will surely die together."

He gave time for his words to travel, then raised his voice.

"Are all the chiefs agreed?"

"We are," said one, then another, until they had all given voice and agreed.

"And you men," he said to the legion of spirit warriors around him. "Are all men agreed?"

Their response was immediate and unequivocal, a shout that filled the night.

He raised his knife over his head.

"Then we go!"

Chapter 25

Moon When Ice Starts to Form, Waxing
Four Years after the Cloud Fell
South of the White Water
Alliance Territory

George rode back with Storm Arriving and the newly-arrived chiefs. Not only had they brought thousands of men, but Two Roads had brought some of the captured explosives they had used so successfully against the railroads. George had the perfect use for them in mind, if the situation was right, but for the moment none of that concerned him. Right now, he could think of only two things: Speaks While Leaving was dead, and he would have to tell Mouse Road.

In truth, all of the men—soldiers and chiefs alike—were grim, thoughtful, and silent. For the chiefs of the allied tribes, George imagined that being led to war by a dead woman was a sobering experience. But for the men of the People, it was much more. It was as if their window on the future had shut, leaving them adrift. They knew only what today owned, and were unable to see what tomorrow promised.

Of them all, Storm Arriving was the most affected. In the time it took the stars to spin a hand's width across the sky,

George had seen him change from opponent to skeptic to zealous believer. At the end, he had even discarded his mantle of bitter estrangement and ridden toward his former wife like a lovestruck boy at a sweetheart dance. Now, he rode dumb, eyes hollowed, as if some major part of him had been brutally amputated.

For his own part, George's grief had yet to come. Instead, his mind was consumed by larger matters. His world had been tipped off-balance, and his concept of reality was no longer as clear as it once had been. It was one thing to accede to the notion of visions—history was full of saints and seers, of prophecies and foretold doom—but speaking with the dead? As a youth, George had listened as his mother scoffed at tales of mediums and séances, calling them sideshows better suited to a carnival or boardwalk than the upper-crusted parlors of Washington society. These men, though...he regarded the dour gathering around him. These were not impressionable naïfs or grief-stricken hopefuls clutching for one last word of comfort from a dearly departed. These were serious men, most of whom had never met Speaks While Leaving. They all claimed to have seen the vision, and to have heard her voice. That was what bothered George the most.

Visions he could accept, either as a message from The Almighty or as this culture's interpretation of His presence. George thought of the body, back with the soldiers, under its drapery of pelts. Even in the windy night, the smell of decay was strong and unsettling. Were these men just seeing what they wanted to see? Hearing what they wanted someone to say? Were they dealing with willful hallucinations, or with ghosts, spirits, and a vision sent by a dead woman who was so powerful in life that her presence lingered on?

George did not know what to believe. During his time with the People, he'd seen enough to know that the world was not as simple or as absolute as he had thought. *He* had seen the vision. So had Mouse Road. That should have been enough, *had* been enough before, but now it strained credibility to its limit.

Struggling, he went back to his training, to the teaching he'd received at The Point and at his father's side: Remove all distractions; focus on the real problem.

He discarded all his concerns about how the message had been delivered. He could have seen it written on a rock or heard it from a passing pigeon; precisely *how* he heard the vision's message was irrelevant. Was the analysis valid? Did it make sense?

Clearing his mind, he listed the reasons for and against the various paths of action that were open to them. He let the scenarios build, searched for new paths, evaluated the outcomes. Was this the best choice? Forget everything about how they had decided; look at the facts. Was it the best choice?

"Hunh," he said.

"What is it?" asked Whistling Elk, riding beside him.

"This *is* the best choice," he said. "This alliance with the bluecoats. It really *is* the best path."

Whistling Elk smiled wanly. "Welcome to the dance," he said.

George relaxed. One problem was solved. Now on to the next.

He found Mouse Road leaning against his walker, fingers absently stroking the monster's silk-haired skin as she gazed up at the stars. He had played it out in his mind repeatedly, first delivering her the good news, then starting out with the bad. In the end, she looked at him and read it in his face.

"Oh, no," she said, standing to meet him. "What happened?"

The words spilled from him, his grief finally welling up as he told her. He held her as she wept, his own tears falling unchecked. They sat, leaning against the warm bulk of his walker, and looked out into the night together. Clouds began to gather, and the sky darkened.

Quietly, the night progressed until, near dawn, the word was passed: Prepare.

Men rose from their brief naps, ate—or did not, according to their habits—and readied gear and mounts. Down on the plain, bugles sounded the orders, and the air was filled with a thousand grumbling complaints as men and horses were rousted from uneasy slumber.

Storm Arriving, his council, and his interpreter rode up

as George was tying a sleeping bundle to his walker's harness.

"We go to speak with the Iron Shirts," he said. "I thought you might like to join us."

George wondered if he misunderstood. "What will you be telling them?" he asked.

"I will tell them nothing, for I am nothing but a savage. But they will tell me much." He waved one of his men forward. "We brought a whistler for Mouse Road," he said. "The main group will head out and we will bring them our orders once the Iron Shirts have told us what they want us to do."

George smiled. "This should be very interesting."

Storm Arriving's smile was weak, but sincere. "Very."

Whistling Elk offered to escort Mouse Road north.

"Let me tell you about all the soldiers that will be waiting for us," he said, and with a parting wave, Mouse Road put herself in the storyteller's care.

George mounted up and headed off with Storm Arriving and the others. They rode down the gentle slope. The sky was heavy with clouds. To the east, between the wrought-iron land and the steely sky, the black was diluted by the faintest hint of dawn. It wasn't much, but it was enough to lift George's mood. This would be an important day, and he prayed that they would all see the end of it.

The Iron Shirts were waiting, three soldiers held lanterns high around an officer and his aides. They drew back when George's walker stepped from the night into their illuminated circle, but they held their ground.

The officer spoke slowly, as if to a group of children, his exaggerated gestures and supercilious expression showing how little he thought of the native soldiers' intellect.

George followed most of it, but when the Spaniard was done, Little Fox translated it all for them.

"The bluecoats continue up the banks of the Big Greasy. The Iron Shirts plan to cut through the hills to meet them where the White Water meets the Big Greasy."

"They must mean Old Man's Pass to Dead Bull Creek," Storm Arriving said.

"That is what I thought, also," the Little Fox said. "But he speaks like a child and has no name for anything." He went on. "We are to follow the bluecoats along and keep them moving."

Storm Arriving smiled. "They think to catch the bluecoats before they reach the narrowing at the White Cliffs."

"It seems so."

"Tell them we understand. We will follow on the bluecoats' heels."

The interpreter relayed the response, and the Iron Shirts turned and rode back to join their forces, now already on the march.

"They do not know how fast the bluecoats can travel," Storm Arriving said. His chuckle was mirthless, almost cruel. "Suddenly I am glad for our new alliance."

Down on the plain, the pale hint of dawn limned shadowy figures trudging along in dark groups. Lanterns held on poles provided each block a guide to follow until the dawn strengthened. George looked farther, to the second Iron Shirt camp.

"Wait," he said as Storm Arriving turned to leave. The others stopped. "Look," George said, pointing. "Out there."

They all peered into the distance, searching through the faint light for sign of the other camp.

"Where are they?" Grey Bear asked.

As George feared, the other camp was empty; the marine contingent was already on its way.

"When did they leave? Why didn't we know?" Storm Arriving asked.

"They must have left while we were gone," Grey Bear said. "We weren't watching *them.*"

Storm Arriving growled. "They are miles ahead. They *will* be there before the bluecoats."

"With their guns," George added.

"Yes," Storm Arriving agreed. "With their guns." He wheeled his mount. "We go," he said. "Fast."

Storm Arriving gave orders to his men as they rode and when they reached the others, his orders spread like fire through summer grass. In minutes the entire force had stepped up the pace, riding through the blue light of dawn, heading for the banks of the Big Greasy.

George's walker, rested and fresh, kept up easily, and he quickly found Mouse Road and Whistling Elk.

Storm Arriving rode up a moment later and told them the news.

"What can we do about the guns?" Whistling Elk asked, visibly worried.

"I have some thoughts on that," George said, and proceeded to explain.

Storm Arriving listened as they rode, attentive to every detail.

They pushed their mounts to the limit, following the bluecoat trail over the easy land along the banks of the Big Greasy. The river was quiet, flat and so muddy it looked solid enough to walk across. It would rouse itself soon enough, George knew, when the season's rains dumped torrents into its bed. The land they crossed today would be underwater in a month's time, but for now, the river lay sleeping.

George steered his walker close to Mouse Road's whistler.

"All good?"

Yes, she signed. "Whistler riding is easy."

"Good," he said, but still he worried. He was bringing his wounded wife and unborn child into battle. Not even his father would be so reckless. "Keep your eyes open," he said. "Stay back. No fighting for you."

She laughed. "Whistling Elk tells me there are a thousand spirit warriors waiting for us. We will not have to fight."

It was something George had not considered. He wondered if she might be correct.

The sun was still high in the forenoon when they caught the bluecoat force. Rear guardsmen spotted them but, thankfully, Meriwether had given preemptive orders and the first shots were warning shots.

Storm Arriving drew them all to a halt. Above, the sky grumbled with dry lightning and Storm Arriving turned to George.

"Your plan. Your signal."

George clenched his teeth and took a deep breath. He nodded to Two Roads who nodded to the soldiers who were in charge of the cache of explosives they brought from home. One man had a half-charge affixed to an arrow, while the other carried a charcoal brazier. The first man touched the fuse to the embers, let it sputter, and shot it high in the air.

George and Meriwether had agreed on a signal arrow to seal their pact, but they had expected to meet on the battle-field. George did not want any doubts, did not want anyone to think this was an ambush, so he constructed an arrow that could only be construed as a signal.

The arrow hissed upward and the crosswind grabbed it, pulling it sideways away from both parties. It exploded with a sharp *thud* of fire and smoke.

George watched with keen interest, but could not see what was happening. Heron in Treetops peered intently toward the other force.

"Another bluecoat has joined them," he said. "He has gold on his shoulders and white gloves at his belt."

"Meriwether," George said.

"He looks at us with far-seeing glasses,"

George stood in his saddle ropes and waved.

"He takes a white cloth from his pocket," Heron in Treetops said. "He waves it."

"Let us go and meet our new friends," Storm Arriving said, not without a hint of acid in his tone.

Meriwether and his command staff were waiting for them. The rank and file surrounding them looked nervous, having learned a keen respect for what the approaching men could do in battle. Meriwether nudged his horse forward from the group and George and Storm Arriving did likewise. George turned at a sound and saw Mouse Road toeing her whistler ahead as well.

Meriwether touched the brim of his slouch hat. "Mr. Custer," he said, and with a nod to Mouse Road, added, "Ma'am. Good to see you again."

George relayed the general's words and saw Storm Arriving hide a smile and a sidelong glance at his sister. Then George introduced the principals to one another, and they got to the heart of it.

"The Spanish have marched through the night," George told them, "and are waiting for you just south of where the

White River joins the Missouri. They have five field guns and will control the heights. We need to get you past them, if you want to meet them at the White Cliffs."

Meriwether studied George and the others. "You seem to think you know my mind quite well," he said.

George relayed his words, listened, and carefully returned with the response.

"Storm Arriving speaks. He says he presumed you were returning to our starting place. It is a good choice. It is where he would have chosen to meet the Spanish. He apologizes. He thought you were smart enough to see this, also."

Meriwether's smile was broad and genuine. "Please tell your war chief that he is not incorrect. Tell him that as a commander, I have admired his methods for some time, now. I am glad to learn that the war chief Storm Arriving is as appreciative of the power of history as he is of military tactics. And, if he wishes, please ask him what it is he proposes to do."

George told the others what was said and waited for the response. Storm Arriving just looked at George, and then motioned toward Meriwether.

"So?" he said sternly. "Tell him. Must I put every word in your mouth?" Then he smiled. "Go on."

George was unused to such authority in proceedings like this, but he took it up and relayed their plan to Meriwether.

"We must move fast. Your men can cover much more ground than the Spanish believe, but now you must prove it. You must move with all speed."

He set the stage with his hands, blocking out their major movements.

"We will be first past the mouth of Dead Bull Creek. You will follow, as if in pursuit. You must be close to us, so that the artillery will not fire for fear of hitting us."

"And if they do?" Meriwether said. "If they decide that killing me is worth wounding you?"

George shrugged. "Then we all come to harm, but likely not all of us. Enough will survive to achieve our separate goals."

Meriwether nodded. "Continue," he said.

George laid it all out for them, every move and counter-move. If Meriwether had the least desire to betray them, he could destroy them all, natives and Spaniards alike. George tried to measure the general, but his professionalism made him inscrutable. They would have to roll the die and hope.

When George finished, he could see Meriwether going back over the details in his mind, looking for pitfalls. After a moment, he nodded and spoke to his staff.

"Drop the artillery here. Drop everything that isn't absolutely required for the assault. We will be moving quickly, so no formations. Make sure all men have a full canteen before we set out." He pulled a watch from his vest pocket. "Be ready in ten minutes."

His staff moved out quickly and then Meriwether turned to George.

"They will have spotters on the high ground, so don't pass us until we get close to Dead Bull Creek. It *must* look like we are running from you. Until the last moment."

"Yes," George said. "Good luck, General."

Meriwether touched the brim of his hat again. "Gentlemen. Ma'am." Then he returned to his men.

In minutes the two forces were underway. Behind them, the riverbank was strewn with every non-essential item, from pots and sleeping rolls to artillery and wagons. Every available horse was repurposed to carry men, ammunition, or both. Meriwether disbanded with columns and formations, allowing his men to move where the land was easiest to cross.

Sergeants pushed the step up to quick time, then faster. As men began to flag, they traded spots with men on horseback. It was a maddeningly slow pace by whistler standards, but George knew it was as fast as these men could travel.

The bluecoats pushed the pace for hours while the sun slipped downward from the zenith. The great river of the plains slipped by silently on their right while the rising land on their left put on a multicolored jacket of autumn trees. Sunlight dodged around clouds made of shining silver and blinding white, and the air was moist, full of the scent of warm, decaying grass.

It was evening when they saw the first signs of white in

the waters of the Big Greasy, and Storm Arriving called a halt.

"We are nearly there," he said. "Dead Bull Creek is just around that rise. We must let them get ahead of us. This must look like a real raid."

Storm Arriving called Heron in Treetops and his brother. He pointed to an outcrop of stone along the far end of the ridge on their left.

"Tell me when the bluecoats reach that point," he said.

With agonizing slowness, the bluecoats put distance between themselves and the soldiers of the People.

George watched, trying to gauge the distance, trying to judge how close the bluecoats were to the end of the ridgeline. If they waited too long, the bluecoats would run within firing distance of the Spanish artillery. They looked like they were there already, perhaps past.

"Surely they've reached the—"

"No," said Heron in Treetops' brother. The two men were staring out at the bluecoats. "Still a ways to go."

Mouse Road rode up next to George. She reached out and they held hands as the minutes ticked by.

"Ready," Heron in Treetops said.

"Remember, fire over their heads," Storm Arriving shouted to his soldiers. "Go in loud. Whistler's Return is our signal."

Heron in Treetops stood up and his brother did likewise, both men balancing on the backs of their whistlers.

"Almost," the brother said.

"Now!"

"We go!" Storm Arriving shouted.

Whistlers skimmed over the land, devouring the distance to meet their mock quarry. On their right, the water grew choppy and George could see huge swirls of white sediment mixed with the muddy brown, like paint spilled by a titanic artist. The confluence of the Big Greasy and the White Water was up ahead.

Soldiers began to whoop as they drew close, and it was clear they had judged the distance right. The ridge to their left dropped down past the outcrop and George spied the valley of Dead Bull Creek. Beyond, past the creek, the land rose up again into a headland that overlooked the river and all approaches below.

Rifle shots popped and soldiers whooped as they bore down on the bluecoats. Whistlers sang out and then they were on them, everyone shouting and yelling and firing shots overhead.

The moment of truth, George thought. Now we learn what kind of man you are, General.

The bluecoats wheeled, knelt, and returned fire in retreating ranks, just as they had been trained to do. George winced as the volleys went off, but no man fell. Every shot missed its mark.

George said a quick prayer of thanks and urged more speed from his walker. The whistlers cut to the left and slipped between the bluecoats and the headland. Storm Arriving sent his men into two sweeping arcs in front of the bluecoats, riding close to screen them from the aim of the Spanish guns.

The mouth of Dead Bull Creek was nearly dry, and the two forces danced and jockeyed across it. Ahead, the riverbank narrowed as it ran up against the high ground, and ahead George saw the full throat of the White Water pouring its creamy, chalk-thick water into the Big Greasy. Looking up the valley, he saw something else.

"Storm Arriving!" he shouted, pointing.

The vale was filled. A wall of men—marines and Pereira's troops alike—all rushing forward for the kill.

The bluecoats were up against the headland now, below the reach of the artillery on the height. Storm Arriving gave a command to his drake and George heard the long, rising call that whistlers made when members long absent returned home to the herd. The call was taken up, each whistler singing it in turn. The signal given, as one they spun toward the vale.

The bluecoats dashed the other way, heading upriver for the narrow path along the bank, while the whistlers and George's walker headed into the teeth of the oncoming Iron Shirts. The Spaniards balked, surprised by their ally's sudden rush, and then Storm Arriving swung them to the side to push upward, slicing between tree and branch, creating a switch-backed path up toward the high ground.

"Ready the fire," he shouted, and the soldier with the

burning coals prepared the brazier. They had to disable the guns before the Spanish could reposition them to bear on the field beyond the narrow path. They pushed up the slope. Whistlers slipped on slick, fallen leaves but sharp toes dug into the soft earth and they climbed. George set his walker along a more oblique path, giving her a straighter line up the hillside, then turned her back to meet the whistlers where the hill leveled off. He could hear the Spaniards shouting as they wheeled the heavy artillery into new positions. Through the trees, George could see them.

"Five guns," he said, and then Storm Arriving shouted.

"Arrows!"

Five riders set arrows and rode up to the soldier with the brazier. One by one in quick order they touched their fuse to the embers and sped on.

The Spanish did not hear them coming over the chaos of their own shouts and commands. The riders swooped in like a gust of wind, each man loosing his arrow, each shaft drawing a snake of smoke that linked bow and caisson. The riders curved away, the arrows sputtered, and the charges blew.

Caissons, each filled with powder and ammunition, exploded in blasts of fire. Men, artillery, and several trees were obliterated in a blink. Shrapnel hissed across the hilltop and men and whistlers cried out.

Storm Arriving pointed to Whistling Elk. "Bring our wounded," he said, and then rode down the far side of the hill. Branches whipped at them as they plunged downslope, and George held up his arms, keeping low and praying his walker remembered her rider. They reached the bottom with a *woof* of expelled breath and began their run across the flat ground.

Ahead, the White Water dug deep into the chalky hill, cutting a sheer cliff into its side. The White Cliffs rose a hundred feet above the creamy torrent, their heights pockmarked by thousands of small black-mouthed burrows.

Below, on the wide field that filled the space within the ghostly river's curving arm, George saw once more the shards of his first life.

The field was strewn with wreckage amid the low sagebrush. Giant ribs of metal jutted upward from the ground, the pale aluminum gleaming like dried bone. Scraps of cloth—remnants of the dirigible's skin—hung from the spars, flapping in the wind that funneled down the river's course. The wreck of the U.S. *Abraham Lincoln,* last aircraft of the United States Army, and George's last command as a serving officer, lay scattered across a hundred yards and more, a broken skeleton of twisted metal and tattered cloth.

Meriwether and his bluecoats wove through the wreckage, horses and men picking their way between the knife-sharp edges of torn aluminum and snapped steel. Behind them, just now emerging from the constricting riverside path, were the Spanish, each column four abreast, each rank straight. Their commanders moved their men in unwieldy groups like stevedores shifting cargo on a ship's deck, while the bluecoats sped lithely past the obstacles, pouring across the broken field like water.

On the height, new reports boomed as the fire ate through to new stores of ammunition and powder. The flames spread to the trees on the hilltop, and the sun dipped down below the clouds.

The bluecoats met up with Storm Arriving, and their bugles' quick notes called them back into company groups. Meriwether arranged them to either side, one half set on either flank, facing the wreckage and the Spanish beyond.

On their side, the Spanish formed up as well. George sized up the two forces. The Spanish had three times the troops but only a quarter of the cavalry, and that was before he added in Storm Arriving and his soldiers.

On this small patch of ground, hemmed in by river and hillside, impeded by hazards, the Spanish would not have room for their classical maneuvers of squares and columns. He played it out in his mind. It would be a dirty fight, a filthy, savage battle of men and beasts. They would not meet in great groups but in twos and threes. It would be barbaric, and many, many men would die.

Storm Arriving nudged his drake forward. George looked at him. He saw the war chief his friend had become, saw his intense study of the field. Then he saw the glint of orange light along the seven silver earrings that decorated the rim of his ear, and looked up.

George nudged his walker and the beast walked past

Storm Arriving.

"One Who Flies," Storm Arriving said. "What are you doing?"

George kept moving, his eyes straying heavenward.

"Come with me," he said. "One Bear, Two Roads, you too. You and all the chiefs. Come with me."

"What are you *doing?*" Storm Arriving said again, his tone urgent.

"Look up," George said.

They would, he knew. And he knew that they would see what he saw. They would see the clouds above them, colored with burning orange, bloody red, and bruised purple. They would see that sky and they would recognize it.

George heard them gasp. He could practically *feel* the power fill them as they saw above their heads the sky from that final vision. And then he heard them ride forward to join him.

George waited for them at the limit of the airship's wreckage. He glanced over at Storm Arriving.

"We began here, you and I."

"We did," Storm Arriving said. "But we will not end here."

George turned around.

"General Meriwether," he said. "Would you like to join us?"

Meriwether leaned forward on his pommel. "What is your intention, young man?"

George grinned. "I intend to issue our terms."

Meriwether set spurs and brought his horse as close to George's walker as the gelding would allow. The general's eyes flashed with anger.

"Do you seriously think that the Spanish will give up without a fight?"

George heard the whoops from the woods behind them. "Yes, General. I do."

"With these numbers?" he asked, incredulous. "You're mad! Why would they surrender to an army less than half their size?"

"They won't," George said, hearing the war cries grow louder.

Meriwether stared at George. "Then what do you...?" Finally, he too noted the shouts from their rear.

They turned and saw, skimming down from the high ground and spilling onto the plain, thousands of ghostly warriors on pale whistlers. They whooped and howled as they rode, spine-chilling war cries full of ready mayhem. They rode toward them like a flood, weapons held high in chalk-white arms, their eyes painted black in chalked-skull faces, their whistler's camouflage skin all ashen. The spirit warriors rode across the flat and up the middle ground, filling the center. Their cacophony echoed from the White Cliffs to the hillside.

George turned back to Meriwether.

"But with these numbers, General, I think they will listen."

Meriwether was silent, eyes wide as he took it all in.

George started forward. Calmly they began to wend their way across, weaving through the wreckage.

"One Who Flies! Wait!"

George paused a second time and turned. It was Limps, riding in from the rear.

"Riders came in last night. From home. They brought some gifts. For you."

A group of riders came forward with prisoners, hands bound. Through the filth of their travels, George recognized them.

Alejandro, D'Avignon, and Father Velasquez.

George felt no anger at their presence, no rage as he had so often in the past. They held no power over him anymore. They could do no more harm to anyone.

The soldiers made the prisoners dismount, and Limps gave George the tethers tied to their bound wrists.

"The Council sent the rest of the Ravens on their way. They told them to head south and turn right when they reached Big Salty." He laughed, and George could not help but smile.

"These two," Limps said, pointing to the ambassador and D'Avignon. "The Council says you may do what you wish with them."

George gripped the ropes that bound the prisoners.

"I know just the thing," he said.

They crossed the field at a walk. George waved a tattered

kerchief and the Spanish quickly rode out to parley.

Pereira met them at the far edge of the field of wreckage. His commanders were close at hand. George nodded to them, recognizing several from his dinner as their guest. He looked to Storm Arriving and One Bear, but the two chiefs declined.

"Tell them yourself," One Bear said. "It is fitting, in this place."

George turned then to Meriwether. "May I?"

The general nodded. "By all means."

And so, to Pereira he turned.

"What is this?" the Spaniard demanded, nostrils flaring, his mouth a twisted line. "Who are these savages? Who do you think you are? I demand you tell me at once the meaning of this charade!"

"Thank you," George said, his generous mood evaporating. "You have made this pleasanter."

"*¿Que?*"

"General Pereira," George said from his perch atop his walker's spine. "I am come to deliver you our terms."

"Terms?" Pereira sputtered. He put a hand to his ear as if he had misheard. "*Your* terms?" He sat straight. "You can deliver us no terms. You are an ally of Her Most Catholic Majesty—"

George's walker chuffed. All the horses jumped, and Pereira looked as if he had completely forgotten what it was he wanted to say.

"We," George said, indicating himself and the whistler riders. "We now reject our former alliance with the Spanish Crown. We rescind all offers and all privileges granted to you are revoked." He motioned for the prisoners and they were brought forward. He nodded at the prisoners.

"These men abrogated the terms of their stay in our lands. Against our specific interdiction, they set up a mining operation for their own, private gain." He leaned forward to pierce Pereira with his gaze. "In our most sacred lands, they did this." He paused and sat back into his saddle.

"Our alliance with the Spanish Crown is thus annulled, your priests have been ejected from our lands, and these criminals—"

He tossed the end of the tethers on the ground at Pereira's feet. "These criminals we return to you for punishment."

Pereira frowned, but George noted that some of his commanders looked worried.

"We have forged a new alliance that binds the United States of America and the great peoples of the plains. And these are our terms.

"You will march away. You will get back on your ships. You will never come here again. If you refuse, we will fight you. If you tarry in your retreat, we will fight you. If you ever step foot on our soil again, we will fight you."

He swept a hand back to encompass the bluecoats, the chiefs, and the host of spirit warriors behind him.

"All of us," he said.

The clouds began to darken as the sun dipped to the horizon and all along the chalky cliffs, from a thousand burrows emerged a thousand thousand eyes. Diving lizards, their scales blue and gleaming in the fading light, climbed out onto the cliff face, stretched their fine-skinned wings, and leapt up into the air. Men stared as, wings snapping, voices shrill, more and more emerged to fly upward and join the flock, forming a huge, amorphous cloud that twisted and gyred above the moon-white river. The cloud shimmered blue to black, black to blue. It coiled and folded in upon itself, rising high on one side and sweeping so low on the other that men ducked for fear of being struck.

George grinned as the living cloud swung and danced above the field. Their piercing chorus deafened and the thunder of their million wings shook the air until, as the last light of day caressed the soft belly of the skies above, the entire mass folded in and flew off toward the Big Greasy, leaving only silence and gaping men in its wake.

Whistling Elk was the first to laugh, his woman's giggle setting off all around him. The laughter traveled, man to man, growing, strengthening, until it became a whoop, a shout, a cheer of joy, a huzzah five thousand men strong.

But that joy sped no farther than to George, Storm Arriving, and the gathered chiefs.

The Spanish were not happy, but George saw the glances exchanged between the general's commanders, and from commanders to their men. They would not fight.

"Turn away, General," George said. "You do not want this fight. And you cannot have this land. It is our land, from now until the mountains fall."

George's walker chuffed again, and he sensed her growing agitation.

"Now, Pereira. Go now. Some of us grow impatient."

Pereira, eyes locked on George, his newborn hatred a palpable thing between them, spat orders at the others, and his staff eagerly moved to obey. The prisoners were taken away; the Spaniards began to melt away into the gloaming, until only Pereira remained at the parley point, his wounded ego unable to free itself from the source of its injury.

George nudged his walker. Her intake of breath was massive, and the roar she loosed was epic, built of the memories, the joys, and the fulfillment of the hearts surrounding her. She roared, and whistlers sang, and men cheered until Pereira fled the field, until the last Spaniard disappeared down the river path.

When the cheers died down and the allies were alone on the field of their victory, George dismounted and walked over to Meriwether.

"General, if you would follow me please?"

Meriwether dismounted and fell in step beside George as he led him over to the chiefs.

One Bear ordered his whistler to crouch and dismounted. Storm Arriving and the other chiefs followed One Bear's example.

"My General Meriwether," George said in French. "May I present to you One Bear, chief of the Closed Windpipe band and leader of the Great Council."

"It is an honor," Meriwether said, extending his hand.

One Bear did not move for a moment, then reached forward and clasped the wrist of his former enemy.

"*Mon cœur,*" One Bear said, his French thick and heavy with emotion. "*Mon cœur chante,*" he said.

The two men regarded one another, respectful, sincere.

"And this is Two Roads," George said, carrying the introductions along.

Some of the spirit warriors cut scrub-wood for a fire. Some bluecoats produced a harmonica and a jaw-harp. Shields became drums, stores of jerky and pemmican were

240

passed around. Songs were sung and dances were attempted.

As the stars came out in a broken sky, and while the army of the Iron Shirts retreated toward the coast, two nations set aside their generations of war and met each other for the first time.

George awoke to the sound of the ocean. He looked up and saw dark blurs streaking against the pale sky. He blinked and the blurs sprouted wings, grew from a few to many, from many to a multitude.

"Awake, I see," Mouse Road said. "Finally."

She sat nearby, resting against an aluminum spar, a bluecoat horse blanket wrapped around her shoulders to ward off the chill.

Above, the diving lizards were returning from their night's hunt, streaming back to their cliffs and their tiny caverns, their wingbeats and their chittering calls sounding like waves rushing up against a graveled shore.

He looked around and saw he was not the only one who had been able to sleep a bit. In amongst the broken girders and metal ribs, men roused from sleep, scratching their heads and rubbing at dream-crusted eyes.

George saw plenty of soldiers wearing a bluecoat jacket and saw just as many shirt-sleeved bluecoats with a war club or shell-beaded vest. Other, less explicable trades had also been made, but George's memory of it all was one of firelight, drumbeats, and grinning faces.

"Sleepy-head," Mouse Road chided him as he came over to her and nuzzled her neck.

"Couldn't sleep?" he asked.

"You snored," she said, then shoved him away. "And you smell."

He sat by her. "It has been a long few days." He raked fingers through his hair and scratched at the stubble of his beard. Then he stood, stretched, and lent Mouse Road a hand as she rose. She opened her arms and wrapped them both in her blanket.

"What will we do now?" she asked.

He pulled her tiny frame close.

"First, we must see the Iron Shirts to their ships," he said. "And then..." His gaze drifted across the field of groggy men and sleeping whistlers. They littered the entire field except for one spot, a place to one side where no soldier, no bluecoat, no whistler had slept. An empty circle in which lay a small, fur-draped bundle on a pine-log travois.

"And then," he said, "we have one more stop to make."

Chapter 26

Moon When Ice Starts to Form, Waxing
Four Years after the Cloud Fell
Near Kansa Bay
Alliance Territory

The trip south was slow and uneventful, though not as slow as George was sure the Spanish would have liked it to be.

Meriwether had offered to ride along, but all the chiefs insisted that he and his bluecoats go home, across the Big Greasy.

But when Storm Arriving and One Bear asked the other chiefs if they also wanted to return home, no one took that option.

Storm Arriving's habit of sending small squads to harry those lagging behind kept the Iron Shirts motivated. And so the Spanish found themselves dogged all the way to Kansa Bay where their ships hung at anchor.

When the last Iron Shirt was crammed aboard the last ship and the last sail disappeared into the weather that hung over the Big Salty, George felt as if his heart was both buoyant and heavy.

One more stop, he told himself.

The entire army—all the chiefs and all their soldiers—rode west with One Bear, Storm Arriving, and the rest of those Speaks While Leaving had called friends. Such a funeral cortege was unheard of in the history of the People. Even when they brought Three Trees Together, one of their most venerated chiefs, here to this spot, George could have counted the attendants on both hands.

This, though...this was different.

The body of Speaks While Leaving on its travois was pulled by a lone, riderless hen. Storm Arriving and One Bear led the way, while Limps rode next to the hen, having put himself in charge of the body's safety. George, Mouse Road, and the rest of her close friends came next, but there ended all similarities.

Behind George rode the chiefs of a dozen nations and their gathered solders, many still streaked with the pale chalk of their spirit paint. They sang as they rode, now a song from the Crow, then one from the Cut-Hair People, each group tying their song to the end of the one before it, each tribe singing of love, of victory, of the spirits, and of the land, all as their mood decreed.

But when the burial grounds came into view, where the sage-studded dunes were replaced by empty air, and fern-encrusted cliffs fell hundreds of feet to the seashore below, all singing ended. In silence, the army of the allied tribes watched as Little Teeth, lizards the size of a man with wings twice that size, hung on the updrafts like monstrous kites held by invisible string. These winged beasts would tear open the body of their loved one, releasing the spirit to fly down the star-studded waters of the Big Salty and up the star-strewn river of the Milky Way to reach Séáno and the Spirit World.

As the mourners turned the travois into a burial scaffold, George doubted the Little Teeth were needed. If anyone knew her way from here to the Spirit World, it was Speaks While Leaving. She had lived with one foot beyond the veil almost all her life.

There were no words when they lifted her body and placed it on the scaffold. There were no fancy speeches, no orations. Her friends, her family, the soldiers and chiefs, they all merely stood in reverent silence until, at the back, a soldier from the Little Bowstrings society began to sing.

Nothing lives long,
Only the earth
And the mountains.

George held Mouse Road's hand as the lonely voice sang the song once more.

Then, nothing but the wind, the dull thud of the surf below, and the croaking call of the Little Teeth.

Storm Arriving stared up at the body for a while, then turned.

"Come," he said. "Time to go home. Time to see what this new world holds for us."

Chapter 27

Friday, October 27th, AD 1890
Aboard the *Catarina Michaela*
Gulf of Narváez

The warships, their decks jammed gunwale to gunwale with the unexpected weight of not one but two retreating armies, rolled heavily against the swell as they sailed west toward the safety of the Tejano coast.

But safety was a relative term for Alejandro. He stood on the foredeck, sweat stinging his eyes and the taste of bile twisting his gut. His hands, bound now by iron instead of rope, were swollen from the infection of his festering abrasions. His fingers ached at the joints and burned with fire where the skin had split.

Nearby stood Pereira and two of his officers, but they paid Alejandro no mind. Their attention was on the priest, Velasquez, who stood on the steps below them.

"And you swear this to be true," he asked as he leaned over the rail, looking down at the man on the deck, his chief witness.

"Yes, Father," D'Avignon said. "On the Bible I swear it. On my life! Don Alejandro wanted the gold for himself, to restore his family's good name, he told me. He held a grudge, a long bitter grudge, because of some dishonor back during the Tejano War. He said to me, 'The Crown will get their lands; the priests will get their souls. Why shouldn't I get their gold?' His words. I swear it."

Alejandro closed his eyes and smiled. The rogue's performance was letter perfect.

"Father," Pereira said. "Do you vouch for this man's character?"

"Indeed," the priest said. "He has been a devout member of our flock, and has studied under my tutelage. He has faithfully attended Mass and taken the sacrament. He told me of his suspicions. I only wish I had given his words more credence, instead of trusting in the reputation of the accused. If I had, this appalling disaster might have been averted."

Pereira scowled, but Alejandro knew it was just for show. The little vice-princeling must have been gleeful at having such a scapegoat so expertly served up to him.

"I have heard enough," Pereira said. "Gentlemen, are you satisfied?"

The two officers agreed readily, and the three held a brief, whispered conference. Then Pereira turned back with the verdict.

"Guilty."

Alejandro wanted to laugh, but could not summon the energy.

Other words were spoken, but he did not hear them. A rope went over a boom and was made into a crude noose. A table was brought and put against the foredeck rail. Then calloused, thick-fingered hands took hold of Alejandro's arms, made him climb up, and held him steady as he looked over the drop.

"Does the condemned have anything to say before sentence is carried out?"

He considered it. He considered denying it all, but D'Avignon had sprinkled just enough truth on his concocted tale, had mixed in just enough plausibility, that it was simply a matter of who was the more credible. And, of course, D'Avignon had seen to that, as well, with his devotions and his catechisms.

He considered leaving some last words for his wife and

family, but the final thoughts of a convicted traitor would mean nothing to them, even if they were delivered intact.

Briefly, he considered piping up with some bit of patriotic pabulum, but tossed the idea in a heap with the rest.

He was done. Manipulated by politics, outmaneuvered by a scoundrel, and betrayed by his own ambitions, he was done.

He looked out over the blue, sun-spangled waves and smelled the fresh, salt air.

"At least I am not seasick," he said.

The loop of the noose was put over his head, the rope rough against his skin and its slack length a prickly weight across his shoulder and back. As Velasquez gave him a final blessing, Alejandro scanned the faces below him.

Most of the men looked satisfied that justice was about to be done, while some were eager to see a high-born man hanged. A few had more charitable souls, and bowed their heads in prayer along with the priest. And then there was D'Avignon, head down, lips repeating the words of the Latin benediction in perfect unison with Velasquez's gravelly baritone.

The priest finished his prayer and D'Avignon looked up, his face sorrowful, penitent.

Alejandro felt the hand on his back, ready to shove him over the edge.

D'Avignon winked.

Alejandro fell.

Epilogue

Hatchling Moon, Waxing
Sixteen Years after the Cloud Fell
Eastern Province
Alliance Territory

The clouds above had been building for hours, stacking one atop the other, building immense, steely towers, like pillars of heaven. George and Storm Arriving rode quietly, heading east toward the American border.

It had been a long day out on the range, checking on the herds. They'd been on the move since sun-up and George's stomach was grumbling for food.

"The calving numbers look good," he said.

"Good?" Storm Arriving said. "They looked very good. The winter wasn't too hard this year, so percentages will be high. Very good for the next few years, probably."

They rode around the shoulder of a knoll and the whistlers fluted, picking up their pace, knowing home and a night's rest was not far away. Ahead, toward the river where the land dipped slightly, the town of Wewela lay quiet, settling in for the evening. It was an odd collection of buildings. Square wood-frame structures fronted the straight path where some traders and Americans had been given sanction to set up shop, but surrounding them were the hummocks of the Earth Lodge Builders who brought their families south to farm, and a handful of the conical buffalo skin lodges raised by those who came to this borderland town for a visit or to trade.

But the whistlers were not interested in Wewela. They knew that, for now, home was a bit farther along the trail, beyond the pastures and fields with acres of new-sown crops. Soon they could see it, the little grey house with a large garden out front and a lodge set up next to it.

The wind picked up, bringing the scent of rain. George looked to the west. He judged it likely that the weather would hold off until midnight. No longer than that, though.

"Are you sure you will not stay the night?" he asked.

"No," Storm Arriving said. "I need get these reports back to the Council soon. They are already drawing up the numbers for the summer hunts. You will be coming for the hunt?"

"Of course," George said. "We will only be here for a few more weeks." He thought for a bit. "If we had a telegraph, you would not have to leave so soon. When you meet with the Council, talk to them again about the telegraph. Now that we've repaid the Americans—"

Storm Arriving laughed. "I will, I will."

"I am serious. It is a new century. We must move forward with the times or—"

"You are as persistent as a robin in springtime," Storm Arriving said with a smile. "But do not worry. I will sing your song to them once more. First we will build these message wires, and then we will convince them to build a railroad." He laughed again.

"I am not joking," George said.

"I know!" Storm Arriving replied.

"Well. Then, good!" he said, and laughed at himself. "I am too earnest at times. Your sister will be disappointed though, that you will be leaving so soon."

Storm Arriving shrugged. "I know," he said, hesitation in his tone. "It is just that..."

"What?" George prompted.

Storm Arriving growled. "I never know what to say around him."

"Who?" George said. "My father?"

"Who else?"

George laughed, took a breath and laughed some more. "Well!" he said. "That explains why you are so 'busy' whenever we come out to visit them." He laughed again. "You will stay for a meal at least." He raised a fist. "No argument!"

Storm Arriving held up his hands in surrender.

"No argument," he agreed.

The tiny homestead was settled in its dell near a stream. A thin line of smoke rose from the chimney.

"Ah, good," George said. "Mouse Road is cooking. My mother always burns everything."

"Ha!" Storm Arriving said. "No wonder Long Hair is so thin."

George nudged his mount and she sang out with a rising call that ran from her belly to the top of her crest. From the paddock near the house, other whistlers answered. Then the door flew open. Two children ran out into the fenced garden, stood between the rose beds and the pea patch and waved.

George and Storm Arriving waved back and let their whistlers run toward their rest.

When the whistlers were in the paddock, Blue Shell Woman, the eleven-year-old George and Mouse Road named after the infant who had died, ran in to collect a hug from her father. Her brother Black Knife, bearer of his great-great-grandfather's name, was close behind. Then they both turned to greet their uncle.

"Are you staying?" Blue Shell Woman asked.

"For a bit," Storm Arriving said, sleeking her black hair.

"Mama is cooking," she offered.

He scooped her up and flung her over his shoulder. "In that case, maybe a little longer than a bit."

They came around the front of the house and found George's father on the porch, sitting in a rocker, taking a cup of tea.

Storm Arriving nodded in greeting and then took the giggling children out past the garden fence to play Green Monster.

Custer sipped. "That boy doesn't like me much, does he?"

George sat down on the floorboards and dangled his legs

over the edge of the porch. "You...unsettle him."

"Me?" Custer said theatrically.

"Yes. You," George answered deadpan. "He doesn't dislike you. You just..."

Custer sipped. "Just what?"

George shrugged. "I think you remind him of all that went before."

"Hm," Custer said. "I can understand that." He sipped again. "Is he staying for dinner? Your mother isn't cooking."

George smiled. "Blue made sure he knew that."

Custer took a deep breath and let it out slowly. Out in the field, Storm Arriving chased two screaming children with his claw-fingered hands and stalking gait.

"Rawr!" he said, catching Black Knife, only to find Blue Shell Woman climbing on his shoulders. They all collapsed into a giggling pile and then were up for another round.

George noted his father's peaceful smile.

"Go," his father said. "Go inside. Kiss your wife. Help with supper."

George got up and patted his father on the shoulder.

"Right away, sir," he said, and went inside to help.

ACKNOWLEDGMENTS

As always, I gratefully acknowledge the Cheyenne people whose law, legend, and history have been such a continued enlightenment and inspiration. Without them, this series simply would not exist.

My cadre of Second Readers is also due a nod. To the Baker clan (Mike, Kim, & Todd) and K.A. Corlett: your nit-picky "Surely you meant" attitude made all the difference. Thanks for taking nothing for granted, and seeing all the mistakes I couldn't.

To my wife, my undying appreciation for her support during the long years of this project.

But for this final book, I reserve my greatest thanks for my readers (the Faithful Few) who have sent me their thoughts and encouragement over the many empty years between Books IV and V. You guys kept me going, got me started when I had stalled, and cheered me on to the finish line. This book is, in very large part, yours.

All the best,
    k

Cheyenne Pronunciation Guide and Glossary

There are only 14 letters in the Cheyenne alphabet. They are used to create small words which can be combined to create some very long words. The language is very descriptive, and often combines several smaller words to construct a longer, more complex concept. The following are simplified examples of this subtle and intricate language, but it will give you some idea of how to pronounce the words in the text.

LETTER	PRONUNCIATION OF THE CHEYENNE LETTER
a	"a" as in "water"
e	"i" as in "omit" (short "i" sound, not a long "e")
h	"h" as in "home"
k	"k" as in "skit"
m	"m" as in "mouse"
n	"n" as in "not"
o	"o" as in "hope"
p	"p" as in "poor"
s	"s" as in "said"
š	"sh" as in "shy"
t	"t" as in "stop"
v	"v" as in "value"
x	"ch" as in "Bach" (a soft, aspirated "h")
'	glottal stop as in "Uh-oh!"

The three vowels (a, e, o) can be marked for high pitch (á, é, ó) or be voiceless (whispered), as in â, ô, ê.

Glossary

Ame'haooestse	Tsétsêhéstâhese for the name One Who Flies
Bands	Cheyenne clans or family groups. Bands always travel together, while the tribe as a whole only gathers in the summer months. Bands are familial and matrilineal; men who marry go to live with the woman and her band. The

	ten Cheyenne bands are:
	The Closed Windpipe People (also Closed Gullet or Closed Aorta)
	The Scabby Band
	The Hair Rope Men
	The Ridge People
	The Southern Eaters
	The Tree People (also Log Men)
	The Poor People
	The Broken Jaw People (also Lower Jaw Protruding People or Drifted Away Band)
	The Suhtai
	The Flexed Leg people (also Lying On The Side With Knees Drawn Up People, later absorbed into Dog Soldier society)
	Northern Eaters
The Cloud People	Tsétsêhéstâhese phrase for the Southern Arapaho
The Cradle People	Tsétsêhéstâhese phrase for the Assiniboine
The Crow People	Tsétsêhéstâhese phrase for the Crow
The Cut-Hair People	Tsétsêhéstâhese phrase for the Osage
Eestseohtse'e	Tsétsêhéstâhese for the name Speaks While Leaving
Grandmother Land	Tsétsêhéstâhese phrase for Canada
The Greasy Wood People	Tsétsêhéstâhese phrase for the Kiowa
Haaahe	A Tsétsêhéstâhese phrase of greeting, from one man to another
Héehe'e	Yes
Hó'ésta	Shout!
Hohkeekemeona'e	Tsétsêhéstâhese for the name Mouse Road
Hoohtsetsé-taneo'o	The Tree People band
Hová'âháne	No

Glossary

The Inviters	Tsétsêhéstâhese phrase for the Lakota
Iron Shirts	Tsétsêhéstâhese phrase for the Spanish conquistadors
Ke'éehe	Child's word for grandmother
The Little Star People	Tsétsêhéstâhese phrase for the Oglala Lakota
Maahótse	The four Sacred Arrows of the People
Ma'heo'o (singular), *Ma'heono* (plural)	A word that can be loosely translated as "that which is sacred," referring to the basis of Cheyenne spirituality and mystery
Mo'e'haeva'e	Tsétsêhéstâhese for the name Magpie Woman
Moons	In the world of the Fallen Cloud, the names for the yearly cycle of moons are slightly different. The winter-to-winter cycle in these books is as follows: Hoop and Stick Game Moon Big Hoop and Stick Game Moon Light Snow Moon Ball Game Moon (or Spring Moon) Hatchling Moon Moon When the Whistlers Get Fat Moon When the Buffalo Are Rutting Moon When the Cherries Are Ripe Plum Moon (or Cool Moon) Moon When the Ice Starts to Form Hard Face Moon Big Hard Face Moon
Ne-a'éše	Thank you
Néséne	My friend (said by one man to another).
Nevé-stanevóo'o	The Four Sacred Persons, created by Ma'heo'o, who guard the four corners of the world
Nóheto	We go!

Glossary

Nóxa'e	Wait!
The Sage People	Tsétsêhéstâhese phrase for the Northern Arapaho
Séáno	The happy place for the deceased
The Snake People	Tsétsêhéstâhese phrase for the Comanche
Soldier Societies	The military organizations within the tribe. Membership in a society was voluntary and had no relation to the band in which one lived. The six Cheyenne soldier societies are: Kit Foxes (also Fox Soldiers) Elkhorn Scrapers (also Crooked Lances) Dog Men (or Wolf Soldiers) Red Shields (or Buffalo Bull Soldiers) Crazy Dogs Little Bowstrings
To'êstse (singular), To'e (plural)	Wake up!
Tosa'e	Where?
Tsêhe'êsta'ehe	Long Hair (General G. A. Custer)
Tsétsêhéstâhese	The Cheyenne people's word for themselves
Vá'ôhtáma	The place of honor at the back of the lodge
Vé'ho'e (singular), Vé'hó'e (plural)	Lit. spider, from the word for "cocooned," and now the word for whites
Vé'ho'e	The Tsétsêhéstâhese name for the Spider-Trickster of legend
Vétšêškévâhonoo'o	Fry-bread
The Wolf People	Tsétsêhéstâhese phrase for the Pawnee

The Year The Star Fell	In the year 1833, the Leonid meteor shower was especially fierce. The incredible display made such an impression on the Cheyenne of the time, that it became a memorable event from which many other events were dated